The Lobster's Shell

The Lobster's Shell

Caroline Albertine Minor

Translated from the Danish by Caroline Waight

GRANTA

Granta Publications, 12 Addison Avenue, London W11 4QR

First published in Great Britain by Granta Books, 2022

Originally published in 2020 as *Hummerens Skjold* by Gutkind Forlag,
A/S, København

A CIP catalogue record for this book is available from the British Library

9 8 7 6 5 4 3 2 1

ISBN 978 1 78378 755 5
eISBN 978 1 78378 757 9

www.granta.com

Typeset by M Rules in Garamond

Printed and bound by CPI Group (UK) Ltd, Croydon, CR0 4YY

For Ivan and Dunia

‘I’m only pronouns, & I am all of them, & I didn’t ask for this
    You did
I came into your life to change it & it did so & now nothing
    will ever change
That, and that’s that.
Alone & crowded, unhappy fate, nevertheless
    I slip softly into the air
The world’s furious song flows through my costume.’

Ted Berrigan, ‘Red Shift’

MAIN CHARACTERS

THE GABELS

In another world
Charlotte 'Charles' Gabel, the mother
Troels Gabel, the father

Charlottenlund, north of Copenhagen, Denmark
Niels Gabel, the youngest
Phillip 'Cosmo' Tibbett, Niels' flatmate

Copenhagen, Denmark
Sidsel Gabel, the middle one
Laura Gabel, Sidsel's daughter

San Francisco, USA
Ea Gabel, the oldest
Hector Nunez, Ea's partner
Coco Nunez, Hector's daughter from his first marriage

Copenhagen, Denmark
Aunt Elisabeth, 'Efie', Charlotte's sister

THE WALLENS

San Francisco, USA
Beatrice 'Bee' Wallens

Bondurant/Des Moines and on a visit to Beatrice in San Francisco, USA
Seraphina 'Fifi' Wallens, alias 'Fessonia', Beatrice's daughter

Bondurant, USA
Marianne Wallens, Beatrice's mother and Seraphina's grandmother

San Francisco, USA
Mr Pistilli, Beatrice's neighbour
Pita, Beatrice's pug
Pauline Farley, Beatrice's ex-wife
Hudson Farley, Pauline's son

KEY MINOR CHARACTERS

Vicky Singh, Laura's father	*London, England*
William Catchpoole	*Kentfield, USA*
Curtis, a wanderer	*San Francisco, USA*

The Lobster's Shell

*

Charlotte

Yes?

(Who called?)

Well, here I am.

I've come.

Nobody replies.

Silence, bolts of yellow light through fog.

A damp heat, nothing else.

The connection has evidently been broken – if it was ever made?

Perhaps it was a mistake? Some irregularity in the system, although I'm surprised that sort of thing can happen.

No, I'm sure.

Someone was calling.

Somebody asked me to come, or otherwise I wouldn't be here.

And I am here, freshly washed, and with the stiff grass of the meadow between my toes. The air is spiced and hot as a sauna, scorching my nostrils as I inhale.

A few yards away, at the foot of a hill, is a copse of young birch trees. Moving among the thin zebra-striped trunks is an unsteady light. It hops in and out among the trees like a lantern carried outstretched across a courtyard. In a radius of several feet around the trees, the perspective is distorted. The birches arch outwards bow-legged from the middle; higher up they're elongated and thin, their crowns listing, so that the copse gives the impression of a temple or pagoda, with rickety columns and a dense, shimmering roof of green.

I start to walk without hesitation, making for the hill and the trees.

The fog swirls with each step I take, and before long I'm drenched in sweat. My cardigan is sticking to my arms, and my dress rides up between my thighs. A gust of wind sweeps across the meadow, bending broad, idle sections of the grass. I stop short. Pushing the hair back from my forehead, I tie my cardigan around my waist. When I look up, the birch trees are gone. There's no trace whatsoever of the landscape from before.

In its place, stretched taut, is a thing I can best describe as a vast elastic sail.

It expands with the direction of the eye, swelling and subsuming empty space.

There is nowhere that it isn't, and now it fills the sky, or whatever you'd call it. It is everything.

It's billowing. Slack then tight, gliding back into place.

The sight fills me with a piercing longing, as though the thing I'm looking forward to is long past. I tread closer, tilting back my head and letting my eyes skate across the endless surface, chasing along the dazzling whiteness, before I flop down on to the ground exhausted and sit, chin resting on my knees, crestfallen. Like a tourist waiting for a bus in a foreign country.

At the mercy of an obscure timetable.

A different culture's flexible notion of time.

Time like a cupola, a dome in a temple, filled and emptied at the same time.

Or like a loop.

No bigger than an ant on a background of white.

No bigger than an ant compared to an ant compared to an ant against the whiteness's extent.

Yet behind my back, mute, the sail is demanding my attention. It's asking to be examined more closely.

It's hard to say what the material is: it has a matte sheen like the inside of a mussel, translucent but not transparent. Close up, a network of delicate rose-pink veins becomes visible; is it some sort of membrane, then?

Tissue-like and frail.

It's so beautiful.

I wonder if . . . very gingerly . . .

Just with the tips of—

Oh!

It's cold, and damp with condensation.

The surface feels alive against the skin, like a freshly caught flounder.

Afterwards my fingers are buzzing, but there's nothing to see. No marks, not even any redness. For the first time I notice the sound: a low electric crackle. Leaning forward, I turn my good ear towards it. Yes. That's definitely where it's coming from. Pop rizzz pop pop popopop, *it goes.* Rizzz . . . pop . . . rizzz. *The hairs on my temples rise, scenting the air like antennae. I take a step back, and they settle neatly back into place.*

My fingers have left a mark.

The dew has rubbed off where my skin touched the membrane, and underneath the material is clear as glass. The veins are unmistakable: reddish, thread-thin branches.

Rizz . . . pop! RZZZZZZZZ *it goes, when I dab my fingers against the transparent patch.*

There, I whisper, it's all right, it's all right.

And it does seem like the current retreats, leaving only a pleasant prickle on my skin. I rub until I've exposed an area the size of a tea plate, and lean forward.

Darkness.

Silent and dense.

There's nothing to see; but then something happens very far to the right: a pulse, moving threads of light, writhing and forming shapes.

Simple circles and lines to begin with, but soon growing more complex. Images bubble up and elongate, before converging with a bang into a silver ball. The ball hangs in the darkness, trembles a moment, then dissolves outwards and fills the space with a red glow from which the figures emerge, one by one. Fleeting, colourless beings that seem far away and underwater, until everything finds its shape, clicks and swivels. The lens comes into focus – and there's a woman standing on a doormat, saying goodbye to someone. Her ears peep out beneath her short hair. The other person says something, but the woman doesn't hear it; she's already walking down the steps and on to the street. On the front door of the neighbour's house hangs a garland of artificial flowers: blue, Easter yellow and pink roses. She shivers, shakes her sunglasses out of her hair and starts to walk. The woman is clearly in a rush, striding off up a steep road, following the row of sun-warmed cars until she reaches a sand-coloured Ford parked in the shadow of a palm tree. Climbing in, she pulls her sweatshirt over her head – her arms are brown and sinewy as a circus artist's – then puts the key in the ignition and reverses hurriedly out of her parking spot. She turns the car around and drives on to the boulevard.

She flickers.

The image of the woman driving mingles with other images. Like painted sheets of glass thrust on top of others, lit from below by a powerful bulb. Faster and faster it goes, and soon it's impossible to hold on to the individual pictures for more than a few seconds at a time. A waterfall of images, a careening merry-go-round. Light and colours weave in and out.

I press my face deeper into the soft, cold pane, and gradually the projector slows, until it lands back on the woman with a dry click.

She's sphinx-like behind the dark glasses, stuck in traffic. She's not pleased, you can tell by the way she's twisting her ring. Round and round on her index finger. The amethyst casts splinters of light on to the roof of the car. On her left wrist is a tattoo of a coiled snake, and as she leans forward to reach something in the glove compartment I recognise with a jolt my eldest daughter. Despite the sunglasses and the colour of her hair, I'm sure.

The light goes green, but it's the turning lane, and we were both nearly caught out. She exhales through her nose, tapping along to the rhythm of the music on the wheel with the edge of her thumb.

At last the cars in front of her are moving. Her thigh tenses as she steps on the pedal.

Can you hear me?

She's looking straight ahead, at the road, at the car in front. The lights are pale in the afternoon sun, the sky over the city as dull as a glazed eye, and now I remember everything in one nauseating rush. Memory's stake through the heart.

There were three of them.

Two older girls and a boy with wiry curls.

And I was their mother.

Lottemama.

The edges of the picture buckle and burn as though someone's holding a lighter too close to the surface. The horizon quivers like blubber and the houses' pill-coloured facades collapse one by one. Palm trees, which had been hissing in the wind, still their leaves and then, without any warning, the sky lurches inside out and shuts around the landscape like a hand around a stone.

The delicate sound of a bell calls me back.

I sit up.

All is as it was.

The fog.

The warmth. The membrane breathing peacefully a few yards from my feet.

Has time passed?

Not much.

Not much time.

My dress has ridden up, exposing two lumpy thighs.

I get to my feet, brushing loose grass from my arms and legs, and as I do, I see it: an unhealthy colour where I rubbed the membrane. The veins have turned dark brown, in places black.

I brace myself mechanically, expecting some kind of authority to intervene.

Some unveiling.

To be taken away.

Expecting the stern scrutiny of eyes that tell me I should know better – but no one comes.

Nothing happens.

What strange rift, what blind spot have I got myself wedged into now?

Whatever it is, it's a mess.

The moist heat has steamed open the envelopes of the past and scattered their contents around me.

I feel seasick.

Duped and sodden.

I will come forward and have things put right. Make a clean breast of it and ask to be free of this body again as soon as possible. I had forgotten all about the astronomical weight of incarnation, the sense of an iron piston being tamped down, compacting all that swirls free into a tight cake beneath it, the brain nailed to the feet by quivering strings and memory striking up its earworms.

Come forward. Good.

But where? And to whom?

I squint. The meadow is a dusty plane of violet through the haze. There is no horizon, no sense of an ending. All is level, all mute.

I recognised the city at once, from films I suppose; I've never been to America myself. She had got very thin and wasn't really young any more.

That means the boy has become a man, and the middle girl has been a woman for years now.

Well, assuming they're—

But why wouldn't they be?

Let it go! Shake yourself off, like Trille loping back up the beach.

(Grains of sand and drops of seawater flung in a steel-coloured halo around her.)

Curiosity needs nothing to grow; only cress outdoes it in frugality.

The questions sit on my tongue like cherry stones.

Swallow them. One by one.

With the membrane at my back I start to walk: straight ahead, my footsteps firm. After a while I pause and cup my hands around my mouth.

Hello?

My voice lands like a shoe a few yards away, and no one answers.

The bell is back . . . no, wait, I know that sound! It's not a bell at all; it's cheap metal bracelets sliding down an arm and tinkling.

I turn around and there, not two yards away, wearing his usual leather jacket, sits my ex-husband. He's smiling his goatish smile, as though life and some immeasurable amount of death hadn't gone by since we saw each other last.

You're late. That's not like you.

Troels! I say, and after all these years his name still sounds like an accusation in my mouth.

PART ONE

The Lobster's Shell

1

Beatrice

You'll have a glass of ice tea, she thinks sternly, and shuts the front door. She walks upstairs and past the kitchen, into the dining room and over to the corner cupboard where the Armagnac is kept. The good one, the one they usually only bring out at the end of dinner parties that have gone exceptionally well – and after the total flops. Really, Pita needs to stop looking at her that way, with her head cocked and a disconsolate expression in her bulging eyes. She can still feel a delicate current in her palms and the rawness in her chest.

The way Bee Wallens is slumped on the edge of the sofa with a bottle of Baron de Sigognac 1967 pressed against her left cheek, it's hard to square her with the *renowned spiritual expert, intuitive coach and psychic medium* smiling serenely on her website. She needs to get something done about that. Those pictures are over ten years old, so seeing her in person always gives clients a shock straight off the bat, and then they have to waste time getting over their bewilderment as discreetly as possible, just as she has to every morning in front of the mirror. Age struck with the abruptness of a landslide, and Bee would give almost anything to experience again what it feels like to please people with her face alone. Now their eyes flit awkwardly, searching for a place to rest. *Beauty is in the eye of the beer holder!* Pauline liked to say (when she was in that mood). Bee still doesn't know who she was quoting.

'Come on over here,' she says, patting the cushion beside her.

Pita snorts enthusiastically, kicking her forelegs like a fat little dressage pony.

'Stay where you are then, you silly dog,' Bee mutters, pouring until the liquid reaches the brim and spills over. She swears under her breath and leans forward, putting her lips to the glass, which, now she comes to think of it, was Hudson's favourite. The diamond glass, he called it, and he pestered her to let him drink from it even though it was so small you were constantly having to refill it. Hudson, whom Bee hasn't seen for nearly six months. He's a good boy, a good boy down to the bone, and although he was never hers, she misses him.

She slurps until it's safe to lift the glass and carry out the opposite manoeuvre: rim brought to mouth. Then she tips her head back and drains it.

'Aaah,' she gasps, and has to stop herself slamming it down on the table as though it were a bar, as though a buttoned-up bartender were standing on the other side, ready to lend an ear to a stream of complaints, to the endless string of examples that prove she isn't good for anything.

But there's no one there.

No one, her mind sings, no one, no one.

She refills her glass, drinks and, after briefly haggling with herself, knocks it back in two.

It is what it is. And, as she sometimes says when things don't go according to plan, clairvoyance isn't accounting. There are no guarantees in this business. Her job is to hear the unsaid, to sense what's no more than a vibration. Thought as light as a moth . . . But this time she hadn't had the chance to trot out the usual mollifying explanations. The woman had been hell-bent on getting out of there as quickly as possible.

'My dad?' she'd said, jumping to her feet. 'Not a chance. I'm not remotely interested in talking to him. Make him go away!'

Like he was some poisonous creepy-crawly.

'No, that wasn't very popular, was it, Pita, eh?'

The dog has curled up and fallen asleep in her basket. She's breathing heavily through her constricted nostrils, and the sound is reassuring.

'My baby,' she says, suddenly placated, almost touched.

The woman was beautiful, actually, thinks Bee, albeit clinging to the very outermost branches of the tree of youth. Soon they'd no longer hold her weight, and she too would drop.

And things had gone downhill from there, pretty much.

He'd seemed so bloody cocksure, so totally assured of his right to be there. His attitude had fooled her. It's rare for someone to simply come straight through like that. Usually there's a crackle on the line, and she has to sort things out and prick up her ears and fine-tune the signal, but not with this guy. He'd been standing right next to her. Bee had been able to smell him (smoky vanilla and something else she couldn't put her finger on . . . something chilly, pollen-like), and then – directly counter to her client's instructions – she'd let him in.

She shouldn't have done that, of course.

She can see that now.

The woman had made herself perfectly clear: I want to speak to my mother.

He'd been there like a shot the moment Bee opened the channel. It was, she thinks as she pours her third glass, as though he'd been lying in wait. She sinks back into the sturdy embrace of the sofa.

From that point on, things had happened fast.

'My *mom*, I said. Nobody else.'

'I can't quite sense her – it's like he's blocking the way. The channel's pretty narrow, you see, but I'm sure if we invite him in he'll make way for—'

At that she'd actually laughed. A harsh laugh, Bee thinks now.

'Make way? You don't know my dad.'

Bee puts out her hand and switches on the lamp, a gift from Pauline, bought at Christie's at the start of their relationship for a sum she's repressed. Purely because she'd expressed admiration for a similar lamp in the window at Coup d'État, the place run by that dreadful snob (they had refused to support him). Fantailed goldfish, blue and indifferent, circle the porcelain base, and outside the weather has cleared up. Bee has no idea what time it is – it could be anything between two and seven.

She shuts her eyes and the room vanishes, replaced by a delicious orange darkness. The trembling sensation is ebbing away. Normally it passes more quickly, but it was hard to shut down properly with all the ruckus in the room. The client wouldn't let her finish the job, and she had been obliged to stuff him hastily back, the way you shove a mess higgledy-piggledy into the wardrobe five minutes before your guests arrive.

No, the session had certainly not been up to her professional standards. When all is said and done, she's proud of her abilities as a serious practitioner of a generally despised and misunderstood trade. Despite what certain people claim on *certain* forums online, she isn't a fraud. She isn't out to exploit anyone's vulnerability. When there's contact, there's contact. That's all. She has stopped wishing people understood.

Here's a reason to love Pauline: she had no interest in 'proof'.

And, swiftly, a reason not to: Pauline has stopped loving Bee.

I wonder what he did? thinks Bee. Usually they're only that insistent when they're feeling remorseful about something.

Her eyes still clamped shut, she finishes her drink, then slumps on to her side and draws her knees up to her chest.

A few minutes later she's fast asleep.

The bump makes Pita open one toad-like eye. From her basket she can't see the glass, which has landed in the deep pile of the carpet, only Bee's hand, hanging limply off the sofa's edge.

2

Sidsel

The feeling that's been bothering her over the past day or two makes sense at last. Sidsel observes the thread-like creature wriggling in the toilet bowl, one and a half centimetres long, with disgust and increasing fascination. It's quarter past two, and there's nothing to be done. The pharmacies won't be open till morning. If she's got threadworms, then so has Laura, and if Laura has threadworms, then she's not the only one in her class. It'll be like that time with the lice, a democratic plague that brought prohibitions and warnings, and finally separated the sheep from the goats during the treatment phase (who's combing *every* night?). Everybody had them, and the ones who didn't have them got them, and the ones who'd had them got them again, or maybe never got rid of them in the first place. Grown women braided their hair into French plaits, and Sidsel envied the mothers who wore theirs under tight, elegant headscarves. On the other hand, she can't imagine Esther's mother having threadworms, or Ibrahim's dad, who's tall and smells nice and speaks so earnestly even when he says very ordinary things, like good morning and goodbye. Ibrahim's dad, who right now will be sleeping next to Ibrahim's mum, while Sidsel is sleepless and alone in her bathroom, thirty-two years old with worms up her arse.

Is she really that bad at remembering to wash her hands?

Bacteria don't scare her. Never have.

While she was on maternity leave with Laura, Sidsel had carried a bottle of hand sanitiser everywhere she went, because that's what the rest of her mums' group had done. She'd never used it, and her changing bag had smelled of limoncello for ages after the cap broke off. She'd stopped boiling the dummies after only the first month; she just stuck them into her own mouth, and if there was sand on them she spat it out.

She reads online that the adult worm embeds itself in the first part of the large intestine, where it is loosely attached to the mucous membrane. Pregnant worms crawl through the anus on to the surrounding skin, where they can lay up to 10,000 eggs. This often happens at night.

Sidsel puts the phone on the edge of the sink and flushes.

There it is again. The sensation that a person is writing with a fine-nib pen on the inside of her rectum, embroidering on a teeny-tiny pillow.

Fetching a chair from the kitchen, she climbs up, pulls her knickers down around her knees and spreads her cheeks in the mirror. From this angle, wrong-side-out and glistening, her arsehole looks like an organ, like something that should be much deeper inside the body. She kneads her palms either side, opening it even more. When she sees something, a glimmer of white, she lets go with her right hand and jabs her finger in. It's cold and dry, and it hurts. She won't catch anything that way, obviously. She washes her hands again, first with soap, then with washing-up liquid, before she goes back to bed and tries to cry with eyes that feel like two sun-baked stones, because more than anything else, this is stupid.

Next morning Laura is excited.

'What's *this* doing in here?' she calls from the bathroom, louder, because Sidsel didn't answer the first time.

'I used it yesterday,' she yells, rolling up the blind. It's still raining, and on the other side of the street the lights are off in all the windows except the one that doesn't count. The old man with the geranium and the red candles always leaves a single lamp lit overnight. It's only just gone six, and Sidsel has slept a total of four hours. A headache flicks through the left side of her skull and all the way down to her hand as she bends over to pull on her jeans.

'But I can't get round it!' whines Laura cheerfully.

'Then move it,' says Sidsel. 'No, hang on. Leave it, I'm coming.'

'Were you trying to reach something?' asks Laura when Sidsel is back in the bathroom. Her thick dark hair has come loose during the night and is hanging down over her face. Sidsel can't remember when they discovered that Laura didn't need a stepstool any more but could jump up by herself. Finding a hairband, she gathers Laura's hair into a high ponytail.

'No, don't want a bun. Braids.' Laura shakes her head violently.

'We'll do them later,' says Sidsel. 'After breakfast. Laur, I need to ask you something—'

The girl looks up at her, sensitive to the change in her mother's tone. Like many children, she has this seismographic capability.

'Have you noticed anything in your bottom? Anything itchy?'

Laura thinks.

'No, nothing like that.'

'Not yesterday, when you were going to bed?'

'No.'

'All right, call me when you've finished.'

'You promised to do braids.'

'After breakfast, I told you. Give me a shout, don't flush.'

'Why not?'

'Because I need to check something.'

Sidsel actually goes so far as to poke at the poo with a chopstick she finds in the kitchen drawer, but there's nothing to see. Laura is hopping up and down behind her, elated by all the twists and turns the morning has already had to offer. First a chair in the middle of the bathroom, and now this: her mother hunched over the toilet, hunting for something secret in her poop!

With a grunt, Sidsel tosses the chopstick into the shower

cubicle and peels off the plastic glove. Sometimes she's glad that it's just her and Laura after all – that there are no witnesses to these dark and jumbled mornings.

There are eight numbers before hers, and as she waits among the shelves she keeps thinking of more things she needs: deodorant, heel cream, Decubal for Laura's cheeks, vitamin pills – why the hell aren't they taking those already? At least. And cleansing milk. For ages she's settled for water and a flannel, but a routine would do her skin good. Cleanse, tone, moisturise; and a wide headband to hold the hair back from her face.

When the pharmacist has totted up all her items, it's such a struggle to hide her dismay at the price that Sidsel nearly forgets the pills.

'Oh, and I also need something for threadworms.'

'It's Ovex you need, then. For how many people?'

'One child and one adult.'

'Right.'

He's typing in a very businesslike manner, thank goodness.

'And there are no other adults in the household?'

Sidsel hasn't thought about that.

'Basically, everybody who has regular access to a household with threadworms needs to take the medication. Otherwise you'll just end up cross-infecting each other and you'll have to start again from scratch.'

Cross-infecting.

'Right,' says Sidsel. 'I understand. That wouldn't be very good.'

'So just two then? A child and an adult?'

'Give me three. Two adults and one child.'

'Sure,' says the pharmacist, sniffing contentedly. 'And just be extra careful about hygiene, and make sure you wash your bedding and towels regularly for a while. Might also be a good idea to cut your nails short' – he holds up his own hand – 'because the eggs get underneath and transfer to your mouth, and then the whole rigmarole starts up again.'

She doesn't remember the paracetamol – which should have been carrying her along on a light, numbing cushion – until she's locking her bike to the iron railing outside the museum. Oh well, no help for it now. On the other side of the road, a narrow strip of lawn separates the staff entrance from the pavement. Usually, letting herself in through the oak door – with a seasoned nod to the glass security booth – gives her a special kind of thrill, even after six months, but not today. She's late, and her frustration overwhelms everything else. Inside the lobby, Sidsel takes off her rainproof trousers and runs a hand through her hair, which is short and dark blonde. It never went back to normal after the pregnancy, and on her hairdresser's recommendation she chopped it off a few years back. She's come to like the hardness the cut gives her face because, unlike her siblings, Sidsel hasn't inherited her father's features. Her skin is pale and sensitive, running to softness along the jaw. There's no trace of his cheekbones, his chiselled Cupid's bow or broad, straight nose; instead, she has their mother's personability. People have always *liked* Sidsel. She puts them at ease, unlike her siblings, who both – though for different reasons – take more getting used to.

Avoiding the mirror in the cloakroom, Sidsel hurries towards the workshop, where she should have been ages ago.

'Sidsel!'

Vera is hanging over the banister, looking down at her. They're around the same age, and Sidsel gave up competing with her the moment they met. Today, the art historian is wearing a mandarin-coloured turtleneck and a suede skirt that would have made Sidsel look like she'd gone temporarily nuts.

'Birthe asked me to find you. She wants a word with you about something.'

'Did she say what?' asks Sidsel, following Vera to the first floor. Birthe has never asked her up to her office before.

'Not really,' says Vera, ushering her down the corridor and through an open door.

Sidsel places the bag from the pharmacy on the floor and smiles at the two women on the sofa. One is Birthe Käszner, curator of the museum's collection of antiquities, and the other introduces herself as Jeanette. Sidsel recognises the henna-dyed braid and bejewelled scrunchie from the cafeteria.

'Excellent,' says Birthe, nodding towards the empty chair opposite. 'Take a seat.'

The room smells of cardamom, at once new and old, but mostly just pleasant. At one point it was at least twice the size, but cuts have meant that most administrative areas have been subdivided into smaller and smaller chunks. Even so, there's still something effortlessly majestic about the office: the walls are painted with mustard-yellow distemper, and the ceiling's got to be about five yards high. Sidsel rarely finds herself on the first floor. All contact with the staff goes through Nana, the head conservator and Sidsel's boss. It's only Vera she speaks to day to day, when they're down in the courtyard for a smoke. Otherwise Sidsel concentrates on her statues, her stones and reliefs. On the table between them is a Thermos and a stack of cups, but nobody makes a move to use them.

'Have you spoken to Nana?'

Sidsel shakes her head.

'Fine,' says Birthe, 'I'll make this brief. There's been an accident at the British Museum involving one of our Syrian busts. I'm not quite sure what actually happened, whether a visitor managed to bump into it or whether it was a mistake on their conservators' part, but the upshot is that there's a chip in the Beauty of Palmyra. They rang yesterday, absolutely beside themselves. Never happened before in the history of the museum, they say. They don't want to do anything until we get there, for insurance reasons. But obviously it doesn't look great having it covered up in the middle of their exhibition, so they're pretty desperate to get someone out there. And that was when we thought of you.'

'What about Nana?'

'It's not possible for Nana to go.'

Birthe is not unfriendly, but her manner makes Sidsel feel like a babbling amateur.

'I spoke to her yesterday,' continues the curator, 'and she's happy to send you in her stead. As I understand it, you already have quite a thorough knowledge of the collection?'

Sidsel nods. 'I wrote my thesis on alternative methods of conserving eroded sandstone. I used one from storage as a case study.'

In the weeks before she handed in her dissertation, the Palmyrans' confident stone faces had begun to haunt her dreams, and although it had been a relief to finish, the thought of being that close to the most beautiful of them all made Sidsel's heart thud eagerly underneath her blouse.

'Anyway, if you'd be up for going,' says Birthe, 'you'll set off tomorrow afternoon, and most likely be back home sometime on Sunday.'

The British Museum. London.

She can't.

Sidsel has already leaned too heavily on her friends these last couple of months. When Laura was younger, she didn't mind asking for a little of the time they had in such abundance, but now that they're busy with their own children and jobs and renovation projects, she shrinks from the thought.

Vera, who has lingered in the office out of curiosity, is fidgeting uneasily behind her, and Sidsel realises what's just happened: the management are giving her a chance here. They're taking her out and shining a light on her. It's unexpected, and maybe nobody knows why it's turned out like this. Nana doesn't praise her, but on the other hand she's never expressed dissatisfaction with her work. Now it seems she trusts her.

'I'd love to,' says Sidsel, feeling her head bob up and down long after it should have stopped.

'Great. You're working on the hippopotamus at the moment, aren't you?'

'Yes,' she says, feeling them again. *Enterobius vermicularis.* The embarrassingly pronounced tickle.

'Well, that's not going anywhere in a hurry,' Birthe says, and starts talking about the exhibition, which – apart from the accident – is apparently a smash hit. Through the window Sidsel can see out across the wet chestnut trees, and beyond them the loops of the rollercoaster in the amusement park and the occasional dark red train whizzing along the track. There are only a few riders, their hair whipping around in the dank spring air, and their screams don't reach them in the office.

Of course she can't just pick up and go to London this weekend.

What is she thinking?

Why does she always make things so difficult for herself?

Tie tight knots that she then has to undo?

'The nuts and bolts,' says Birthe, 'the security clearances and so on, you'll go through all that with Jeanette. I don't think I mentioned this, but Jeanette is our registrar. That means she's responsible for the procedural aspects of museum business here and abroad. Insurance, customs, transport, that sort of thing.'

'All the boring stuff,' says the woman in a hoarse voice

whose blue-collar Copenhagen timbre instantly captures Sidsel's heart, 'the paper-pushing. So if you're the one we're sending, then the two of us need to put our heads together at some point today. But for now you'll have to excuse me, ladies. There are some very insistent Frenchmen trying to get in touch with me, I see.' She holds up her phone.

Vera gives a small wave and follows the registrar out.

Their departure leaves Sidsel and Birthe alone with one another and the unfamiliar situation. The sun breaks through the clouds, and the window throws patterns of shadow on the floor, narrow dark blue lines and crosses that are gone a moment later. Sidsel answers questions. Inside she's counting down from a big number – it's an old trick for getting through situations like this. She should just spit it out. Get it over with.

The Golden Tower at Tivoli has risen slowly upwards, plummeted down and hoisted itself halfway up again four times before Birthe lets her go. In the corridor outside she bumps into Vera, who hurries off with an excuse about needing the toilet. Sidsel feels sorry for her, but still – if this is the first time in her life that Vera has felt like the least important person in the room, then it's not a moment too soon.

Later that day, Sidsel is in a better mood. Whatever happens, it's a good thing they asked her. The medication is working, the itch is subsiding, and Vera has turned out to be less mean-spirited than Sidsel had feared. Though she hasn't hidden her surprise, it seems she's genuinely pleased on her behalf.

'It shows they've got tons of confidence in you,' she'd said when they'd gone into the courtyard to smoke after lunch. 'Just imagine if it was a visitor who knocked it over. Shit, and the Beauty as well!' And then she'd laughed and shown her missing back tooth and wide tongue, and Sidsel felt bad for having judged her too harshly. The more she thinks about it, the more she wishes that both of them could go. They're sort of friends by now, after all: it could be a girls' trip. Sidsel hasn't been on one since having Laura. Once they've finished at the museum for the afternoon they could grab a beer and ogle passing men, and maybe open up to one another. Maybe form a bond strong enough that Sidsel, her chest warmed by the Guinness, would decide to tell Vera about her last visit to the city nearly six years earlier: about how she'd walked across the university hall with Laura in a sling, legs shaking and stomach writhing in spastic cramps. She could tell her about the thirty irresolute minutes spent on a padded bench in the faculty corridor before the dash back out into the rain, about taking the Tube to the hotel, fetching her suitcase from her room and asking the receptionist to book a taxi to the airport. Sidsel still doesn't know what she'd thought would happen if she'd taken the final steps to his office and knocked. If without a word she'd opened her jacket and let him see the child's thick brown hair.

Sidsel jumps when there's a knock. Hardly anybody visits the workshop. It's tucked away, accessed only through the courtyard, so if people want something they usually send an email and ask one of them to come up.

'Come in,' says Sidsel, turning in her chair to face the door. In her right hand she's still holding the makeshift swab that moments earlier was being dabbed carefully inside the hippo's red marble nostrils. The sculpture will be loaned to the Getty Museum in Los Angeles soon enough, and it's Sidsel's job to make sure it's transport-ready. As the weeks have passed, she's come to be fond of the big animal, of its stocky fat legs and oversized snout (it's unlikely the sculptory ever saw a live example). The thought of it being packed up and flown across the Atlantic makes her uneasy. It was made to be part of a fountain. Hollow tunnels run from its mouth into its body, making it far more fragile than its compact red form would suggest. It makes her happy turning up each morning to find it standing in the dim light, its right front leg raised in greeting.

Jeanette coughs, and Sidsel hurriedly moves her handbag and shopping off the other free chair.

'Do you have five minutes?' asks Jeanette, still standing. 'Because I don't really think Birthe explained things properly before. It's not just the sculpture you're dealing with here. If you go, you'll be representing the museum in London. Handling curators, managers, the conservators at the British Museum – you'll be the one in charge. Think about it this way: objects can't talk. They can't tell you if they're all right, if they're being looked after properly, if the right measures are being taken. While you're there, you'll be their voice. Your job is to listen to them and make their case. Do you follow?'

Jeanette is watching Sidsel. Her eyes, which are small and bright lavender-blue, are tightly edged with eyeliner.

Sidsel nods.

'You're being quiet as a mouse. Does it make sense, what I'm saying? I just think it would be a shame if you went there thinking you'd been given some cushy job. Birthe can sometimes be a little abrupt.'

'It makes sense,' says Sidsel.

'Is there something wrong? No offence, but you look a bit down in the mouth.'

'It's just finding someone to look after my daughter, really. It's only the two of us,' Sidsel says. 'This weekend,' she adds, and is disgusted with herself.

'How old is she?'

'She turned six in December.'

'She doesn't have any sprightly grandparents who could step into the breach?'

'Not really,' says Sidsel.

Normally she has slicker answers prepared for these questions, but Jeanette has a disarming sort of face.

'My parents are dead,' she says, 'and the others live in England. I'm not in touch with them.'

'Damn. Well, I see the problem.' Jeanette sticks out her bottom jaw and nods. 'You know what, Sidsel? I can just tell Birthe it won't work this time. We'll figure out something else, don't you worry. It was only because Nana seemed so keen it should be you that we thought it might be a good opportunity—'

'I'd like to go.'

Once she's said it, she knows how true it is. Knows it with her whole body. She really wants it to happen. She wants to take the metro to the airport and board the plane. She wants to walk the streets she recognises from before. She wants to be alone a while. To sleep in.

'Okay, then you're going to London. Shall we leave it there for now? Once you've found a solution you come to me and we'll set things in motion.'

Jeanette gives her an encouraging smile.

'Okay,' says Sidsel, feeling tears tug at the skin beneath her eyes. 'Thanks.'

'Of course. Now, why don't you get back to your hippo.'

Above the courtyard the clouds are packed tight, and the room seems very dark despite all the glass. When she can't hear footsteps any longer, Sidsel grabs her cigarettes and pulls a long cardigan somebody's forgotten on a peg over her own jumper. The courtyard reeks of cooking from the cafeteria. A chef jogs down the steps with a stack of empty plastic containers and puts them down without paying her any attention. She smokes and forgets to enjoy it. A few droplets fall on her wrist; she settles underneath the arch and before long it's raining heavily.

Sidsel lights another cigarette – she's freezing. Her breath hangs in the air before her face. Winter is refusing to let go this year.

3

Niels

'On my way home,' says Niels, biting off the other mitten. He's stopped like she asked. Now he gets off his bike and leans it against the park fence. His eyes are narrowed impatiently as he listens to his sister's voice. Even though he's not doing anything – one hand on the saddle, letting her speak – he radiates the kind of raw energy that enables someone to lie down and go to sleep on a bench in any city in any country and wake up the next morning untouched and with all his belongings intact. It's like the world gives him a wide and curious berth. Niels, who knows nothing else and has never doubted this rock-like quality in himself, has found everything around him rickety and indecisive by comparison. He has grown without leaning on the supports and trellises offered. The result is a person tougher than most his age, more solid in structure, and more alone.

There are a few solitary tourists in the park. In places the grass is flooded with rainwater. Last summer he'd lain here with Linn, among the rhododendron bushes and dried seagull shit. Linn, with her big, sunburnt hands and her roller skates. Linn, whom he hasn't seen since December, when he lost . . . or just kind of stopped . . . well, at some point he simply hadn't wanted to give her anything, let alone pretend like he did. Her anxieties bored him, and before long he wasn't much interested in her dreams and fantasies either, or in the details of things – she found it easy to take pleasure in those, much easier than in the whole image, which always let her down in the end. If he concentrates, he can remember her skin: smooth and damp across her shoulders, dry on her upper arms. In summer, in the yellow grass and with the sun above them, she'd tasted pleasantly of the ice cream they'd shared, and she'd cried about something he'd said but had been all right again, the way she always was, swaggering and merry. Where she'd spread out her blanket there's now a long, gravy-coloured puddle, treetops mirrored in its velvety surface. He gazes at the trembling reflection of black branches and the sky beyond, listening to Sidsel. Her voice is harassed and maundering, and it's getting on his nerves.

'What did you want to ask?'

Sidsel inhales.

'Niels, what's that racket? What are you doing?'

He turns around. They're coming down Gothersgade, under the pepper-grey clouds.

'It's the Royal Guards.'

'Can't you move away from them a bit?'

'Not really worth it. It'll be over in a minute.'

The boys have hard, thin mouths, and their noses point

dead ahead. He tries to tell one from another, but it's difficult when they all look so equally stupid. Straps hiding chins, cheeks red on white, plagued by eczema and acne. The wind flattens and ruffles the fur on their bearskins, separating it into partings. Their knees jerk up, up, up, up. The sound of their feet falls in step with the flute and its brief, jarring notes. The melody climbs to hysterical heights and tumbles into a valley, before immediately setting back off for the summit.

'Don't hang up, okay? I'll wait until they've passed.'

He lowers the phone. At the sight of the idiotic procession, the last bit of happiness is wrung out of him. It should depress everybody that something so irrelevant has been allowed to start up again. All those blue trousers that have to be sewn, those new jackets, the effort of buying boots and hats, of recruiting the boys. It's the lack of imagination that bothers him. The priggish inanity. They march in a sweetish fug of decorum, mixed with the rank stench of self-satisfaction. His hands are freezing. He needs a piss. He hasn't eaten since last night, or slept enough in several weeks. And now this, these fucking halfwits.

'Yes?' he says.

'You were the one who was saying something.'

'I asked you what you wanted to ask.'

He can hear how harsh that sounds. It wasn't meant that way. She hesitates, then speaks:

'There's been an accident with one of our loans, and they want me to take a look. Problem is, the bust is in London. If I go, it has to be tomorrow, plus the weekend. I thought about taking Laura with me, but I don't think there's much point. It wouldn't be fun for either of us.'

She's been gabbling, and now she falls silent. She still hasn't said what she wants to say, what she *really* wants to say, but she's too old for a helping hand. It's only when she's plucked up the courage to ask him point blank that he says yes, without reservation.

'Are you sure? It's two whole days.'

He can hear her relief. The tension has left her voice like a dog slipping through a gate.

'Of course. I'm honoured.'

'Oh, Niels, thank you, thank you so much. It so lovely of you to agree to this. I'll tell Jeanette straight away. Is that okay?'

'Like I said, sure.'

He doesn't ask who Jeanette is. Sidsel's gratitude is making him uneasy. Had she expected him to say no? When this trip obviously means so much to her? Once she's finished thanking him, she immediately turns practical and invites him over that evening so they can 'come up with a plan'. The expression irritates him, but he bites back his annoyance.

'Could you be there at seven? Then you can hang out a bit before she goes to bed. She's still talking about playing Monopoly with Uncle Niels.'

'I'm happy to play whatever capitalist board games the child wants.'

Sidsel laughs giddily and thanks him again.

Then they hang up.

Far away, the march is still floating above the soup of noise. Niels lets the distance absorb it fully before he pulls on his mittens and picks up his bike, glancing around for a gate or a back courtyard where he can empty his bladder without spoiling anyone's day.

Niels whips down Gothersgade, crosses the bridge and turns on to the gravel path by the lakes, his back wheel spattering mud. The best things in life are often pretty simple: accelerating, and knowing with each revolution that he can press on. That today is one of those days where there is no bottom to him, and no upper bound.

A few weeks ago, awaking with the same sensation, he walked just over twelve miles, south out of the city and back again, because his legs had wanted to, and because it was needed. Niels doesn't delude himself that he's immune. He loses his sense of proportion every now and then, contending with the same undignified pitfalls as everyone else, the same petty concerns about where he's going to stay and what he's going to live on. What – to use a lax turn of phrase – is *going to become of him*. It's that urge to be buckled into a seat and handed a colouring book and a pack of juicy felt-tip pens. It's middle-classness, plain and simple, which diverts attention from the real like an existential lightning rod, offering quilted warmth and arithmetic in its place. He's lucky: usually he spots rising weakness in himself in time to react. On the walk out of the city he had cast it off; he had stood stripped once more before existence, tender-skinned and pure, ready to scratch and claw at reality, while the ties that bound him to conventional thought seemed more illusory than ever. Uplifted by this new lightness, he had thrown his arms wide and walked cross-shaped, suffused, along the edge of the road. After only a minute or two a car had pulled up alongside him, and the woman had rolled her window halfway down to ask if everything was all right. She was caught off guard by her own softness of heart, and Niels felt like scaring her, but resisted. There was an acquired strictness to her face that he liked. Definitely a teacher of some kind. Hell yeah, he answered. All good with *you*? The woman nodded, a flurry of quick little nods behind the glass, which glided up and into place with a tight *shoop*. He kept waving both arms until the car turned the corner. On the ride home he stopped at the harbour. He ordered meatballs with pickles and a beer at the sailing-club cafeteria, then found a table by the window. Four elderly men with knobbled faces and the stiff hair of alcoholics noted his presence but did not approach him. He was left to eat and drink in peace. No one felt the need to say a word. The unfamiliar was no better than the familiar. No grander. Why point it out? They were fishermen. Between them, invisible, hovered something that kept them connected. Like a herd of animals, they seemed to communicate via charged silences, shifting stares and low grunts. He couldn't take his eyes off the men, and all at once it dawned on him that he loved them. That was the emotion he was feeling. Niels chuckled behind his bottle. He had to keep it to himself, of course, but throughout the meal the secret lit him from within. He glowed, Niels Gabel, sitting there contented as a pumpkin. After the meal he left without a word to the men, without even glancing in their direction, and made his way down to the waterside for a smoke, his legs hanging over the edge of the dock. It was a clear day, cold as bone, but he was dressed for it. For reasons neither wholly principled nor wholly practical but a mishmash of both, Niels owns very few items of clothing. He is, however, quite picky when it comes to fabric. Pure wool or linen; a silk shirt or two for special occasions. The tomato-red hat, and the scarf that shines green as a duck's throat if the light falls on it right. The bridge that day had been crisp in the plain, frosty air, and he could count the cars as they crossed over the fairway. He had assumed it was spring – that oncoming warmth he had sensed like coiled metal in his chest – but he was wrong: in the middle of April, after a few weeks' break, the frost had returned in the night, and he'd had to bring out his thermals and shell jacket again.

It's still cold. The plants are hard and withdrawn in their beds at the park, but there's something else, too . . . he noticed it last night, when he was out putting up posters. A smell of onions rising from the earth, and in the buds on the beech hedges, barely distinguishable from the smooth branches, the leaves crouched like guests at a surprise party. Probably wouldn't take more than two or three properly sunny days for everything to crack open with a downy *toot*. But right now it's raining, or it's started raining again, first in spatters, but then with real determination. A chilly, slanting rain that beats against his cheeks and forehead. Niels slows down and tugs his jacket up around his neck with one hand. Crossing the Triangle, he presses on northwards along soulless Østerbrogade.

He didn't say anything about Saturday, and if it doesn't occur to Sidsel then he sees no reason to bring it up tonight. By now Niels thinks of their aunt as his own personal problem. Sidsel gave up a long time ago, and Ea is out of the picture. He's had the presents lying around for months. Efie is getting a salt lamp and a bottle of port. She's got no intention of quitting, so she might as well drink something decent.

No. He's not asking anyone's permission.

As he cycles through Hellerup, he can smell the rotted dragon's breath of the sea. He's hot now, the woollen thermals sticking to his lower back, and he can hear himself in his ears. The pulse is regular and joyless as a church bell.

*

Charlotte

We've agreed to keep our distance.

Neither of us fancies a performance from the shadow puppets of our past.

Some way away from me, half-hidden in the steam leaching from the membrane, Troels is walking with his hands deep in his jacket pockets and his shoulders hunched, like he's thinking or investigating something important.

We've already established that neither of us knows how we ended up here, or how we get out.

Is he humming?

He's humming.

I catch a few scattered notes, but never enough to reconstruct the tune.

Out of habit I start glaring furiously at his leather-jacketed back and flat arse. I strain until my eyes feel like lumps of ice and my mouth like a burning bush.

Hey, I yell, keep a lid on it, will you?

4

Ea

On the way upstairs, she prays that Hector isn't home. This has nothing to do with him – Ea just needs to be alone. Shaken by her visit to Beatrice Wallens, she drove straight to Patti and Afshin's house in Inverness. She told them what had happened, and afterwards they ate some food cooked by Afshin, good as always, and shared two bottles of wine. Patti called clairvoyance a load of late-capitalist horseshit, and they drank to that. The two of them had seemed happy and in love, although only a few weeks earlier Patti had been talking about leaving him. With a dark look she had confided to Ea that she was struggling to want him still. She focused on the parts of his body she liked most. Chopped him up into little pieces so she could enjoy the act. Yet the memory of that conversation had not made the evening any less fun, and Ea had ended up spending the night. The older she gets, the more other people's relationships confuse her. She took a picture of Afshin making up the bed for her in the spare room and sent it to Hector. He replied immediately, asking her to say hello. Patti had come in and kissed her on the forehead with her cool mouth, saying, Promise me you'll forget all about it. It's bullshit, we all agree. Complete and utter bullshit designed to separate people from their money.

Remember, it was Sand who recommended her.

You know Sand, Ea.

She laps that shit up.

I just wish she'd stop forcing her perverse inclinations on to other people. I'm surprised you fell for it.

Ea nodded, as though to say *me too*.

But when she woke up this morning, it was still there. It?

A fidget in her body. A nasty buzzing dot behind her forehead. She lay listening to their getting-ready-for-the-day noises and smiled politely when Patti stuck her head around the door, said goodbye and asked her one more time to forget 'the whole thing'.

It's quiet in the apartment. Ea slips off her sandals by the mat and waits, palms against the wall in the corridor, which she decided to paint a few weeks ago. She's pleased with the result, and it makes her happy every time she comes home. Just as she had pictured, the dusty orange looks great with the ivory edging around the door frame and the skirting boards.

'Hector?'

Silence. So they did go out today, then.

Ea drinks a glass of guava juice before walking into the bedroom and flinging herself on to the bed. The pillowcase smells pleasantly of his hair: a mouldy, melonish scent.

Through the double doors she can see into the living room; she can see the sun snag on the bits of dust and fluff under the table, making them glint. She'll take care of that tonight, when they're there to see. Ea doesn't mind being the one who does the cleaning, but she makes sure to remind them that the work isn't done by discreet elves while they're out. She tries to approach the chores with a cheery ease, to set an example for Coco. The girl is a slob, and has inherited her father's fondness for objects: tiny figurines, parts of things, bits and pieces. The first time Ea saw the place she felt like she was walking into a messy, grubby version of one of those stores that specialise in kitsch and knick-knacks. There was nowhere for the eye to rest, no quiet plane. The wooden floorboards peeped out between trampled rugs and woven plastic mats, the walls bulged with Coco's drawings and Polaroids, and the fruit was growing fur in bowls. Books competed for space on the shelves with glass skulls, wizened hanging plants and tennis trophies. The floor was covered with everything there wasn't space for elsewhere, heaped into swaying piles that toppled every so often with a whoosh.

Ever since Ea moved in she's been mucking it out, carefully, one room at a time. She doesn't want to cause offence, but it was impossible for her to feel at home in the shambles that had engulfed the two of them. With Hector's reluctant permission, she had filled one trash bag after another, and what she didn't throw out she gave away or sold for cheap. She mopped the floor several times, sent the rugs to the cleaner's, emptied drawers and changed dented lampshades; she cleaned out Cashew's terrarium and bought him a hollow piece of wood at a pet shop. The lizard showed no sign of gratitude. Still, as she had hoped, buried underneath the grease and dust and all the bric-a-brac was a two-bedroom flat with high ceilings, bay windows and original features dating back to the late nineteenth century. They'd never be able to afford anything like it, except that Hector has been on the lease since 1993. They're incredibly lucky to live where they live, what with their jobs and non-jobs and the stuff in between. In the last year or two, the rent has gone up by several hundred bucks, but that's nothing compared with the rest of the city. When she hears what people are paying for their basement rooms, she's shocked. Property prices on this part of the West Coast are absurd. The tech boom has driven up the cost of housing to the point where hardly anyone can keep pace, and in the last few years, tent encampments have sprung up in several places in the Mission and the area around Market Street. Miserable improvised cities within a city. People make love and sleep and shit and quarrel and die there, because they have no place else to do it. Ea read somewhere that more than eighty per cent of America's homeless live in California, attracted by the long summers and mild winters. Many of those Ea saw when she arrived nearly ten years ago have moved on. To Albany, Piedmont, Mountain View.

San Francisco isn't a place where people grow up.

That's what Bianca had said before she sold the shop and moved to Portland. Ea had found the comment tasteless, but now she's starting to worry she was right. There's an air of the enchanted funfair about the city – maybe that's what her friend had meant? This summer Ea will turn thirty-five, and although she assured Patti and Afshin that her visit to the medium wasn't an age thing, that's exactly what it was.

An age thing.

A death thing.

Lately, Ea has been more afraid of making bad decisions. She has this constant, oppressive sense that the years are arranged like a funnel, and that the widest, most open part of her life is behind her.

If only someone could tell her what the best thing is, the right thing, and how to get there.

Some days that's how she thinks.

And then she'd bumped into Sand, and Sand had seemed uncharacteristically well-balanced, chattering about her visit to Beatrice Wallens in a way that made it sound less desperate than it felt a few weeks later, when Ea found herself holding a cup of mint tea in the medium's oddly empty living room with a view over Buena Vista Park.

Is there anyone in particular you'd like to get in touch with?

She was surprised how clearly the urge had arisen. Like thirst: powerful and impossible to ignore.

My mother, she had said. I'd like to speak to my mother.

Face to face with this woman who claimed she could channel the spirits, Ea had been gripped by a suffocating longing she had thought was ancient history. It felt like someone had stuck a ladle into her guts and was stirring round and round and round.

Your mother . . .

Beatrice had sat quite still, leaning forward slightly, her mouth open. Her eyes were fixed on a point eighteen inches to the right of Ea.

The memory of what happened next fills her with unease, a mild dread smeared thin across her body.

Hector has left the living-room window open. A draught is making the hanging chair with the peacock-green cushions turn slowly on its chain. There's a piece of paper in the typewriter – from here it looks blank. Every morning he writes a poem and puts it in Coco's lunchbox.

Ea rolls on to her side, pulling the bedclothes with her.

The smell.

If it hadn't been for that, she could easily have dismissed the whole thing, shrugging off Beatrice as the fraud she almost certainly is. But how could she have imagined a smell? It had filled the room in an instant.

Eau Sauvage.

The cologne was unmistakable; and beneath it, the cool leather and the packet of yellow Bali Shag.

The smell of her father coming home after a long day.

Beatrice had been unambiguous: a man, not a woman, early fifties, possibly a bit older, quite tall, dark hair. Perhaps a beard, was that right? Did he wear jewellery?

Maybe her mother simply couldn't cope any more? Maybe she didn't care.

The thought of Charlotte's posthumous rejection hurts, and in an attempt to shake off the pain, she repeats Patti's words of yesterday, mimicking the self-assured, indignant tone.

'Spiritual claptrap. Late-capitalist bullshit. Money machines.'

It really does help.

Ea looks down at her body: legs sticking out of denim cut-offs, knees, the veins on her thighs obvious in the morning light. On the bedside table are the flowers she picked yesterday, their silken lilac muzzles already beginning to sag: four tired ruminants resting their heads against the rim of the jam jar.

It's hard to live knowing that everything rots, bleaches, breaks and gathers dust. Ea is overwhelmed from time to time by the urge to find somewhere shiny and smooth and clean and new, where people don't smell, where things don't spoil or digest, where hair, nails, diseases and lumps do not grow. Something like the spaceship in Kubrick's film: an environment that can be hosed down.

She once tried explaining it to Hector. He had looked at her with genuine concern and said it was the opposite of life, what she was describing.

It was death she longed for.

Sadly, she's not sure he's right. That things will ever come to a perfect standstill. It's not even eleven yet, and Ea's trying to remember what time Coco gets out of school on Thursdays. She's been the girl's stepmother for nearly seven years. On Sundays they go swimming together, and the weekends when Coco is with her mum, Ea misses her so much that the smell of chlorine brings tears to her eyes.

Sometimes the biggest mystery is simply that things are the way they are.

~

The rice has been rinsed, and Hector isn't replying to her texts. It's been half an hour since Ea sent Coco for a wash, but she still hasn't heard the water come on. She doesn't understand how the girl manages to get so dirty in a single day. What *was* that in her hair? It had smelled spicy and caramelly, like barbecue sauce, but the child is denying everything.

'Coco?'

'What?'

'You're not in the bath.'

'I'm getting round to it.'

'Can I come in?'

Coco is sitting on the edge of the tub, reading a manga. She looks up at Ea when she hears the door open, her face at once watchful and expressionless. There's a hole in her right sock, and two toes are peeping out.

'Come on, get it over with – we'll be eating in twenty minutes.'

'Twenty minutes!' Coco drops the comic, wriggles off her leggings and socks, and turns on the tap. Water gushes out in a lumpy jet.

'You won't have time for a bath today,' says Ea, turning the knob the other way. The jet disappears from the tap and hammers down from above instead. Coco sighs and steps under the shower. Her fine, curly hair is soaked, clinging to her cheeks and forehead. She's put on weight. Her belly is protruding like a baby's, but her nipples are dark and swollen.

'You're welcome to borrow my good shampoo,' says Ea.

'Which one is the good one? I can't see anything.' Coco flails her outstretched arms. Ea hands her the bottle, sensing the familiar urge to fix things. To cut her nails and split ends. Even to pluck some of the dark down between her eyebrows, maybe. When you're a little kid, you can get away with looking like a forest troll: in the earlier grades, Coco had been the teachers' favourite, self-motivated and attentive, quicker on the uptake than the other children, but at nine, nearly ten years old? It won't be easy for her. Childhood is an island sinking into the sea. Sooner or later you've got to leave, and you'll only be as ready as you get yourself ready for it. Before long the teasing will begin, she's sure of that. It's clear that Coco is different from her peers, but Ea can't put her finger on precisely what makes her stand out.

'Can you manage?'

Coco nods, eyes closed, and Ea leaves the door ajar. On the kitchen table, her phone lights up. Hector's on his way. Traffic. She had a curry in the freezer, but it's smaller than she thought, so she hopes there's a tin of coconut milk lying around somewhere. She walks into the pantry. Although the windows are always open in here, the room is full of the sweet, heavy scent of the hemp she uses to make her lube. It's really just an extract concocted from the top of the plant and shea butter, mixed with essential oils and poured into glass bottles with a homemade label, but people will happily pay the fifty-five dollars she's decided it costs. To begin with she only sold it to her friends and acquaintances, but these days she gets orders from people she's never even heard of. Last week she was at the post office twice, dispatching six bottles in all. It's not a living, of course, but with the tattooing on the side she makes ends meet. Ea moves Hector's bike and stands on her tiptoes. Lentils. Chickpeas. Corn, more corn, but no coconut milk.

The bathroom floor is dripping, and the mirror is foggy with steam. Ea pushes the window open and gropes the hair out of the drain.

'Coco,' she shouts, 'I'm just nipping out to pick up some things for dinner. I'll be back in fifteen minutes.'

'Got it.'

Coco is bent over something at her desk, naked apart from a hoodie she must have fished out of the laundry basket. Ea bites her cheek. Why doesn't she get dressed properly? Why *is* she like this?

'See you,' she says. 'I'm bringing my phone, if you need anything.'

'I'm doing a drawing for Seven. It'll be really uniquely Seven-ish, I think.'

'I'm sure he'll like that.'

'Of course he'll like it.'

Ea takes the steps two at a time. Sometimes it feels like her worrying about Coco has no beginning or end, like one of those balls of elastic bands – a tight muddle of thoughts and nightmare scenarios. Every so often she shares them with Hector, who always asks her to stop.

Quit worrying!

As if it's that simple, as if you can just choose not to.

She nudges the light lattice door open with her shoulder and hears it click back in place behind her.

Worrying. Love.

Coco is Coco, he says. She's clever and funny when she wants to be, she can be a real hoot, and she's creative. Look at all the stuff she makes. And it's true. The girl is constantly occupied with something or other – you never see her hunched over a tablet or whining for entertainment. Her imagination is rich soil, a nesting box for the oddest thoughts and ideas. Quite often Ea genuinely wants to put the paintings Coco does in art class on the wall. There are the seeds of something brilliant in there, Ea has no doubt. And Hector is probably right: Coco will be fine. Still, she should have a word with him about the deodorant. Maybe tonight, even. The last couple of months, Ea has noticed that Coco smells of sweat when she comes home from school. Not the sweet scent of a warm child, but acrid adult sweat. Dads don't know about stuff like that – stuff that's crucial, or can be, before you know it.

Her own didn't, anyway.

A couple has pitched a tent in the square outside the church. The woman is sitting on the broad steps, eating a sandwich. She's younger than Ea, and beautiful in a fox-like way. They can't have been on the streets very long. The dog lying between her legs lifts its head and growls as Ea passes. It has a red bandana tied round its neck, like a dog in a film. She can hear the woman bawling at it behind her. Shut the fuck up, Alfie. Stupid animal. Ea runs the final stretch to Bi-Rite. They're too expensive, but closest, and she only needs the coconut milk.

'Hey!'

Sand must have stepped out of the shop only a moment before. Now they're face to face, and Ea can't come up with anything to light-heartedly fend her off with before Sand has pulled her into a hug. Her suede jacket smells of spruce needles.

'Ha! Twice in less than a month. How'd it go?'

'Oh,' says Ea, pulling her jumper more tightly around her, 'I don't really know. It ended a bit abruptly. We didn't finish.'

Sand's eyes goggle.

'What do you mean, didn't finish? Did something happen? Oh no, don't tell me something happened.'

Ea clocks the misunderstanding after a beat. Last time they bumped into each other, she was on her way to a mutual friend's home birth.

'No, no, that went great. I misunderstood you. It was such a beautiful experience!'

Ea gives as many details as she can bring herself to, and listens to Sand complain about a colleague at the bookstore who's on long-term sick leave.

Afterwards, when they've said goodbye and Ea is heading back to the apartment, coconut milk in one hand and her purse in the other, she feels guilty. She would never have talked so openly about her friend if she hadn't been terrified Sand was going to ask about the visit to the medium.

How inconsiderate. How typical of her to use another person's vulnerability to shield her own.

The square outside the church is empty. No sign of the tent or its occupants.

But she can hear them, can't she? Their voices.

Ea stops and listens.

Yes, someone's talking.

Too far away for her to hear what's being said. Like a radio on in the farthest room in the house.

She turns around. The street is deserted, the church's heavy doors shut and chained. A little way up the steps, the cling film from the girl's sandwich is skittering in the evening wind.

Behind the white wall is the churchyard. When Coco was younger, they'd go inside the church sometimes and pay five bucks to ring the bell. They both loved to set the heavy metal tongue high above them in motion, to watch the clapper beat against the sides and hear the strokes rain down over the neighbourhood like a telling-off.

Perhaps they went inside for some peace and quiet?

It's late, and the gate is locked.

They could have jumped over.

Though unable to explain why, Ea feels very strongly that this is her business.

Their decision, their disappearance.

A car goes past at high speed on the road, and the noise drowns out the voices for a few seconds. She has reached the gate when it dawns on her that the conversation is going on inside her head, and is in Danish.

That it's the sound of someone arguing.

Not passionately or loudly, but with the particularly bitter tenacity she remembers far, far too well.

*

Charlotte

Do you hate me?

The question takes me by surprise, but only because I thought he was asleep. It's been so silent. Silent as the grave – so perhaps I nodded off myself. The air feels heavier than ever, and behind me the membrane is slack, as though it's resting.

I keep expecting to see a cow come sailing out of the fog, complete with a bell around its neck and jagged-ridged hips. Or a herd of goats.

The surroundings make you harbour such hopes, and yet there are still no animals here.

Charles?

He's the only one who calls me that. I've always liked it.

Are you asleep?

No.

So you did hear my first question?

(Yes, but I was trying to dodge it, you dope.)

You disappeared, I say. It's hard to hate someone who isn't there.

The leather creaks as he sits up.

Does that mean you tried?

(Fine, if he's going to insist . . .)

I can't say I definitely wouldn't have hated you if I'd had more time. Mostly I felt sorry for you. I felt like you were missing out on so much. All the swarming bustle of life.

He's quiet for a long time, and when he speaks again it's in a voice that sounds like it's kicked off its blanket and is freezing:

The life you're talking about: I didn't see it, any more than you see the colonies of bacteria on your skin. In the last years of our marriage, I felt like I was trespassing. When I woke up in the morning, often I had no idea where I was. I'd lie there in the dark, waiting for the smell of smoked roe and boiled potatoes, lighter fluid, the sound of dogs outside the window. I stared at your sleeping face, but no name crossed my mind. The house was closed to me. A hard bud that opened for the rest of you each morning.

We could tell, I say. We knew you were in your own world. A world of snow and cold that we didn't know, that you couldn't explain in a way that satisfied you. The children acted differently when you were home. They went quiet and self-sufficient. It took days after you'd left before the house felt like itself again. We aired it out and played loud music, cursed and swore and chucked our shoes into a pile in the hall.

Christ, he says, and he looks genuinely upset. You're making it sound like an exorcism!

And what if it was? You did look like a ghost during those years. Every time you came home, you were leaner than before.

I was on a pretty narrow diet. Anyway, uncertainty affects the appetite.

Until at last you chose your river and your Evenks, I say, and allow myself a short, bitter laugh. That must have been a relief.

It was, but . . .

He clears his throat.

But what?

My river? My Evenks? I know what you mean, of course, but that way of putting it makes my skin crawl. I was there to help them, Charlotte – they never belonged to me.

The bracelets clink, affronted. I had completely forgotten those sensitive academic toes, always bristling and ready to be trodden on.

Neither of us says another word. Troels resumes his humming, now beating time with his shoes. Clunk, clunk, *sing the leather soles. I remember them well: the square toes and the exclusive nougat brown of the uppers are the same, although by now they're very worn. The man who sold them to him was just a boy, really, willowy as a reed, with his dark hair slicked back. A little while in, after Troels had already tried on several different pairs that for various reasons weren't right, the boy dropped down on to the carpet and, leaning forward on his young knees, took Troels's foot in both hands, as though it wasn't a sweaty piece of flesh but a precious treasure. His left hand slid around the cracked heel and underneath the arch, while with his right he bent and stretched the toes so that the joints clicked and cracked. The purpose, he explained in lilting English, was to form an impression of the shape of the foot. Its strengths and weaknesses. I couldn't bear to watch, so I excused myself and left the shop to wait outside with the kids, who were idling in the shade with their melted ice creams . . . and as though reading my mind, he says:*

Didn't you take that to Sicily?

I glance down. The yellow synthetic fabric is printed with blue and pink flowers, tulips as well as something that might be peonies, joined up by dots and thin lines.

That's right, I say. Well, no, actually. My suitcase never turned up, so I bought it during our first couple of days there.

Oh yeah, you did. We gave them your name and kept thinking they'd find it any day now. It took forever. The kids coped fine, although it wasn't the best start to a holiday. We were proud of them, do you remember? That was a good trip.

I nod.

But wait.

Wait.

Was *it a good trip, really?*

I remember the day Ea borrowed the dress. It suited her springy fourteen-year-old body so much better than mine that I was ashamed to put it on that night, and when we finally found a restaurant we all agreed on I only ordered an appetiser, even though I was starving and wanted pasta with a creamy sauce. I remember Niels drinking instant hot chocolate in yellow packets until he threw up, and Sidsel chatting to a group of local fishermen who let her keep a freshly caught squid. It sucked on to her arm with such force that she had rows of small circular bruises for weeks. She didn't cry, but she was pale when she came back from the harbour and told me. The fishermen had laughed, she said, and I felt like an irresponsible (insane) mother to let her go wandering off alone in a foreign city, among people whose minds I still didn't understand. I remember the glossy dogs and the enormous turds they left in the kennels at the hotel, the packets of stiff marmalade at the breakfast buffet, the shadow of leaves on an apricot cotton tablecloth.

Were we happy?

What a useless question.

The word has long since lost all meaning.

An adder's slough among the heather.

I have no idea.

That day in the shoe shop, I say, now spoiling for a fight, you should have seen yourself. You looked like such a tyrant up there on your throne. I remember looking at you through the window and thinking, Troels, I thought . . .

I fall silent, for now the anger subsides, it just dissolves, giving way to mild indifference.

What did you think, Charles?

Nothing.

He looks at me, astonished.

Nothing?

Yes.

5

Beatrice

The buzz of the intercom tugs her out of sleep like a hook round her neck. Standing up, she feels a rush of blood and grabs the corner of the sofa. For a few breathless seconds she sees nothing. The parquet seems to bend beneath her feet.

'Coming!' she shouts. Futilely, of course, because the person who woke her is a whole floor away. Judging by the light in the living room, it's late afternoon. Bee has been asleep at least twenty-four hours. One cheek is whirring.

'Hello?'

She jams the white plastic receiver hard against her ear, trying to stabilise herself.

'It's me.'

A shot of undiluted horror: it wasn't today, was it? They'd said Friday, plus the weekend. How does she always let things get mixed up like this?

'Just a minute. Can you hang on? Two seconds, okay? Then I'll let you in? Is that okay? Can you—'

'Of course.'

She just has time to hear her neighbour, Mr Pistilli, asking in his powdery voice if she got through, and Fifi answering just as sweetly that oh yes, yes, everything is fine, before Bee slams down the receiver and hurtles into the living room. Her forehead feels like a bowl of shifting marbles as she swiftly clears away the bottle and knocks the pillows into shape. She grabs a wrinkled apple from the fruit basket and takes two big bites, rolling the juice and flesh around in her mouth, then throws the rest into the bin.

Moments later, for the second time in the nearly eight years she's lived in that house, she lets her daughter in.

'Fifi!' says Bee, taking her by the shoulders and drawing her slender body close. 'My little sweetheart.'

The scent of perfume is overwhelming. She tries to calm Pita with her foot – the dog's going crazy and doing lopsided little skips on the spot. They let go, and for a minute or two Seraphina concentrates on the pug. She kneels down and lets it bore its smooth black head into her belly. She strokes its back and chest, praising and encouraging it.

'She's still alive,' says Fifi, getting to her feet.

'Pita? Oh yes, fit as a fiddle. She needs a walk, by the way – just let her run out into the garden. Oh, hi there, Mr Pistilli. This is my daughter, Seraphina.'

Mr Pistilli, whose ingratiating good manners soon turned out to be hiding a dubious and unstable personality (he shouts insults at the people who deliver Bee's food, and she suspects him of deliberately pushing bicycles over), waves from his sun deck. Bee turns to Seraphina.

‘I was expecting you tomorrow.’

‘I texted yesterday to say I’d been rebooked on to an earlier flight. Didn’t you get my message?’

Bee isn’t entirely sure right now where her phone has got to.

‘Must not have gone through,’ she says. ‘If I’d known I would have prepared, of course, I would have got everything ready for you. Has it been a long journey? You must be absolutely exhausted.’

Seraphina pulls off her thin fur-trimmed gloves and places them together in one hand. ‘Not that bad,’ she says, ‘I got some rest on the plane.’

Only now does Bee catch sight of the suitcase on the garden path behind her. A Samsonite, its shade of dove blue matched to her daughter’s trench coat and shoes. She looks like a fairy – no, it’s Thumbelina she reminds Bee of, from the fairy tale. Her blonde hair is in chic ringlets that reach the middle of her back, and a Swarovski crystal glints on each of her small earlobes.

‘Come in, come in,’ says Bee, carrying the suitcase up the stairs. It’s heavier than she was expecting. ‘Would you like a cup of tea? I just put the water on. I’ve got white tea and green tea and a few different fruit teas. One with berries of the forest and quince. Are you hungry?’

‘White’s good,’ says Fifi, looking around the living room. ‘Did you change the layout? It’s bigger in here than I remember, wow.’

Pita is weaving in and out between their legs, and Bee gets an irresistible urge to kick her out of the way.

'Pauline moved out,' says Bee, putting the suitcase up against the wall in the dining room, which hasn't been used since the separation. 'She had so many things. Big things, and all the stuff on the walls, of course. That's probably what you're noticing. The place seems bigger when there's air around the furniture. The Buddha over the fireplace is mine, and the pouffe there. Remember that from the old days?'

Seraphina nods, and Bee feels like reaching out and touching her cheek, which is smooth with a muted sheen, like a piece of watered silk.

'Nanna told me about you and Pauline.'

Bee shakes her head. Not that, not now.

'Listen, I'm fine,' she says, taking Fifi's hand. 'Why don't you tell me about your life instead. That's much more interesting. Come on, we can talk while I'm getting things ready.'

Seraphina follows, hopping up to sit on the kitchen worktop with a natural ease that's at odds with the years that have passed since the last time she was here.

'Nanna's on top form, anyway,' she says, though Bee hasn't asked about Marianne, or perhaps that's exactly why she says it. 'Did you know she'd started a book club?'

Bee shakes her head. Her conversations with her mother are practical in nature, about either Fifi or money, and if they're about Fifi then, in the end, those are always about money too.

'She decides what to read,' says Fifi, 'and when, but in return she lets them use her house. There's cake and wine for anyone who shows up. Last time they were talking for four and a half hours, although mostly not about the book! Two of them nodded off, and one of them, Joan – you might remember her – got so drunk I had to call her husband, even though she only lives around the corner.'

Seraphina laughs, making her curls bounce. Suddenly the thought occurs to Bee that the hair isn't hers. Not entirely, anyway. The lowest layer seems thicker and less fluid than the rest.

'I thought you'd moved out,' says Bee, thinking irritably of how immensely self-satisfied her mother would be about welcoming people to her book club. 'Marianne said you found a place in Des Moines. An apartment you were sharing with some other people?'

'Yeah, but I've still got my room at Nanna's. She's kept it for me, and she says I can come over whenever I want. Which has been pretty often lately,' sighs Fifi. 'I'm afraid my new roommates aren't always that considerate. I need it to be pretty quiet when I make my videos, but they don't get it. Or they do, but they just don't care. Don't ask me how come they have time to hang around at home all day. Shouldn't they be in class or in a reading room somewhere?'

'Your videos?'

Seraphina's heels thump against the cupboard door as she talks. It started a few years back with make-up tutorials and unboxing. She gained a lot of followers in a short space of time, but gradually she realised that what people responded to most was her voice. They left comments saying it relaxed them, that it gave them a pleasant physical sensation. After repeated requests to make an ASMR video, she googled what it was, and from that point on things happened fast. Within a year, Miss Fessonia has become one of YouTube's most popular ASMR channels.

'A-S-M-R,' says Fifi, before Bee can ask. 'Autonomous sensory meridian response. I make sounds that people find calming.'

'Hang on. You make sounds?'

Nodding patiently, Fifi explains to her mother – who has forgotten all about the tea infuser, held open with her right thumb and forefinger – how every day thousands of people all over the world listen to her whisper, brush, click, breathe and gently scratch into a microphone. Demand for new videos is high, and always very specific.

'Different people have different triggers,' she says. 'Make one with the sound of rain, of plastic bags, one with candles and shades of blue, nails, ear massage, a whispering video, one where you make breakfast . . .'

'Breakfast,' interrupts Bee, with more scepticism than she'd intended, 'why *breakfast*?'

Fifi throws out her hands.

'To each their own. It's a bit like being a mom. I follow them into their dreams,' she says, 'my voice is the last thing they hear before they fall asleep. That's why I'm here, by the way. Some guys are developing an app for people who suffer from insomnia. They might want to use my voice.'

Bee isn't sure what her daughter has just told her. Videos? Plastic bags? It sounds decidedly weird.

And not just that. It sounds wrong, and scary.

Like a slippery slope.

Bee can feel her face stiffening with all this feigned enthusiasm, but Seraphina doesn't seem to notice.

'Anyway, we'll see. This stuff doesn't always lead to anything, although it might be fun if it did. They say there's money in it.'

'Well, there could be!' says Bee, dropping the tea infuser with a smack. 'It all sounds very exciting, Fifi.'

Bee will call Marianne as soon as she gets the chance. She doesn't want to stick her oar in – for once she's not going to be the one who ends up feeling guilty – but she will simply demand to know what the hell is going on.

'I'm just trying to think of it as an experience,' says Seraphina, shrugging her shoulders, which glint like mother-of-pearl in the slanted light. Her banana-yellow halter dress looks like it has floated straight out of a summer in the fifties. Bee feels cold just looking at her. San Francisco is sunk in a chilly fog this afternoon.

'Yeah,' says Bee, 'you should. When are you meeting them?'

'Saturday.'

'This Saturday?'

Bee pours the boiling water into the teapot. A gift from a client, it is shaped like a strawberry and has an elf on the top. You lift the lid off by holding the elf's hat. She hates it. Always has. Why didn't she chuck it out ages ago? In case the client comes back, she supposes, but it's been two years since she was here last. A different type of person from

Pauline would have refused to drink her Earl Grey from it, but she contented herself with dubbing it The Pissing Strawberry.

'I hope you don't mind me sleeping over here? Anywhere's fine.' Seraphina nods towards the living room. 'I'm happy with the couch.'

'You don't think I have a room for you?'

Bee can hear how she sounds: huffy and cross.

A stinking black dollop in the room.

It isn't what she intended.

Frankly, none of this is what she intended:

Pauline and little Hudson Farley.

San Francisco.

The fully renovated Victorian townhouse, which made it possible to attract a type of customer Bee had never dreamed of before. And yet it happened. Just as though she'd planned it all scrupulously from the beginning.

'I won't be here much,' says Fifi. 'There's loads I want to see while I'm here. I just need a place to sleep.'

'Hudson's room,' says Bee, taking two mugs from the cupboard. She should have said guest room, of course. 'Let me show you where it is.'

While Seraphina unpacks, Bee prepares the tray. Her hands are as nerveless as withered leaves as she fills a bowl with almonds and puts some wizened blueberries in another. She pours mineral water into a carafe and drops in two slivers of cucumber, cuts an apple into wedges and drizzles them with lemon juice. That's a trick she learned from Pauline, who specialised in making the most ordinary things feel fresh.

In the living room, which really does feel massive now that only a fraction of the furniture remains, she sets the tray down on the coffee table then hovers irresolutely beside it.

'Are you hungry?' she calls. 'If you're hungry we can order food. I'd have been happy to make something for you if I'd known you were coming.'

'Did you say something?' Fifi is in the doorway. She has changed her dress for a black velour tracksuit. Her hair is braided, hanging in a golden rope over her shoulder.

'Have you eaten?'

'I bought something on the way here. Tea's fine, Mom.'

The door is shut again, not hard.

She looks like herself.

For some reason Bee finds it heartening that Fifi looks like she stopped developing around the age of fourteen. She's not too thin, just unnaturally small. More than petite, but too well-proportioned to be confused with a dwarf. Bee has often tried to recall Fifi's father's height, but his body, like his name, has faded over the years. Arms, legs, nose, mouth, hands. The whole thing is gone. Only his laugh, which was shy and rarely sincere, has endured.

During the fourteen days he stayed at Esalen, they were together only once. Bee, who back then was working as a yoga and meditation instructor, noticed him because he was alone, and did not seem to be enjoying his stay at the institute. He refused to wear comfy clothes, wandering around in khaki slacks and a shirt instead. Arriving late for the communal breakfast, he'd bring a newspaper with him and immediately start to read. That way you couldn't strike up a conversation without explicitly disturbing him. The few times he showed up for one of Bee's classes, he always left without a word before they reached the savasana. So when he called to her one morning on the steps leading down to the beach, Bee would never have guessed what – only slightly flustered – he was about to ask her.

The cabin was set back from the main building, behind a row of weather-beaten pines, and there was a view from the terrace over the Pacific Ocean, which broke against the jagged black rocks along the coast. He had bought ingredients to make gin and tonics, and Bee felt at ease in his company. He was so different from the men she usually went for, less tanned and – like herself – from the Midwest. They drank their G&Ts and ate Cheez Ballz he'd brought with him from home, and he told her about his job as a programmer at a start-up. A few months earlier he'd got pretty sick, and his boss had urged him to take it easy. The company was paying for his stay at the retreat, and because he didn't want to lose his job he'd agreed to go. The truth was he was longing for his office in Menlo Park, for his coding and his colleagues. They were on the verge of something. A breakthrough of some kind. At the time, Bee had listened to him without really understanding much of what he said. The year was 1995, and it was the first time she'd heard of the Internet, just as she'd never heard of anyone 'burning out' before.

As Bee welcomed her class the next morning, she felt a pang at the thought of the man who would soon be retaking his seat in front of a screen a few hours' drive up the coast. Just three weeks later she came down with diarrhoea and sweaty palms, and it was obvious she was pregnant.

At no point had she doubted the right thing to do.

Bee strove to live in harmony with her body and the rhythms of nature. The nice young man had spoken the foreign language of technology, a new lexicon of alienating words she did not understand.

Besides, he was bound to have a girlfriend – maybe even a fiancée – back home in Palo Alto. They usually did.

No. The child was hers.

Born out of a flower.

Bee delivered Seraphina in an inflatable pool in a room in Esalen's staff wing. Iris, a bird-like German woman who taught yin yoga, acted as doula, and for the first six years of Fifi's life, the retreat – clinging to the rocks south of Monterey – constituted her entire world. They really were, as the saying goes, one big family. When Bee had classes to teach, there was always someone around to take care of the baby, and if they'd had a rough night, one of her colleagues would generally look after Fifi while Bee slept. Seraphina became a sort of mascot for the retreat. She toddled after the cleaners and the gardener. On cold days she visited the kitchens, where she helped blanch almonds or wash salads until she lost interest and wandered out into the park to feed the squirrels with leftovers from breakfast. Fifi was an easy, quiet, and strikingly beautiful child. The Girl with the Starry Eyes, they called her.

When she was old enough to understand that fathers existed and to enquire curiously about her own, Bee decided to tell her she was donor-conceived. Her father's identity was protected by law. All she knew about him was that he was born in Missouri.

So that was that.

As Bee sits down on the sofa, her socked foot bumps against something hard and light. Bending down, she already knows what her fingertips will find. The familiar smell of caramelised prunes and aftershave still lingers on it. Straightening up, Bee shoves the faceted glass between the backrest and the cushion, quick as lightning.

'It's so nice in here,' says Fifi, who walks into the living room at that very moment. 'It doesn't matter that it's a bit empty.'

'You don't think so?'

'You remember what it's like at Nanna's, stuff everywhere,' says Fifi, perching on the opposite end of the sofa. 'Honestly, I prefer it here. How big is it?'

'Nearly two thousand square feet,' Bee says evasively, 'maybe a little more.'

The house is 2,345 square feet. It has seven rooms, with potential for a loft extension, and it costs in property taxes what Bee earns in a really good year. Bee knows this because last week a burly Latin American man, his fingers heavy with rings, came by and took pictures of the place, and two days later all the information was online. In a fit of self-torture, she looked up the ad. Pauline is a fair-minded woman, but she's not a charity.

Bee has six months, then the house will be put up for sale. The bridging loan has run out. Bridging loan. Interim financing account. Words like these come to Pauline quite naturally, even though she didn't get rich till late in life.

Some people learn fast.

Some people let go and fling themselves into a new romance with the triumphant, death-defying confidence of an acrobat.

Bee is the dangling trapeze in this metaphor, which is probably about right. She pours the tea and hands her daughter a cup. Fifi has lifted Pita on to her lap; the dog looks at once satisfied and inconsolable.

The photographer had been nice, as it happened. He took the time to drink the glass of white wine she offered him (she'd thought about only opening it after he'd gone, but something about him stirred her slumbering instinct for hospitality), and before he left he wished her luck in a way that felt sincere.

I hope you find a good solution, ma'am.

Yeah, thanks. She should have started thinking about possible solutions a long time ago.

She's well aware of that.

The problem is that they all lead to the same stomach-churning place: the first floor of her mother's villa in the fairly nice part of Bondurant where all the elderly couples and widows live.

She can hear them talking already. Has Marianne Wallens' daughter come home *again*?

Has anybody seen her? Have you spoken to her?

I heard she's a lesbian *and* divorced.

'Ugh, she sheds like crazy!' Fifi holds out her palms, which are indeed covered in Pita's shining fur. 'Can't you do anything about it? Give her a supplement or something?'

'She's a dog,' says Bee. 'They shed.'

Fifi smiles, bringing out the dimple in her right cheek, and she looks just as she does in the photo on Bee's bedside table. Seven years old, brown as a nut.

'No offence!'

Hudson used to say that Pita had a crying face. It's still the most precise description Bee can think of.

'Let's go out to eat,' Bee says, making a gesture that's too large and rapid. The blanket slips to the floor. 'I know an Indian restaurant where you can always get a table, and it's much better and cheaper than the one where you never can. It's a bit of a trek, but it's worth the walk. What do you think?'

'I think that sounds great,' says Fifi, kissing Pita's flat muzzle. 'You know I love Indian.'

Bee didn't know that. Now she does.

6

Niels

Niels parks his bike in the racks outside the Strandlund housing complex. Biggo has expanded his patch to include Vesterbro and Kongens Enghave, and he can feel the miles and the countless extra strokes of his pasting brush in every muscle. He's battered and hot, but that's okay. Maybe for once he'll actually sleep when he goes to bed tonight. Out over the sea, the clouds break apart in the tulip-yellow afternoon sky. The sunlight hits the metal handle of the front doors and the handlebars of the bike, making them glimmer as though drizzled in syrup. Stuffing his hat into his pocket, Niels opens his jacket. His hair is short, cropped close at the neck and sides, and a few millimetres longer on top. You can't tell, but if he let it grow out it would flop over his ears and forehead in wiry honey-blond curls that he's never come to terms with. He thinks they're vulgar, and as soon as he was old enough to have a say, he asked his mother to get them chopped off.

The blinds in Barbara's study are down but the window is

ajar, and through it Niels can see the contours of his friend's long body under the duvet.

'Cosmo?'

He doesn't move.

Niels whistles, an insistent tune that he repeats until Cosmo's bony hand scuttles searchingly across the duvet, as though to find the source of the noise and choke it. Niels steps back from the window, but doesn't let himself in straight away. Lowering himself on to the steps outside number eleven, he chucks stones at the upturned flowerpot where they usually stub out their cigarettes.

Sitting here, the sun on his face.

Things are good.

Simple.

Down by the water, the ducks are loudly cursing the unscrupulous gulls.

Plink. He hits the terracotta.

Plink. Plink. Plonk – that's the table.

Not one of them goes through the hole.

Niels had not meant to stay at Strandlund for much more than a week or two. Cosmo had offered to let him sleep on the sofa at his grandma's flat while he waited for Evald and a guy they called the Paracetamol – because his skin was such a chalky white – to clear out the attic on Frederikssundsvej. He could live there for free, they'd said, no problem. But it did turn out to be a problem. A stray cat was found dead in the roof space, and after a visit from the council it turned out the level of asbestos was so high that they advised against any unnecessary activity up there. The residents had teamed up to sue the landlord, and Niels was once again homeless. He'd never really settled since returning to Denmark late last summer, and had considered going back on the road. Saint Petersburg, maybe, or southern Spain – but the timing was all wrong. If he'd left Copenhagen after only a couple of months of putting up posters for Biggo, he'd have been branded unreliable and barred from a profession that suited him better than anything else he could think of. Hard physical labour didn't bother him, as long as he could choose his own hours and was paid cash in hand. Sidsel would have offered to let him move in, of course, but her place was cramped as it was. She'd deny it, but he would have been a burden. Anyway, by that point Niels had realised that Cosmo was suffering from something more serious than the usual bout of despondency. It didn't seem to be passing by itself, and Niels was afraid to leave his friend to his own darkness.

The upshot was that Niels had moved in with Cosmo at the beginning of March, staying in the sheltered housing formerly assigned to Barbara's husband Hugo's previous wife, now deceased, and which Barbara and Hugo (thanks to a combination of his contacts at the local authority and her clout) had been able to keep as a kind of summer residence. They spent most of the year in southern Portugal, in the old farmhouse that Barbara had bought with her first husband. Amid this peculiar symmetry of property and dead spouses, they are, according to Cosmo, on cloud nine. And Barbara did sound genuinely happy and relaxed on the phone when

Niels called to put himself forward as another off-the-books tenant.

As long as you keep a low profile, she said. They could always work out the money side of things later.

After the call he had gone inside and taken Barbara's debut novel off the shelf. It was hard to square the voice on the phone with the young woman on the cover whose dazzling prune-black eyes met his gaze with a look that was distinctly flirtatious. Cosmo wasn't lying when he said his grandma had been terrifyingly beautiful once.

At the sound of footsteps on the gravel, he looks up. It's Arvid, their neighbour on the right-hand side, coming up the path. The rain has darkened the shoulders of his jacket.

'Good evening, Niels,' he says, and stops, because that's what they do here.

'Good evening,' says Niels, getting to his feet. This is the effect the residents have on him. He doesn't like to feel he's wasting their time. Arvid sets his shopping bag down on the ground between them and straightens back up with difficulty. The breath is rattling and whistling in his lungs.

'You've been out in it too, I see? I got caught in a shower on my way home from the shops. At first I stopped under an awning to wait it out comfortably, but there was no telling how long it would last. I could have been standing there all night, so I thought, well, I'd better get off home to Tove, or she'll be cross. Now isn't that silly?'

Standing on the gravel path in front of the widower, Niels has nothing to say. He's unforgivably healthy and alive.

'Anyway,' says Arvid, who obviously wasn't expecting an answer, 'how's it going with your flatmate? It's been ages since I saw him. Is he away?'

'Oh no,' says Niels, 'he's home.'

'Fine, fine.'

'But I can always ask him why he keeps skulking round without saying a proper hello to anybody.'

Arvid looks away. 'I didn't mean it like that. He can do as he likes.'

'I know, I was only joking.'

'But he *is* all right?'

'I think so,' says Niels, realising that Arvid knows perfectly well Cosmo isn't away. It's so easy to underestimate the elderly. Like with children.

'Is he busy at the moment? Barbara told me a bit about how hard it is to plan anything in his industry. It's so hand to mouth, just awful.'

After a brief pause, Niels answers simply, 'Yes.'

'Glad to hear it. I'm pleased.'

Arvid has grasped the handles of his bag.

'Do ask him to drop in when he gets a chance. Good evening.'

'Will do.'

Niels watches Arvid shuffle off uncertainly towards his front door. His shoulders are drooping now that their breadth has become useless and burdensome, his body visibly loose at the joints, grinding in places where the parts once acceded smoothly to the whole. At last he reaches the door, and now he has to fit in the key, which is as small and slippery as a fish between his fingers. Niels drops back down on to the step and lets the hedge swallow the sight of Arvid struggling to carry himself and his shopping the final stretch. Shielding his eyes from the sun with his right hand, he picks up another pile of pebbles with his left, cranks his arm backwards, hurls it forwards and opens his fingers. The stones move in an uneven hailstorm through the air in the direction of the upturned pot, hitting and not hitting, hitting and hitting and not hitting and not and not and not.

When he walks into the living room, the smoke he could smell in the hallway is darker and denser. Niels presses his hat to his mouth, breathing through the damp wool as he runs back and forth, opening windows at both ends of the flat. He takes the pan off the hob and puts it in the sink. The metal seethes and buckles a couple of times, then there's silence. The smoke is sucked out of the window in one long tail, and after a while the living room is back to normal. He straightens up and listens for an alarm, for someone ringing or calling through the door. After all, they're surrounded by staff who are employed to keep people alive and in a good mood. But nothing happens. Nobody has noticed smoke billowing out of a flat in the red-brick buildings for several minutes on this Thursday afternoon.

From inside Cosmo's room comes the sound of blithe American female voices, of background music rising and falling in intensity but never absent more than briefly. Niels imagines flinging open the door and marching up to the figure on the bed, half dissolved in the blue light, grabbing his bony shoulders and shaking as hard as he can, shaking and shaking. Instead he puts the milk back into the fridge, screws the lid on to a jar of beetroot and wipes the kitchen table. The beetroot juice leaves a ring, a shadow in the wood. He knocks the blackened fried egg into the bin and fills the kettle with water. Once it's boiled, he pours it into the pan. Flakes of soot stream over the edge along with the water, collecting in a dark heap in the sink strainer. He turns down the radiators, which are working at full blast in the draught from the open windows. While the current tugs the clammy sea breeze through the living room like a pipe cleaner, Niels fetches his rucksack and empties it on to the table. Not a massive haul – the best stuff was already gone. One of the four courgettes is slimy under the plastic, but there's nothing wrong with the others. As with the apple juice and the shallots, their flaws are cosmetic. He puts the food in the fridge, which is empty apart from a box of eggs and the beetroot. There's enough for a couple of days, maybe three. Biggo owes him pay for March, but Niels isn't going to pressure him. Not yet, anyway. He doesn't want to give people the wrong impression. Of course he can wait, and the money will come. He knows that from Evald, who's been working for Biggo since he dropped out of school. He's keeping an eye on you at the moment, Evald had explained when they bumped into each other on Nørrebrogade, which is Evald's patch, and has been for years. Seeing if you're reliable, if he can work with you. He breathed on his rough hands. That's what really matters to him. Niels can be relied on, Biggo will twig soon enough. He's quick to learn and careful, and it doesn't occur to him to complain, even though he's been living on oatmeal and lentil soup for a month. Apart from the nights he eats at Sidsel's.

Niels puts the coffee machine on to brew and hangs his sweaty clothes over a chair in the dining room. He's been looking forward to this moment ever since he set off into town. Long, scalding showers under the dinner-plate-sized shower head are one of the few luxuries he has embraced during his stay at Strandlund.

The air in the room – he tries not to think of the room as his, but already considers it sacrosanct – is clean and cool, and Niels is grateful that he shut the door behind him when he left yesterday. The room is the smallest in the flat, but east-facing, and from the window – one big sheet of glass – there's a view over the Øresund. Barbara has good taste, and although Strandlund was clearly designed with crumbling bodies in mind, she has managed to drown that out with a mixture of expensive furniture, art and textiles picked up on her travels over the years. Only in the bathroom, where grab rails have been drilled into the wall in the shower cubicle, are you reminded that this is sheltered accommodation.

He drinks his coffee standing up, naked, one hand resting against the sill. Between sips he presses the cup into his chest, which, apart from a heart-shaped island of fair hair, is still as smooth as a boy's. He watches the sparrows from the window, bathing in a puddle on the gravel path. The sun gilds his neck and shoulders, and when he turns and takes a few steps into the room it falls on to his back, where the muscles are growing more visible beneath the skin. Niels puts down the cup and rolls his head around on his neck. He doesn't like his body to look at, but he enjoys its reliability; he enjoys using it and feeling it lean into the movements as it slowly grows accustomed to the awkwardness of working with the brush and paste bucket.

To make room for Barbara's desk, which Cosmo wasn't using except as a dumping ground, Niels has pushed the bed against the wall. Here, facing the sea, is where he reads, and as he does so – laboriously, tirelessly – he builds whole cities of knowledge in his mind. There is so much, so infinitely much he's still missing, and there is no adequate excuse. In the current pile, from bottom to top, are Georg Lukacs's book on Goethe, two editions of a journal issued by the Tiqqun collective, volumes 3 and 4 of *Das Kapital*, some early Heidegger, and Alfredo Bonanno's *Armed Joy*, which his friend Luken Garate sent him. The package also contained a piece of A4 paper on which the words NE TRAVAILLEZ JAMAIS were written, with what Niels guesses was a piece of charcoal.

The words aren't Luken's – they're a quotation from Guy Debord. He wrote them for the first time on a wall along the Rue de Seine, four years before he helped found, in 1957, the Situationist International, a group of Marxist intellectuals and avant-garde artists. If you google Debord, you find – besides the articles about his spectacular suicide in 1994 – a picture taken on a sunny, windy day in Cosio di Arroscia. In it he is flanked by his first wife, the author Michèle Bernstein, and a laughing Asger Jorn in a long-sleeved woollen jumper. Despite his smile, Debord looks like a surly, fat-arsed lawyer.

Niels has tacked the note on to the wall above the desk, because although it's easy enough to obey Debord's imperative when a hefty quantity of euros is transferred into your account by Papa Garate every month, he appreciates the gesture. Anyway, he doubts that his friend – who is too intelligent to be hypocritical – is unaware of the obvious contradiction in a self-declared anarchist being supported by his parents, whom he keeps suspended in perpetual terror that he will one day make good on his threats, leave the University of Tübingen, and join a self-sufficient collective in north-eastern Spain.

Niels met Luken by chance last summer, outside the grocer's in a lethargic Italian village a few miles south of the Swiss border. He'd bought a bag of oranges, which he was eating in the shade, having already offered some to two men who were wearing hiking boots like his and carrying modest backpacks. By that point Niels had been walking for three and a half weeks, broken only by a four-day stay at a monastery, and he needed someone to talk to, but the two men turned down his offer and answered his questions curtly before resuming the conversation he had interrupted. It was their aloofness that made Niels decide to join them. The walkers he'd met so far on his journey through Italy were usually so chatty that after a mile or two in their oversharing company he wished he'd never acknowledged them. A couple of the women on the road had seemed interested in more than just company, but weeks of solitude had turned Niels's desires inward, sharpening his senses. He was enjoying the experience too much to let himself be carried away by fleeting pleasures. The reserve of these men felt refreshing in comparison, tempting, and for the rest of the day Niels followed them around the countryside, drinking when they drank and eating when they ate, without repeating the mistake of offering them any of his own food. They neither asked him to leave nor made any effort to invite him into the conversation. Not until night fell and Niels proved his usefulness by breaking the lock on an old barn door did the two warm to him, explaining that because of his size and wide-set eyes they had assumed he was North American. It went without saying that the fact he *wasn't* North American was a pleasant surprise. The next day they set out together, not parting ways until a week later, when Niels's route led him east across Romania and Luken and Simon continued north in the direction of the Czech Republic.

He never heard from Simon again, but his new Basque friend answered Niels's email after a couple of days with one twice as long, together with a reading list of indispensable works and the draft of an article about the postmodern fetishisation of handmade goods, which he asked Niels to read and comment on.

They've kept in touch ever since, and it's Luken whom

Niels is hoping to hear from when he opens his computer and finds an email from his eldest sister. It was sent an hour and a half earlier – in the morning, where she is. The subject line reads: HOW DO LOBSTERS GROW? Niels stares at the capital letters, his brows knitted. Last time he heard from Ea, it was his birthday. She said she was sending him a present, and he didn't have the heart to tell her that he'd not had a fixed address for nearly two years. Whatever she planned on sending, it would never be received.

He opens the email and clicks on the link. Rabbi Dr Azriel Tobin is being filmed from the chest up against a backdrop of dark brown fabric that is slightly crumpled on one side. His cheeks are hollow and his beard is mealy white and thin, like his hair, poking out in airy tufts from underneath his skullcap. The expression on his face is kindly and concerned as he talks about lobsters, whose shells are inflexible. They don't grow with their wearers, so eventually the lobster will feel so uncomfortable, so pinched and squeezed, that it will start searching for a place to discard its shell. Once it has found a suitable rock or crevice, it crawls into the darkness, casts off its shell and waits – naked and vulnerable – for a new, better-fitting one to grow. Now imagine, says Rabbi Tobin, leaning forward, that the lobster didn't go looking for a place to hide, but went to the doctor instead and got a prescription for Xanax or Prozac or Zoloft. Imagine, says the rabbi, holding up a trembling right hand, that the lobster kept trudging along on the seabed, out of sorts, but not realising because it was drugged. Niels understands the metaphor, of course, but still he sits there and lets the rabbi tell him that periods of discomfort are a sign of spiritual growth, and that we shouldn't fear pain but welcome it. Pain is growth, says the rabbi, leaning back in his chair with a transfigured smile on his thin lips.

The email has been sent to him and ninety-seven others. It's a chain letter. Each recipient is supposed to forward it to their contacts, who will forward it to theirs, and bit by bit the people behind what the original author refers to as Big Pharma will be revealed as the unscrupulous poisoners of society that they are. The brief text is full of exclamation marks. Spread the word! Don't let them drug you! We need to get the truth out there! Pain is growth! All well and good, but the wording is touchingly banal. Niels would never forward this kind of thing. He doesn't know anybody, except maybe his eldest sister, who would be interested.

Ea has no idea who he is. And how could she? He was eleven when she left. A silent boy, he had swapped his childhood home for his aunt's flat in Østerbro with no fuss at all. Niels had known they were expecting a reaction. Efie and his sisters, the psychologist, the teachers they'd kept in the loop. He wished that even one of them had believed him when he said it wasn't coming. Not because he didn't feel anything, but because it made no difference what he felt. No, he sees no reason to blame his sister for anything. He'd have done the same thing in her place, and in fact he did, as soon as he got the chance.

Hey. It's me. Miss Fessonia.

Niels feels a shiver slip down his neck and along his spine, spreading into a tingling warmth across his lower back.

The voice is very close: a hoarse, intimate whisper.

He didn't press pause, and the next video has started automatically.

The girl can't be more than seventeen or eighteen. She's sitting on a bed, in what could easily be her own room. On the wall behind her is a string of purple heart-shaped fairy lights.

And today it's all about you.

She smiles, leaning towards the camera. Pretty, but in the way a Disney princess is pretty, smooth and unreal, with radiantly blue eyes and dainty teeth.

Okay, friends, let's begin.

She holds up an empty plastic bottle and taps it with her nails – not rhythmically, but not quite at random either. She shuts her eyes, as though the tapping demands all her concentration.

Niels can't move.

It's not arousal he's feeling, but something like it. It feels as though invisible hands are pushing him back and down, into the chair.

She stops tapping and starts to lightly scratch the grooved lid.

The feeling from before returns even more powerfully: an intense prickling delight that starts at his neck and glides in waves throughout his body, until every single muscle feels perfectly soft and relaxed.

Miss Fessonia puts the bottle down and raises a powder

brush to the microphone, which is positioned in front of the camera.

Using tiny movements, she strokes its hard, pitted surface, and the sound that reaches Niels is intoxicatingly dense and dry.

Her lips have parted; he can hear her breathing.

Niels puts a tentative hand in his lap, but he's flaccid.

The pleasure isn't localised.

It's moving from his feet to his forehead, down over his cheeks and throat, chest and hips, guided by the sounds the girl on the screen is making.

Maybe you're feeling sleepy? You deserve a rest. Just let it all go. Let it go, she commands.

Niels gets up and lies down on the bed. The back of his body is red-hot against the sheets, and around him the room contracts and expands with his breathing. He can feel a breeze on his right cheek and the baking evening sun on the top of his head. The girl's voice murmurs and scrapes, rustling across his eardrums; she's sending swells of contentment through him, and with each one he feels more heavy and open. Rolling on to his side, Niels lets his eyelids yield to the strange weight.

7

Sidsel

Scanning the pile of clothes, Sidsel changes her mind yet again. She replaces a petrol-blue shirt with a thin sweater and stuffs an extra book into the outside pocket of the suitcase, then zips it up and puts it on the floor beside the bed. Jeanette has sent her an email with her boarding pass and a smiley face. The plane leaves tomorrow at half two; the return flight she has to book herself. The plan is to meet with the head conservator of stonework, Loretta Barry, the following morning and start working on the bust. It's all happening – not right now, but soon. Sidsel goes into the bathroom and surveys herself in the mirror. She takes off her earrings and combs her hair, first to one side and then to the other. She wishes she looked as new as she feels, but you never do. Running the cold tap, she rinses the dust off the sink with the flat of her hand before heading into the kitchen and emptying the drying rack. It's half past eight, and Niels has just texted to say he's on his way. She had been getting nervous. It's not like him to be late, and when she finally got hold of him he sounded dazed. Just hopping on the bike now, he'd said in a voice that came from the bottom of a well. Kiss the Larva good night from me, and tell her we'll play Monopoly this weekend. Sidsel has no intention of doing so. There's no point reminding Laura that her uncle didn't keep their agreement. Like most children her age, she has an easily kindled sense of injustice and a long memory for anything she perceives as treachery.

Laura has taken the news about London with supreme composure. Am I coming too? she asked, of course, but when Sidsel explained that this was work, that it wasn't a holiday, and that Niels would look after her in the meantime, she accepted it without complaint. The girl loves her uncle with the passion that children sometimes feel for people they see more rarely than they'd like. She ate two helpings of dinner and took no longer to fall asleep than usual. Maybe the tears will come when she's dropped off at preschool the next day, but Sidsel doubts it. Laura's personality is robust and straightforward, and more and more often these days it's Sidsel who has to steel herself in order to meet her daughter at her own level. A couple of months ago, when Laura stopped her in the middle of brushing her teeth to ask why she didn't have a grandma like the other kids at school, Sidsel had been tempted to counter with an innocent question: What made you think about that? Who at school has grandparents? Do you remember when we were reading about a grandma in a story last week? What happened to her? But something in Laura's eyes made her think better of it, and Sidsel explained that she did have grandparents, but two of them were dead and two of them lived in another country. Laura replied without hesitation that that was too bad, because grandparents picked you up earlier than regular parents, and then she opened her mouth for the toothbrush and let Sidsel finish the job. No tears, no further questions.

Of course, this won't be the last talk they have about it, but it's a start, and not one Sidsel needs to feel ashamed of. She told it like it is.

Fifteen minutes later, Niels still hasn't shown up, and there's nothing else to do in the flat. Everything has been tidied away, wiped down, hung up. Sidsel finds the cigarettes at the back of the kitchen drawer and opens the window a crack. The street is deserted and wet. She imagines her little brother hurtling at full speed along the coast, hunched over like a projectile aimed at the city, his long legs pumping up down, up down. In the flat opposite, a young woman is aggressively rubbing her hair dry, and when she's finished she lets the towel drop to the floor. Her friend comes into the room and sits down on the bed. They talk as the first one gets dressed, and when they leave the room it's the second girl who bends down, picks up the towel and switches off the lights. Even though the women have been living in the flat for nearly a year, Sidsel can't be certain about their relationship or habits. They come and go at odd times, sleeping in late or heading out on to the street before the sun is up. They have guests often, but never when you'd expect. Then the rooms are filled with young men and women drinking tea and beer, chatting in front of the large mirrored wardrobe. Another life. Days that turn imperceptibly into nights. She's nearly forgotten what it's like to live that way. Stubbing out her cigarette on the windowsill, she lets it roll over the edge and into the street, where it will stay until the residents' association tackles it. She usually volunteers to sweep the road, worried that someone will notice the conspicuous number of cigarette butts underneath her window.

The laptop is at the bottom of the case, and it takes a deft manoeuvre to slip it out from underneath the folded clothes. Pulling it out of its sleeve, she sits down on the edge of the bed and opens it.

The light has an eerie effect in the dark room.

This isn't the moment.

Niels might be locking up his bike outside right now, and in a few seconds the doorbell will go.

It's not a moment at all, it's just a thin indifferent sliver of time between something and something else, and maybe that's exactly why she's doing it now.

The cursor appears and disappears, flashing, waiting.

How long has she known she would end up here?

All along, of course. She has known all along.

The name is at her fingertips, a familiar choreography, and instantly the blood comes in a rush, shooting out of her chest and into her face, stinging and pinching her scalp.

Something inside her gives way when she clicks on the first link. A structure in her chest noiselessly collapsing.

She's hardened herself for so long, and now she's defenceless. He's still working at the university, still a lecturer, and the picture is the same, taken for work. His hair is shorter and he isn't smiling, but the lack of a smile doesn't make him look unfriendly.

It's another office, another floor. The same small, low-set ears.

She goes back to the search results. In a picture taken at a seminar last October, Vicky Singh is seated between two female researchers on a panel discussing *The Mutations of Socialist Modernity*. He's leaning forward over his crossed legs, his hand at an awkward angle on his wrist, as though the weight of the microphone has twisted it a half-turn round. The name tag is pinned askew to his lapel.

Sidsel swallows something compact.

Her guts are churning, and she's feeling sick to her stomach, but it's impossible to stop. Memories are bubbling up and breaking through in a jumble of detail: his chest hair, as bristly as his beard (crackling under her hand), crawling out of the neck of his shirt to meet it halfway. His narrow lower back, his strong knees and elbows. The way he didn't swing a scarf around his neck like most people, but raised it over his head and let it fall with the precision of a pastry chef. His rolling gait, and the way he dumped his bag in a corner of the lecture hall, far away, as though it were a sack of rubbish. The strange scent that lingered on his suit after cleaning, mixed with wind and the sandalwood that burned on a chipped saucer in the kitchen window at his flat.

The cigarettes and the wine in the kitchen window.

The overgrown, rain-soaked garden.

A magenta sheet, a turquoise sheet, one cobalt blue. Never a white sheet.

Never an ordinary meal. It was try this, taste this relish, have a cracker with cheese and quince jelly. This sausage is a delicacy in Poland or Greece or the Czech Republic.

The wardrobe: the scent of him, intensified to the point of unbearability.

The obscure and time-consuming methods of brewing tea, which he pursued like a hobby.

His hands, the taste of his saliva, the hard, crooked cock.

Sidsel was twenty-five the first time she saw Vicky Singh, and she wanted him then and there, fiercely and without reserve.

She had just got out of a two-year relationship, one year of which had been a waste of time. Even so, it wasn't until he was sitting opposite her at Café Dyrehaven one day, talking about the size of brunch eggs, that Sidsel realised it couldn't go on. She broke up with him a few weeks before she went to London, where she would be living and studying for the next six months. Sidsel had felt out of place on her previous course (she wanted to touch, not read about, the pieces, but it would be several years before the penny dropped), and a friendly adviser had suggested she test the waters, try something else, some other subjects, in another city. And so there she was, in the imposing main hall of the university, having arrived in London a week earlier, entirely clueless, ambitious, free.

The first time Sidsel stepped into the auditorium and saw the lecturer, she was so disorientated that she turned around and went to find the Student Information Centre, where a member of staff explained that the room she'd come out of was indeed the right one. She'd assumed from the name that the lecturer was female, so already she felt wrong-footed, trailing two steps behind. In the six months Vicky was her teacher – and the three and a half he was her lover – this did not change.

Dr Singh was one of those promising academics whose talent had somehow slipped through his fingers, and with Sidsel he distanced himself from what he referred to as 'the pallid illusion of academia'. He did, however, love to teach. You could be petty and remark that he'd missed his calling as an actor, but he was an inspired and dedicated teacher whose natural charisma had condensed over the years into a more concentrated form. It was impossible to be unmoved. Students of both sexes hung on his every word, laughing at his jokes and going to great pains to formulate their questions and responses. Sidsel had asked him once what that felt like. Taken aback at having to explain something that had been part of his life since his teenage years, Vicky replied that some days it felt like being bathed in warm milk and others like a stone was rolling over him. Recently, he was sorry to say, it had mainly been the latter.

Perhaps it would have been simpler if he'd been good-looking. Vicky was small and rather spindly, with a short neck and stooping shoulders, and although his mouth was nicely shaped, his lips were dry and hid a set of neglected teeth. His hair was the only part of his appearance that seemed a natural extension of his personality: it was luxuriant and bluish black, except for the broad streaks of white that began at his temples and spread throughout its length. He wore it in a low bun, and Sidsel had only twice seen him without it tied back. Once was when he'd used her shower (which he only ever did that one time), and the other was when she happened to catch sight of him on the street with his wife. Abigail wore flares and a cloth cap, Vicky a tight-fitting suit the colour of lead. His dark hair was fluttering in the wind – they looked like a band! Sidsel had hidden behind a woman with a pram at the bus stop. This was a few days before she knew she was pregnant, and a couple of weeks before she was due to go back to Copenhagen. Later, as she wondered what to do (always in her tiny, overlit kitchen, always with a big glass of red wine and salt and vinegar crisps, which she ate from a bread basket), that image of them popped into her head. Its vividness and clarity quashed any vague thoughts she might have had about a life with Vicky and their illegitimate child. The more she thought about it, the more certain Sidsel became that the right thing was to keep out of it.

Dear V, I don't think we should see each other anymore, she began the email, to get it out of the way. *I hope you know that I am grateful for the experience of meeting you and since I am leaving soon (in less than two weeks as it is), I feel like this is the best way to go about it. I will miss our afternoons.* Missing their afternoons was another way of saying that she would miss having sex with him. Sex with Vicky was different from anything she had experienced before. His cock felt – as silly as it sounded – more alive than others. When he entered her, the undivided attention of his whole being seemed to rush through her body, and the fierceness of his presence made her cling to him. He kissed her eyelids, ran his fingers through her hair, stroked and gripped her face, and adjusted the angle of her pelvis. She often felt as though he could read her thoughts before they were any more than murky, prelinguistic needs. When she came, she came hard and long, and afterwards it felt like there was a little more air and light between every single cell in her limp, grateful body.

He tried to call, but only once, and left no message. It's possible he'd had his own fledgling fantasies about another life with another woman, but if so they were as frail as Sidsel's, crumbling easily in the face of reality, which after all was the reality of an actual, living wife. The last time they saw each other, Sidsel was six weeks pregnant and so nauseous that the other examiner asked discreetly if she was all right. Vicky was wearing an ironic floral-patterned shirt with a big collar, and looked like a man who'd rather shoot himself in both thighs than live through the next thirty-five minutes fully conscious. Having been allowed a breath of fresh air, Sidsel returned to give her presentation. It was toneless and uninspired, but she made no mistakes, and managed inexplicably to give satisfactory answers to their probing questions. After a deliberation that seemed to last for hours, Vicky emerged into the corridor. He shut the door behind him with exaggerated thoroughness, and gave her a mark of eighty and a firm hug. Sidsel could have whispered it to him then, she could have let him into the empty house of her secret, but she didn't. She kept silent, and it was he who spoke first. We can't get confused now, he said, caressing her cheek. Exactly what he meant by those words Sidsel never discovered, but she assumed it was something along the lines of *This isn't love, but I admit it's something like it.*

Back in Denmark she booked an appointment with the doctor, who referred her to a gynaecologist. He examined her, then gave her the necessary information, some long, thick pads and two different kinds of pill. The first, which she was supposed to take at the clinic, would terminate the embryo. The second, a suppository, would do the rest. There was medication for pain and nausea too, but not everybody needed it. The gynaecologist talked about the procedure in a hearty, careless way that made what she was planning to do seem pleasantly banal. Sidsel liked him, but when she still hadn't swallowed the tablet after ten minutes, he asked her to go home and come back in a week.

It's twenty to ten when he rings the bell. Sidsel stands in the doorway, listening to him climb the stairs and feeling like she's had too many shots at a party where she knows no one. Niels is taking the steps two at a time, she can hear it, and when he appears on the landing she's hard put not to run towards him. His face is wet. There are beads of rain in the fabric of his hat and in his eyebrows.

‘Hi there,’ he says, ‘sorry I’m late.’

Every time she sees him, he looks a little more like their dad. As if the older man’s face is working somewhere beneath the surface. The new job has made him thinner, more sinewy. He’s dashing around on that bike for several hours a day now, and almost certainly he isn’t eating enough. Sidsel has always envied her siblings their ability to ignore bodily needs. She’s the exact opposite: a slave to her whims and desires.

‘It doesn’t matter. Honestly.’

She puts her arms around him. The material of his jacket feels pleasant against her groggy head. They stand in silence until the light goes out with a click, and Sidsel pushes him into the narrow hall, which smells of her and Laura.

8

Beatrice

Bee has made a list. It didn't take that long.

So far it consists of eight names.

With a small sigh she picks up her pen and leans so far forward over the tabletop that the ends of her hair graze the paper. The tip of the pen hesitates over David R. (Dave). The last Bee heard from David, he had needed a place to sleep – something to do with a seminar in town. She didn't answer. She forgot, or she avoided thinking about it until it was too late anyway. That must be three years ago now. Pauline didn't have much time for Bee's past, and wasn't interested in her friends from the old days. Hattifatteners, Pauline jokingly called the people Bee knew from her years in Monterey and Carmel: round-shouldered and fanatical and as joyless as the Methodists she'd come to California to escape. So Bee forgot David's email, and just as quietly she forgot David, too.

Until now.

All right, seven names.

Twenty years on the West Coast, and this is the sum total.

She could die laughing. Bee suppresses the urge to bang her forehead against the table, folds the list down the middle and walks over to the window. The floor-length curtains with the gingko-leaf print cost a fortune, but Pauline left them up when she moved out. Bee made the mistake of thinking it was to make her happy.

The living room doesn't look as bare that way, Pauline explained when Bee mentioned the curtains. I want potential buyers to picture this having been a home once, so they can picture it being a home again.

A sales ploy near-identical to compassion.

Bee has been living in this once-a-home for the last seven months. It's gone well and sometimes less well, and now the whole thing is almost over. Last week 18 Park Hill Ave. went up on woolhouserealestate.com. In his adverts, Gabriel Woolhouse is smiling like a wolf in a children's book, and according to Pauline he's famous for his swift and frictionless deals. Nothing less will do, not now their home is being exchanged for the millions it has apparently been worth all along. Pauline thinks Bee has found a solution (because Bee said she has found a solution). She isn't worried about her – she 'knew she'd manage'.

Up close, you can see right through the pale green linen. It's still dark outside, but a more silvery dark than even half an hour ago. The street is vacant, the trees in the park a vast huddle of blue below. The window in the room Mr Pistilli rents out on Airbnb is black. There isn't even a jetlagged tourist to keep her company.

Bee had woken at quarter past four, unable to fall back to sleep. As far as she could tell, nothing in particular had roused her. She lay in the dark, feeling bewildered and well-rested. A couple of minutes passed before she remembered she wasn't alone. A few doors down, Seraphina was asleep in Hudson's old bed. The thought was exhilarating, and after a few breathing exercises that made no difference, she got up and dressed as soundlessly as possible.

It had seemed like the perfect moment to tackle the list, especially after the surprisingly successful dinner with Fifi. Alone in the frail dawn, which was still virtually night, she had made a pot of tea and lit two candles, which she placed on the table in front of her. She had set to work feeling good, with an open mind. But after only the first three names (two of which were former boyfriends), it was clear that she had precious few people to choose from.

The rope that was supposed to lead her out of the cave was too short, and now she was standing in the pitch black with the frayed stump in her hands.

'I hope you find a good solution, ma'am.'

How had she answered the friendly photographer, leaning against the door frame with the bottle of wine in one raised hand?

You always do, don't you?

You just do, somehow. You know?

Something casual and nonchalant. With airy aplomb, like someone sure of being caught as she lets herself fall backwards.

Into a forest of arms.

An obliging network of hands.

The problem is that good solutions require good friends, and for many years Bee left that part of her life to Pauline. She won't lie: it was an extraordinary relief to shrug her past off her shoulders like a shabby winter coat and step into the world that her relationship with Pauline Farley had opened up to her. Her wife's friends were sophisticated and fun, and despite the fact that they were in their late forties, Bee always sensed that their lives were lived right at the centre of things. That they *were* the centre. Half the group were what Pauline used to call creative artists. Things grew from their hands and brains that Bee did not always understand, but whose value she learned not to question. Sometimes, a few of them would get together and open 'a place' (Bee and Pauline kept the invitations in a heart-shaped noteholder on the kitchen table), and they never got discouraged, not even when trade was minimal or non-existent and a few years down the line they were forced to close. The rest of the group operated behind the scenes, turning the art into money, and the two wings alternately nourished and were nourished by each other. The friends made up a cybernetic ecosystem of artists and patrons, wild ideas and capital, and although most people would probably have feared otherwise, the specimen Pauline had imported had thrived from the very start. Bee felt at ease in their company. Nobody asked about her past, and if they did, they always stopped before they reached the teenage daughter she had left with her mother in Bondurant (back then it never occurred to her that their restraint could have been Pauline's doing). Among those open-minded people, her job was considered exotic, and although Bee sensed that to them clairvoyance was more performance art than a real profession, she felt both liked and respected.

Yet no matter how close they got, none of them had ever been Bee's friend. A couple might have been, perhaps, if she'd made an effort. That would have meant knowing the names of their children and dogs. She can recall the smell of their entrance halls, the feel of their hair and beards against her neck as they gave her a hug, the jangle of their rings as they took a glass and raised it in a toast. She knows where they take dance classes and where their families have a holiday home you can borrow. She has a reasonable sense of what wines they prefer and who doesn't eat what, but she could never, ever imagine calling them up and asking for help.

She lost that right when she lost Pauline.

That's the way it goes.

One bulb dies and the whole chain fizzles.

Pita has woken up and comes toddling over the carpet on legs that are stiff with sleep. She does a few sniffling, tail-wagging laps around her owner, but when Bee doesn't return her greeting she gives up and slinks back to her basket.

Down by the wrought-iron gate outside the park, two garbage men in overalls and high-vis jackets have appeared.

It's officially morning.

Once more, my soul, the rising day—

Beatrice's silhouette is narrow against the dull light

flooding the living room. A cold shiver makes her tremble, and in a reflexive gesture her hands dart fast as lightning over her belly and hips, running over her arms and shoulders, as though she wants to make sure she still exists and is a whole.

Bee straightens up and looks around enquiringly, but nobody has said anything. Fifi is standing with her back turned, laying the table in the front room. Now she pivots and gives a friendly smile. She's wearing glasses, which somehow make her look younger, not older. Like a child on the back of a cereal box.

'Well hey there. Good morning.'

Bee untangles herself from the blanket, which her daughter must have drawn over her as she slept.

'What time is it?'

Fifi shrugs.

'About half nine. Want me to check?'

'No, no. It's not important, and you've already been to the grocery store. You didn't need to do that – we could have gone together.'

'I woke up early,' says Fifi, going into the kitchen. 'I was absolutely starving, plus you looked so peaceful I didn't want to wake you. I just ran down to the corner. I took Pita – I hope that's okay?'

'Why wouldn't it be?'

'She had diarrhoea.'

Bee licks her finger and rubs it around the corners of her eyes. She listens to the poignant sounds of another human being moving to and fro. Cupboards opening and closing, drawers, the tap.

'Full disclosure – I didn't even bother trying to pick it up. Don't worry, nobody saw me. Your reputation in the neighbourhood is unblemished, if you're into that stuff.'

'Ha,' says Bee, pulling her hair into a clip and folding the blanket into a perfect rectangle.

Fifi has laid the table nicely. There's a dish of sliced fruit and a basket of toast, two soft-boiled eggs swaddled in a tea towel and a carton of orange juice. Milk in a jug. Bee doesn't usually eat anything until after midday. She has no appetite in the mornings, not since Pauline moved out.

'Do you have any coffee?'

'In the cupboard above the sink,' replies Bee, immediately remembering the list from yesterday. The pad and the candles and the pen – all are gone. Her diaphragm contracts into a quivering string. Fifi must have moved them when she set the table. There are the pillar candles, on the mantelpiece beside the cat-eyed monk, but Bee can't see the piece of paper anywhere.

Fifi is stooped over the coffee machine. She's wearing the dress from yesterday, but has pulled a white mohair cardigan over it. Her damp hair is gathered into a wobbly bun on the top of her head.

'I haven't used these before,' she says, tapping the Nespresso machine with a long nail. 'Nanna has the old-fashioned kind. Where do I put it in?'

Bee lifts the metal flap, slots in the capsule and presses

the button. The machine rumbles, and Fifi makes an excited noise as the caramel-coloured jet hits the bottom of the cup.

'It's just like in the commercials!'

Bee doesn't answer. She's caught sight of the pad. It's on the window frame, and on top is her folded list. The dark scribble over David's name has bled through to the other side of the paper.

'Do you want a cup too?'

'Same as you, please. Was it cold outside?' asks Bee, walking over to the window.

'A bit. Aren't mornings here always cold? I think you told me that once.'

'True,' says Bee, coughing as she tucks the piece of paper into her back pocket. 'They are. Cold, the mornings. It's the fog. It comes in from the sea.'

'All right.' Fifi holds up the cups in front of her. 'Let's eat.'

Her appetite surprises her. Bee eats half a grapefruit, several slices of melon, and two pieces of bread with butter and jam, and when Fifi offers her a soft-boiled egg she doesn't turn it down.

'Ah,' says Fifi, clicking her tongue in annoyance. 'Egg cups.'

'I don't think we have any of those.'

Bee isn't sure any more who the 'we' refers to, and she wishes she could stuff it back in her mouth.

'I think I saw some. Hang on a minute.'

Fifi comes back with two wooden egg cups. It was a friend of Pauline's who lathed them in her workshop and brought them as a gift for the hostess one night two thousand years ago.

'Are you having a party?' asks Fifi, handing one to her mother.

Bee's birthday isn't till December, and she has no intention of celebrating it.

'Party? What do you mean?'

'Or a dinner?' Fifi knocks a hole in the egg with a flick of her spoon. 'I recognised most of the names on the list. Iris and Janice, of course, I *loved* Janice. John, Ocean. Dawn I don't know, but you could set up a really good dance floor in here if you moved the table and couch into the other room. It's a pity the yard isn't bigger, or you could eat out there.'

Fifi takes a big sip of juice and looks around, as keen as though she's been hired to take charge of the whole project.

'I don't have anywhere to live,' says Bee. 'It's a list of the people I thought I could call and ask.'

Fifi puts down the glass and stares at her. Bee hasn't noticed the fake lashes until now. The weight of them makes each blink a fraction slower than normal, and the glasses enlarge her already big eyes, giving her the look of an insect.

'Are you moving out?'

'The house was put up for sale last week, and I promised Pauline I'd be out by the end of the month. The names on the list are the people I thought I could bring myself to ask for help. But lots of them I haven't spoken to for years. I've got no idea if Iris is even in the country. She always talked about moving to Mexico.'

Fifi takes a bite of her egg.

'I wish I *was* having a party,' says Bee, and tries to laugh.

'But why didn't you say anything? Of course you don't have time for guests if pretty soon you won't even have a place to stay.'

Bee can't remember seeing this expression on her daughter's face before.

Does Fifi feel sorry for her?

'Don't say stuff like that! It's really nice you came. I'm glad you're here. I'll figure something out.'

Bee knows exactly what Fifi is thinking. She should just say it. Bee deserves the twinge it will give her in her chest. Pita grunts under the table, and Fifi picks up the pug and starts scratching between her ears.

'Have you thought about going home?'

Bee takes a breath, struggling to stay calm.

'Of course I have.'

'But you're not going to.'

'Not if I can help it. Anyway, I don't think Marianne would be exactly thrilled to have her adult daughter sleeping on the couch again.'

'She'd still let you live there!' exclaims Fifi heatedly.

'Of course she would. I know that,' says Bee. 'But it's not the same as it is with you two, Seraphina. There have been too many disappointments and misunderstandings. It wouldn't be much fun for either of us.'

Fifi looks out of the window. The curtains have been drawn back. The sky above the treetops in the park is hazy and blue. Soon the sun will break through the thin cover of clouds.

Fifi's hands are stroking Pita's back absently, and Bee feels uncomfortably full.

'What about William?' says Fifi. 'He was still in the country last I checked. Maybe he can help.'

'William? William who?'

'Seriously?'

'Seriously what?'

'You seriously can't remember his name?'

'If I don't know who you're talking about, it's hard to say if I remember the person or not.'

'I'm talking about my father,' says Fifi. 'About William Catchpoole.'

Bee doesn't know how she could have been so naïve.

Of course Marianne told Fifi everything she knew.

They've been living together ever since Bee turned up on her mother's doorstep that January morning in 2007. Seraphina was eleven years old. They'd been driving all night in a rented car with nothing but the bare essentials. Bee had written a two-page letter, which she stuffed into her pocket at the last moment and replaced with a piece of paper that simply said:

We've gone. Don't try to contact us. B.

The note was on the kitchen table beside his tobacco. She had put a stapler and a coffee cup on two of the corners to make sure the draught didn't blow it away when he opened the door, hassled and irritable after his night shift.

Twelve years have passed, and she hasn't heard from him.

For once, he has done as she asked.

It had snowed all night long, and if you overlooked the bulky sacks of garbage strewn across the pavements, the neighbourhood had looked like something out of a fairy tale. Fifi was taken in.

It's so beautiful here, she sighed, as Bee turned down Cedar Street.

Like a true hippie's kid, Bee's daughter has been drawn ever since she was a little girl to anything and everything suggestive of petit bourgeois orderliness. Marianne opened the door in her nightdress and fleece, and said she'd got the upstairs ready for them.

Afterwards she asked only the most necessary questions (Do you owe him money? Did he do it to the girl too? Are you pregnant?) and concentrated on Seraphina. She bought her piles of new, warm clothes, set her up with a place at the local school and put her into treatment for the epilepsy Bee had hoped to cure through diet. Once the essentials were sorted, Marianne signed the girl up for Bondurant's hockey club and booked an appointment at the hairdresser's, and Fifi's matted and sun-bleached hair was chopped off just below the ears. For a long time she couldn't walk past a reflective surface without turning in amazement to stare at her mirror image.

From the very beginning, it was clear that Fifi was in her element in the suburbs.

She loved the peace and the rhythm, the neighbours who drove home at the same time each day, Marianne's meat- and milk-based cooking and the sound of lawnmowers and leaf blowers. All the things that had suffocated Bee now made her daughter unfurl and blossom. Fifi quickly acquired a big group of friends, and at school she set to work uncomplainingly, filling in the gaps left (and in some cases caused) by her mother's and stepfather's homeschooling. Bondurant was everything she had dreamed life could be. It was only ice hockey that she never really got on with, and after a couple of months she started doing jazz dance instead.

Bee made an effort, and for a while things actually went quite well.

She was glad to see her daughter happy, and the relief at having escaped Rodney and the village was enough to keep her going for a long time.

Three nights a week she taught yoga in a space at Fifi's dance school, and Marianne's friend's sister got her a part-time job as a receptionist for the same dentist she'd seen as a child. Now and again she did private sessions (always at the client's house – Marianne did not want *that* in her home), but it wasn't something she advertised. People would hear something through the grapevine, and then, after stewing for a while, would pluck up the courage to call and ask if they had 'understood correctly'. Within a year, Bee had saved enough money for a deposit on a ground-floor flat with a garden in the north-eastern area of Bondurant.

A few days before she was due to meet the landlord for a viewing, Pauline turned up in the dentist's waiting room. Bee was refilling the dispenser on the wall with plastic cups, next to a poster of a tooth riding a skateboard and wearing a backwards baseball cap.

The tall woman was the first patient of the day, and her presence and distinctive perfume filled the otherwise empty waiting room to the brim. Bee greeted her, and the woman – who did not look like someone who lived in Bondurant – gave her such a familiar smile that she was confused.

'Do I know you?' asked Bee, and regretted it the moment the woman looked back up, because clearly she did not. 'From the old days, I mean? Are you here from the city?'

Pauline cocked her head. 'Old days? I don't think so. I'm just visiting. And I got a toothache. That's my sob story.'

She tapped her cheek with a long finger. Bee apologised and turned her attention to the cups. There was a certain knack to getting them all into the tube and making them stay there. As she worked, she could sense the woman's eyes on the back of her neck, and she could smell her body long after 'Pauline Farley' had been called in. Something warm and root-like that lingered. Bee made sure she was busy with something in the back room as Pauline left the office, but when she re-emerged to change the bottle in the water cooler she found her still sitting in the waiting room, wearing her outdoor things, engrossed in an article in one of the old interior-design magazines the dentist's wife had donated to the clinic. A swell of shiny hair was visible between her hat and her scarf. Her mouth was lopsided from the anaesthetic. Bee headed for the water cooler and started unscrewing the empty bottle without a word.

'Do you think they'd mind if I took this with me?'

Pauline held up the magazine.

Bee was about to look over her shoulder, but caught herself. She nodded and said, 'Just take it.'

'Great.' Pauline got up and put the magazine in her bag. 'I found an article about one of my potential clients,' she explained. 'It's always good to have some background information when you're persuading people to give you money.'

'Sure,' said Bee, and nearly dropped the heavy plastic bottle of fresh water as the neck slipped, making a loud noise. Pauline didn't offer to help, but nor did she leave.

'Dr Lodenstein told me you teach yoga?'

Bee hadn't told Kent Lodenstein about her other job, but of course he knew. Just as most people in the neighbourhood knew by now why she and her daughter had moved back to Cedar Street after having visited Marianne only once in the last five years.

Man trouble.

A bad marriage.

I heard he was an addict. Marijuana.

Aren't they all?

A self-sufficient village? (What kind of person wants to be back in the Middle Ages?)

'Yes,' said Bee. 'I do.'

'What kind?'

Bee started explaining the principles behind Hatha yoga, but Pauline interrupted her. She really just wanted to know when the next class was being held.

‘Tomorrow night at eight,’ answered Bee, ‘in the big hall at the dance school, in the community centre. There’s a poster. You don’t need to sign up.’

Pauline thanked her, patted her leather bag twice and left the room. Not until Bee heard the outer door bang did she dump the infuriating bottle on to the floor and sink into the chair, which was still warm from Pauline’s buttocks. Laughter bubbled up inside her and dissipated. It was ages since she had felt light in this particular way.

Months.

No. Years.

‘Everything all right?’ called Dr Lodenstein from the other end of the corridor. He wasn’t used to hearing his new secretary laugh.

Bee could smell her perfume throughout the class, and underneath it, like a promise, the scent of her skin and hair. She made sure to distribute her time and attention equally among the students, but she was constantly aware of Pauline, casual in cropped trousers and a loose white T-shirt. Bee noticed the fluidity of her movements, admiring the freckled calves and big, well-manicured feet, the curving nails painted a dark red. The woman from the waiting room filled Bee with an emotion she couldn’t immediately pinpoint, so when Pauline invited her for a beer after class, she said yes without quite understanding why. It wasn’t the first time since coming back to Bondurant that Bee had been asked out, but it was the first time she had accepted.

They sat at a table in the corner of the Irish pub and took turns getting a round at the bar. Pauline was only in town for a couple of days, visiting a dying aunt. Bee was surprised that a woman like her would have relatives in Bondurant, and she was surprised how easy it was to talk about her years in Twin Oaks, about the house that was never finished and never would be finished, and her ex-husband's awful, gradual transformation. All the things that had felt like a dark tangle inside her, like barbed wire and shards of glass. They chatted until the owner appeared at their table and asked them to wrap up so he could close shop and go to bed. Outside, a few streets further on, they said goodbye.

You remind me of someone, said Pauline, tilting her head in the way Bee was already started to like, but I can't remember who it is.

The kiss felt simple. Pauline had a forthright, burning tongue.

Bee couldn't help laughing, the same untroubled laughter as in the waiting room.

They kissed again. Deeper, longer. Then they said goodnight and goodbye.

After maybe ten yards Pauline turned around and yelled, Kristin Scott Thomas! In *Under the Cherry Moon*, my first lesbian crush. To a T.

The first time, Bee only stayed a couple of days, under the pretext of attending a yoga workshop.

The second time she stayed a week without making any excuse.

Pauline lived in a duplex apartment with two men, one of whom was the father of her child. There was, as far as Bee could tell, no unpleasantness involved. Hudson was an easy, happy boy who loved his nanny, a young woman by the name of Delia, who arrived each morning before Pauline went to work and didn't go home until he had been put to bed.

After the third trip to California, Bee told Marianne she wasn't planning to sign the lease on the flat.

Fifi had already left for school.

The two women sat opposite one another at the kitchen table.

The same crocheted doilies were there, and the same moss-green lampshade as when the sixteen-year-old Beatrice Wallens had plucked up her courage and announced she was moving into a camper van with her boyfriend, ten years older. The only difference was that this time her father's chair was empty.

Bee put forward her case: she and Fifi would move back to California. It was there they had spent their best years, at Esalen, near the coast, among people who were broad-minded and curious. Twin Oaks had been a mistake, she would admit (here Marianne turned her face decorously away), but that didn't mean Bondurant was the only solution, did it? There were lots of places where you could lead a good life, and lots of different paths. There was enough money that they could start over properly.

Marianne had listened without interrupting, and when she finally said something, it was only a whisper.

You can do as you like, Beatrice. Seraphina stays here.

There were many things Bee could have said in reply. This is my child, my life, what right do you have to interfere? What do *you* know about happy childhoods?

Instead she nodded and said, Fine.

You can come as often as you want, said Marianne, and Fifi can visit you, but Bondurant is her home. She deserves a home after what she's been through.

There was nothing more to say. That's how the truth works.

A few months later, Bee flew to California with two light suitcases. She moved in with Pauline, and the two men moved out. Delia no longer came every day; Bee could look after Hudson, drop him off and pick him up, and after a while they used her only in the evenings when they were going out to dinner, or at weekends if they needed to get away. Fifi stayed with Marianne, as agreed. In the first couple of years Bee visited once a month, but with each trip back to Bondurant she felt more and more superfluous. Nanna and her grandchild had their in-jokes and routines. Bee reminded them of something they didn't want reminding of, and as the years went by, her visits became fewer and further between. She adapted to the guilt, learning to live with it the way you learn to live with a bad hip.

Ever since Seraphina was a young teenager, Marianne has functioned as her primary carer, her confidante, and yet all this time Bee has imagined her mother is loyal to *her*. Unlike Bee, though, Marianne hasn't forgotten his first name, and according to Fifi it didn't take more than a bit of light detective work to find the right man.

According to the register, three Williams checked into the Esalen Institute in the summer of 1995. One was seventy-two years old, another eighteen. William Catchpoole was born in St. Louis in 1967, two years before Bee.

Today he lives in Kentfield, one hour's drive north of San Francisco. As far as Fifi can tell, he's the only one at the address, and very well-off, judging by the height of the wall around his house.

'Do you want to see him?' asks Fifi, already taking out her phone.

'How – do you have a picture?'

'I can find one,' she says triumphantly, her thumb gliding over the screen, which responds to her touch by lighting up.

'Wait,' says Bee. 'Wait. How can you be sure it's him? Maybe you found someone else. Some random man we think we know all about. It's a bit weird, isn't it?'

Fifi lowers the phone and looks at Bee. Then she reaches across the table, past the juice and the empty plate, and takes her hand.

'I promise you he looks completely normal, Mom. No horns.'

PART TWO

For Fire for Warmth

9

Elisabeth (and Ida Marie)

The sun is shining, but they're probably right: it'll be too cold to sit outside. Anyway, the table inside is already laid. The desk, which under normal circumstances stands in the corner opposite the bed, has been dragged into the middle of the room, making it look cramped and messy.

Efie opens the door and pokes her head out. At the end of the corridor, she recognises Ida Marie's waddling gait. She doesn't want to ask her again – she can be terribly short-tempered and snide. Especially at weekends, when she'd rather be out shopping and drinking coffee with her friends. The locum turns the corner and disappears. Someone starts a machine running in the laundry room. Efie loiters in the doorway for a few more minutes, but no one walks past. They're probably in the rooms, getting everybody ready for lunch. She shuts the door and returns to her vantage point by the window. From here she can keep an eye on the bike racks and the entrance.

The pastries, which she ordered from the baker's herself,

seem daft this close to lunch. They're already serving up in the kitchen: steel dishes are clanging, and the aroma of cold cuts and buttered bread soon creeps in under the door and makes her belly gurgle. Leaning forward, she rests her head against the glass. The buds on the roses in the flower bed have lifted, and a cluster of poet's narcissi have unfolded their yellow flounces next to a severed root. A magpie hopping over the lawn takes flight and lands in the lower branches of the sycamore tree. When she opens the window, she's struck by the raw smell of earth and cold, and the wind lifts the curtain. If only she had a summer birthday! She envies the people who can hold their parties on the terrace. She has asked them to put the drawsheets and support blocks away while she has guests, and not to ask about toilet visits or pad changes.

Efie has been looking forward to this. Unlike a lot of other people, she's always liked birthdays. She enjoys celebrating, putting on a spread and getting presents. She's wearing her best shirt and clean black leggings. Her good shoes. Her hair is freshly trimmed in the grannyish style she's gradually got used to, and she has stayed away from her local for nearly a week. Anker dropped in to see her the other day. We were really worried you'd popped your clogs, he'd said, visibly relieved to find her safe and sound in her room. Efie, touched, was tempted to get in the car with the old man, take her regular spot among her friends and stand them a round, but instead she told him she was taking it easy because of her eczema. The frost and the dry air made it worse. She sent her love, and he promised to pass it on. She wished somebody had overheard their conversation. They were always so disappointed when she slipped up. And they hadn't been making up that stuff about her skin – for ages Efie had thought it was strategic, a way of getting her to drink less. It's your own fault you're itchy! Just look at that, see how bad that's got. But now, after only a week, the mottled patches over her breasts and back aren't as rough. Wow, that's looking great, Fatou had said as she smeared her with moisturiser after yesterday's bath. Keep it up, Efie! We might be able to drop the prednisolone altogether. Efie was pleased. She doesn't like them having to change her bedding and cut her nails because she's scratched herself bloody in her sleep again. She hates being a burden. Efie can never bring herself to surrender to the attendants' care. She can't get used to it. After two and a half years, she still shrinks from their practised hands. Most of them act like they don't mind bathing and changing and turning her, but Efie doesn't believe them for a second. She's a millstone, and apologising doesn't make it even the tiniest bit better. Yet the stupid bloody word is on her lips morning till night, ready to land like a dead mouse at the feet of anyone who enters her room in a white coat.

Sorry.

Sorry.

Sorry.

Efie shuts the window.

He did reply to the invitation, didn't he? Suddenly she's not sure. Her head is acting up – it's getting worse. The gasses of the past are seeping in through invisible cracks in the present, spreading chaos and confusion. Every morning she writes out her schedule in the diary, crossing out the bullet points as she gets through them. It's always in the same place, open at the current date, on the bedside table beside the bronze sculpture of Ganesha that Leif brought home from one of his trips. She consults the list regularly, some days multiple times an hour, and without it she feels like an astronaut she once saw in a film: free-floating and alone in space, a silver dot against a background of infinite darkness. The glue in her brain is getting brittle; the images are coming loose and disappearing.

Efie goes through the messages in her inbox. It doesn't take long to find his reply. The date and time are correct. He's looking forward to celebrating with her, he writes. Until then, behave yourself. Her heart stops racing – he must be on his way, then. She puts the phone down on the napkin, which Ida Marie has folded into a slapdash triangle. She adjusts the flag, standing wonky on its base, and tugs at the poppy-seed twist so it's resting against the almond pastry. What will they think if her one guest doesn't turn up? They'll bring it up at the staff meeting and try to put a positive spin on it. They'll do their best, and she'll act like it helps. Efie has never thought of herself as lonely. She has a knack for making people laugh, and as a younger woman she was always part of a crowd. If she wasn't the host, she was somebody's guest; but ever since Leif was hit by a car, there has been silence. He was the linchpin in their circle of friends, and the one who knew her best. René and Ulla she never hears from – they're busy with their grandchildren and allotments. Sus drops in from time to time, but her daughter's illness has changed her. The people down at the Five and Lime are either dead or too ill to visit, and her former colleagues, too, have gone quiet. At first they sent joint cards on her birthday and at Christmas, but it's been years since she had anything like that.

What made them decide to stop?

Niels is the only one Efie doesn't have to fight to keep hold of. He visits a couple of times a month, sometimes more often. They chat for a bit, then he sits at her table and reads while she watches TV or takes a nap. If the weather's good, they borrow a rickshaw bike and go for a ride around the neighbourhood, or he takes her to a proper pub, where they drink a single beer before he trundles her back home. When he went travelling last spring, she didn't expect to hear from him (he was on an adventure, after all), but after only a week she received the first long email. It contained detailed descriptions of people he'd met and places he'd seen. There were the names of cities and rivers, precise distances and altitudes, and thoughts about his next move. Efie typed the information into Google Maps and stared entranced at the grey-and-green mass, as though somewhere between the treetops she might spot her nephew, plodding through the forest in lonely majesty. She replied with anecdotes from her day-to-day life (adding a fictitious death or squabble here and there), and soon afterwards she received an email from somewhere else in the world, a little further south or east than before.

Efie understands Niels; she persuades herself she does. Something about him reminds her of her own younger days:

his mistrust of the establishment, his idealism, the recurring urge to get away, to move on. As a young woman she'd set off travelling as soon as her parents let her. First to France and Greece, like so many others her age with fire in their bellies, but later, when she got a job and started earning real money, to Asia, South America and the Balkans, with various friends, in groups or alone. Efie still feels the restive sense of premonition conjured by the name of a foreign city. She had imagined her pension would go towards seeing the places still on her bucket list. It hasn't turned out that way. There comes a point when life does what it wants with you, and this is why time after time she encourages Niels to go, even though when he's away she misses him so badly it hurts.

And there he is—

Walking up the tiled path, hand in hand with a little girl.

The girl says something, and he stops and kneels so their faces are level.

Efie feels instinctively offended.

Who is this child?

And why is she coming to her birthday?

How typical of Niels to be so impulsive.

So tone-deaf to other people's feelings.

Getting back to his feet, he whisks off the girl's balaclava, the movement as exaggerated as a magician's. Her dark hair flops forward over her face, and she pushes it back with both hands, laughing.

Efie watches them through the chink in the curtains; then comprehension dawns.

Sidsel's daughter.

The crinkled infant she had been the first person to visit on the maternity ward.

The child to whom she had imagined she might be a kind of grandmother.

Screwing up her eyes, she makes an effort, but the name eludes the sweeping floodlights of her memory.

Charlotte's grandchild.

Has Sidsel changed her mind? Has she been forgiven?

Efie cranes her neck, but there's no one by the bike racks, no one by the entrance to the park. It's just the two of them, and now the automatic doors are closing behind them.

Moments later she hears their voices in the corridor: Niels's low and muffled, the girl's clear as glass.

Efie still remembers how stunned she was when her niece called. It's just a couple of hours, said Sidsel, and she'll probably be asleep most of the time. Efie agreed without checking her diary – she didn't even pretend to think about it. Whatever plans she had, they could be cancelled.

Afterwards, once they'd said goodbye and hung up, she remained sitting in the car. It was the height of summer. Her shopping was sweating in its carrier bags in the back seat, but Efie didn't want to open the door and get out. She wanted to hold on to the feeling.

She made a mental note of the moment as a step in the right direction.

A sign that she was returning to the life she knew and had loved so much.

The following week, as she locked up her bike outside Sidsel's block and rang the bell, she was jittery in the same exhilarated way as a student in the days leading up to the prom. The intoxicating aroma of sun-warmed fruit and spices streamed out of the greengrocer's, and she was sweating profusely in her light blouse. The antidepressants had rapidly made her body bloat to twice its size, and her face was as round as a ball. She was unrecognisable, but that didn't really matter. The medication was working, and Efie was able to get up again in the morning without gearing herself up to it for hours beforehand. She could make plans and keep them, and she could get through the day without incorporating breaks for tears and sudden exhaustion.

The depression had come after the rehab, like a taunt.

A hard and unexpected shove from behind.

For the vast majority it was the other way round, the doctor had said.

In her case, the void left by quitting alcohol had been filled to the brim without warning by a paralysing and diffuse sorrow.

After the last follow-up session she had been sober but incapable of returning to work as planned. It felt like someone had poured sand in her eyes, ears and mouth then pulled a hood over her head.

They had agreed to extend her leave. To 'wait and see'.

We're all rooting for you, Elisabeth, Aksel had said, giving her shoulder a squeeze, as though she were participating in some obscure competition whose object was grim endurance.

But things were better now. She was returning to the world of the living, taking short, sensible steps.

Sidsel's phone call was the proof.

Her niece opened the door with the baby on one arm, and gave Efie a perfunctory hug with the other.

After going through the feeding and settling routine one last time, she gave her daughter a kiss, squeezed her hand and tore herself away before vanishing out the door and down the stairs at high speed, as though afraid she might regret it.

The child was crying heart-rendingly, but Efie was calm.

She held the girl in her arms as they walked around the flat, looking at things. Efie pointed at a photograph, a cushion, a potted plant, and told her what colour each thing was, what it was called and what you used it for. She let the baby reach out and touch them all.

Yes, she said, that's soft.

That's damp.

Look at that, that's shiny and glowing.

Afterwards, when the baby had calmed down and apparently forgotten all about the pain of separation, Efie put her down on the play mat in the kitchen and warmed the food Sidsel had left out in Tupperware. She lifted her into the high chair and tied a bib around her neck, then patiently helped the pieces of fishcake and potato into her mouth, offered her water from a beaker, and wiped her face with the corner of a clean tea towel.

At seven o'clock she put her into her pyjamas, mixed a bottle of formula, and gave it to her in the darkened bedroom. She burped her and lowered her into the crib.

Good night, she said, putting a hand on the girl's round belly.

The child whimpered and turned her head side to side, spat out her dummy and accepted it again several times, then fell asleep.

When Sidsel came home an hour later, Efie was on the sofa, reading a book she had found on the shelf.

She had done the washing-up and folded the laundry.

Outside the windows, the summer sky was pink.

Did it go all right? asked Sidsel, and Efie didn't have to lie.

A little while later, Sidsel called again. She'd been invited to a close friend's farewell do.

Efie turned up as agreed, and the routine was repeated. The girl cried more insistently this time, as though she understood now what was happening, and Efie had to go back into her bedroom several times to pick her up, sing to her and reassure her, but by half past eight she was sound asleep. Efie made herself a cheese sandwich and sat down with the paper she'd brought, and which she'd neglected to read that morning. Around midnight she heard the key in the lock. Sidsel smelled of smoke and night, and as she stood waiting impatiently for the water to boil, rumpling her blonde hair, it struck Efie that she looked like her mother. They had a cup of tea in the cramped kitchen, and as Efie was about to leave, Sidsel remembered something.

'Hang on,' she said, disappearing into the bedroom. 'To say thanks for helping. I thought it was really pretty.'

The cactus was no bigger than a thumb and had a single fiery red flower.

Efie thanked her, and when she reached her bike she lined the basket with her jacket so the pot didn't tip over on the way home.

She put it on her desk and watered it the way she was supposed to.

That autumn she bought a ticket on a group tour to Istanbul and ordered fizzy drinks while everyone else drank cheap wine and raki. The word *alcoholic* no longer frightened her, and if people asked she gave them a candid answer. Efie saw the Hagia Sophia, struggling up the thousands of steps until her lungs and feet were burning. She took pictures of the scrawny cats and caught a ferry across the Bosphorus.

On Christmas Eve they ordered a gigantic tray of sushi, exchanged gifts and played Settlers of Catan. Sidsel put the baby to sleep in Efie's bed, and Niels stayed over until the following day.

It was at the beginning of the new year that things went wrong. Not long after the girl's first birthday.

Sidsel was going to an open day at the School of Conservation, and Efie had offered to help. There was no longer anything odd about it.

She was about to head over to Sidsel's when Aksel called.

Efie went back into the living room, loosened her scarf and unbuttoned her jacket.

We've been discussing it a lot, he said, and you've got to believe me when I say we've done everything we can to find a solution. I argued your case.

She imagined him pacing around his high-ceilinged flat overlooking Østre Anlæg Park. Efie had visited the headmaster only once. That staff party had gone down in history. Everyone had had a skinful; she was new at the time and hadn't yet drawn attention to herself. The headmaster's wife threw up on the balcony, and the physics teacher took off his shirt and swung it over his head like a lasso.

The way things were looking right now, he couldn't offer her anything. There were too many unknowns. The students were unsure about a change of teacher so close to their final exams. They had come to like the substitute and wanted to keep her. He was sorry.

The original plan had been to return after the Easter break. A fresh start.

Efie said she understood. She was glad he'd tried.

On the way to Sidsel's, she stopped at a corner shop she didn't normally use and bought white wine and a small bottle of vodka. She wrapped the bottles in her scarf and put them at the bottom of her bag, all without letting her actions become thought.

She can still hear the bellow that woke her. Tattered and fearful. Sidsel flung down her key and strode past her into the bedroom, where her daughter's hiccupping, mechanical crying took a long time to subside.

Efie didn't wait for her niece to throw her out.

Getting up from the sofa, she picked up her things with numb fingers.

On the street below, her bike was gone. It was snowing, and she decided to step inside a pub she didn't know to call a taxi. But not until she'd had a glass of wine. Two. Not until she'd drunk herself deep into that starry high, that expansion of her too-constricted brain that she had missed so much. God, how she'd missed it! The velvety sensation. Like a tightly bound string had been undone somewhere deep inside her head.

I've been looking after my grandchild, she told anyone who cared to listen.

I look after her from time to time. Help out where I can. Her mum is alone with the girl.

Two days later, Niels came by with her reading glasses and the scarf she'd forgotten. He said not a word about what had happened, although Sidsel must have told him everything. He tidied up and put a load of laundry in the machine, and he took the empty bottles and the rubbish when he left.

Laura, yes! A sweet and somewhat ordinary name.

She takes the little hand and smiles.

'My name is Elisabeth,' she says, 'but people call me Efie.'

The girl looks at Niels as though for confirmation, and he shrugs and nods.

'Are you ill?' she asks, looking at the wheelchair.

'Mostly in my legs,' says Efie. 'There's nothing wrong with the rest of me.'

'Many happy returns,' says Niels, giving her a kiss on the cheek.

'Thanks, but I think we'll need an extra plate.'

'I'll find one,' says Niels, and is out the door before Efie can protest.

She looks at the girl. A pretty child, but aren't most children pretty at that age? As fresh as newly minted coins.

'Don't you want to take off your snowsuit?'

Laura nods, but doesn't move.

'Shall I help you? Come over here, then.'

She unzips the snowsuit and peels it off. Out of the teddy-bear shape emerges a slight frame in a glittery skirt and striped top.

'Gosh, don't you look nice,' says Efie, clapping her hands. 'Just look how that catches the light.'

'My mum bought it for me. It's got sequins. I have two. But the other one is green.'

'It's lovely. Are you hungry?'

Laura snuffles, but doesn't answer.

'Do you like Danish pastries?'

The girl turns uncertainly towards the open door, just as Niels enters with a folding chair, a plate and a jug of yellow juice.

Once they've eaten and sung, Efie lets Laura climb on to her bed and press the buttons. The child squeals with glee every time the motor whirrs and the mattress bulges and rises beneath her.

'Last time,' says Niels, 'then that's it. It's not a toy. Ideally Aunt Efie will be able to use it when you're finished.'

Laura nods and holds down the button until her matchstick legs are sticking straight up in the air. The mechanism clicks threateningly a couple of times and stops.

'Can I do it just one more time?' she asks, rolling over and up on to her knees as though it were nothing.

'Nope,' says Niels. 'A deal's a deal.' He hoists her down from the bed, puts her back on a chair and pours her a glass of juice, which she immediately begins to drink. Maybe it's her colouring, but Efie can't see Sidsel in her. The narrow face and wide mouth, those radiant black eyes – the child doesn't look remotely like her mother. Without him even knowing, her father's genes are busy recreating his image in this new person. Efie admires her niece's decisiveness. She herself spent the better part of twelve years waiting for the right man and the right moment to show up (all while her friends, one after another, settled for the wrong one on both counts) before she realised neither was going to – and certainly not at the same time.

Laura puts down the glass, coughs violently and wipes her mouth on her sleeve.

'Niels, please can I go into the hallway for a look?'

'What do you want out there?'

'Just a look.'

'Can you find your way back, do you think?'

The girl nods, jumps down from the chair and slips out through the door. Niels follows, her shoes in his hand.

Efie was thirty-eight when she understood she wasn't going to be a mother. It happened a few days before Christmas, at a café in Seville. It was a warm night for the time of year, and starry; she had eaten and drunk well. She was smoking as she savoured her coffee, waiting for the bill, and it was there, between two cigarettes, that the thought popped into her head: it won't happen. Not because it was physically impossible, but because it was not to *be*. A premonition. A vision. In a way, it was a relief. Unlike her sister, who was shackled to the house and her children's wildly differing demands during the increasingly frequent and lengthy periods when Troels was away for work, Efie could do as she pleased. Apart from her teaching, which she loved, she was free; she wasn't worn thin, like so many women her age, on the family grindstone. When Charlotte fell ill and Niels moved in with his aunt, Efie had expected that taking responsibility for the boy would awaken some maternal instinct in her. That didn't happen. From the first, their relationship was one of equals, and in the years after his mother's death they were more flatmates than anything else. They took turns cooking and doing the shopping, and Efie only meddled in his life when it was strictly necessary. In return, he did not judge her when she went on one of her binges.

'She found the TV room,' says Niels, shutting the door behind him. 'Lost to the world.'

'Well,' says Efie, 'it must be pretty boring in here for a six-year-old.'

'Not necessarily. I think she's finding it thrilling enough. Laura would say something if she was bored.'

Efie smiles, but things aren't the same. The girl has changed the way they speak, the way Niels feels in her room. The salt lamp he gave her is on the desk, glowing with an uncanny coral-red light.

'Would you like any more coffee?' she asks, already reaching for the pot.

'No thanks.' Niels leans back in the chair and stretches. 'Fifty-six. You're holding up pretty well.'

'Oh, give it a rest!'

But she can't help laughing.

He says no more. The sun is on his neck, making the short hair glimmer like the surface of water. Is he bored? Efie casts around for something to offer him. She'd like to give him something – she wants them to stay longer. The thought of them leaving makes her feel blackened inside. It's nearly two; they ought to be going. At some point people always have to be going. She's learned to live with it, not to like it. But she doesn't want to cry, not on her birthday.

'I haven't said anything to Sidsel,' says Niels.

Efie didn't ask, but the thought had crossed her mind.

'What if Laura says something?'

'I'm not going to forbid her to talk about you, Efie.'

He looks straight at her. God, it's crazy how much he's come to look like Troels as he's got older. The eyes, the long cheeks. She needs to make sure she doesn't get mixed up, let the old anger take hold and flare up. How she despised that man, and Charlotte's insistence, to the very last, on defending him! Efie took the news of her former brother-in-law's sudden illness and death in north-eastern Russia without much emotion. In her eyes, his three children had long been de facto orphans.

'Did you hear what I said?'

He's put his hand on her arm.

'Yes,' she says. 'That's good.'

In the room next door, Jonna is complaining in long chains of vowels. Niels dabs poppy seeds from his plate and sticks his finger in his mouth.

'Sidsel won't change her mind.'

'No,' says Efie, and smiles by mistake. 'I know that.'

Ida Marie returns the bed to its neutral position and gathers the plates and cups on to a tray as quietly as possible. The flag last, draped over the top plate. Elisabeth has nodded off in her chair. Ida Marie lifts her warm head with one hand and tucks a pillow between her shoulder and her ear, then squats down, puts her arms around Elisabeth's legs, and shifts her knees forward and into the middle, so that her weight is better distributed. The large woman smells pleasantly of shampoo and camphor lotion, but her pad is heavy at the front. Ida Marie shuts the window and turns off the lamp, which has been placed on the bedside table. The photograph of the two girls catches her eye and, cautiously, she picks it up. She's not normally like this. Many of the other staff members give in to their curiosity. They poke through cupboards and drawers, read old letters and diaries, rifle through things that don't concern them – and afterwards they gossip about what they've found. Not Ida Marie, not normally. She respects the residents' private lives, just as she hopes hers will be respected one day when she's too old or too sick to protect it. The girls in the picture appear to be in their late teens, wearing light shorts and colourful T-shirts with the name of a resort town emblazoned across the chest. Elisabeth's tight curls are a cloud around her head. The other one – she must be a sister or a cousin – has sleek blonde hair gathered into a ponytail. Arms around each other's shoulders, they're laughing at the photographer, both of them sweaty and exhausted, bronzed in the way Ida Marie associates with the seventies. The total absence of any connection between the girl who once stood on a tennis court and the woman snoozing in her wheelchair makes time itself seem like a cruel magic trick. Shuddering, Ida Marie puts the photograph back. She throws the wrapping paper in the bin and takes the tray with her when she leaves. In the office, she finds Elisabeth Gabel's daily schedule and adds a note for the evening shift:

Needs changing when she wakes up; didn't want to disturb her.

10

Ea (and Curtis)

It's early, but there's a line at El Farolito. Ea watches Hector's bulky shape through the fogged-up pane. He's reached the counter now, and puts in his order. She doesn't need to hear him to know what he's saying, or how he's saying it. They parked in the sun. She didn't realise it would take this long. A man is pushing a shopping cart piled high with his belongings up the sloping sidewalk. One of the wheels is turning round and round, squealing. Ea keeps an eye on him in the rear-view mirror. He keeps having to stop and hitch up his pants, which are held in place with a length of nylon rope. His beard is the same nicotine-yellow as the wool around a sheep's tail; his forehead is shiny with sun. She recognises him. He hangs around down at the park. Ea isn't used to seeing him upright and in motion, but there's no doubt it's the same man. When she walks past him with Coco, he greets them with a courteous *Ladies*. Long after he has turned the corner, she can still hear the wheel. Ea pulls her purse into her lap and rummages for a bottle of water she knows perfectly well isn't there, then dumps the bag back on to the floor. On the door of the SECOND CHURCH OF CHRIST, SCIENTIST there's a note in Spanish and English to say that the church is permanently closed. The cross and crown hovering against a background of fleecy clouds, the looping red letters. She has always liked that church sign. Ea rolls down the other window and opens the glove compartment. Apart from the candy wrappers and neglected comic books, it's full of the cassette tapes her ex-boyfriend made for her, which he presented to her in a shoebox after she left him. *So you'll think of me while you're running away from me.* In a sense, it works like a charm. She thinks about him every time she puts on one of the tapes, and feels relieved. Ea finds *The Modern Lovers*, slots it into the deck and presses play. Jonathan Richman's baritone voice closes around her chest and squeezes. She's felt like crying ever since her visit to the medium, but when she tries to, nothing happens.

Ea hasn't told Hector about Beatrice Wallens or about the voices. The way they felt at once close by and too far away for her to hear what was being said. She knows exactly what he'd say: mediums are experts (to a greater or lesser degree) at reading people. The voices are a symptom of overtiredness – she's in shock after having been confronted with a woman who claimed to be in contact with her dead parents.

And now, when the physical world seems compelling in all its overheated, fetid might, Ea is inclined to think he's right.

'Can you tell me what all these people want with burritos at half ten in the morning?' asks Hector, bringing the smell of

El Farolito into the car. 'What's this crap you're listening to?'

'Just switch it off.'

'I was on the verge of giving up. That really wasn't a fun experience.'

Ea strokes his hair.

'Did you remember to ask for extra guacamole?'

Balancing the polystyrene containers in his lap, he fastens his seat belt.

'What if I didn't?'

'Then you'd have to go back in.'

'I forget how mean you can be.'

He sticks his whole head out the window like the dog he reminds her of, big, with long black fur and droopy eyes.

'Why aren't we driving?'

Ea gestures towards the cars on their left, spread like a string of pearls. Other people have had the same idea.

'By the way, did you see the church is closed?'

'Is it? Hm. I never understood that comma, and now it's too late. No one to ask.'

Moments later Ea indicates and pulls out, and they can finally join the northbound traffic on Mission. It was his idea to take a drive. Normally it's Ea who drags the three of them out of town (excursions during which father and daughter spend half the time whining about having to leave and the other half not wanting to go home. Coco: 'This is my Happy Place', and so on), but not today. Hector mentioned it again over breakfast, as though afraid she'd forget and make other plans. This time they're alone. Coco was picked up early that morning for yet another one of her countless cousins' birthdays. Ea suspects Lola of inventing relatives in order to see her daughter beyond their agreed days. Hector says paranoia doesn't suit her.

He's put on Roberta Flack, and Ea sings along unselfconsciously. After all these years, the sight of the bridge and its lobster-red harp strings can still hit her hard in the chest. Happiness! Bam! Above them the sky is cloudless, the Pacific glittering dark blue. For a few moments, everything is simple. They're nearly halfway across the Golden Gate Bridge when he suggests a detour to the Headlands Center for the Arts. The fort, situated in the national park in Marin, runs a residence programme and exhibition space for practising artists.

'And give Sausalito a miss? Is something happening up there?'

She turns her head. Between the beard and the sunglasses there's only a narrow strip of face, impossible to read.

'Damian has a residency there. I said we might drop by. We'll stop real quick and say hi, then we can head over to the waterfront and eat.'

'If you want.'

She'd rather not.

Damian Roo is a reasonably well-known art photographer she had a thing with shortly after arriving in town, when she desperately needed a way to connect to the place. They never slept together, but it was a close call. He travels for much of the year, so when he's finally back in San Francisco he's obsessed with the idea of 'rallying the crowd' and celebrating things. Let's celebrate – it's the last Tuesday of the month, the moon is full, so-and-so's got a job, we're all here together! Last time he came to dinner at theirs, he managed eventually to persuade Ea to get out her needles. He'd already chosen the one he wanted from the folder of Coco's drawings. Most people tend to flip through the nine-year-old girl's designs, sigh and point and go, gosh, how cute, and look at that one, she's so talented, but when it comes down to it, nobody chooses them. Until Damian did. He pointed at *Eye in Hand* (Coco names her designs very laconically, and this one depicted a hand with an eye in the middle of the palm), pulled up his shirt and puffed out his chest. The others whooped. Ea felt too drunk, really, to start such a challenging piece, but she soon settled into her rhythm, concentrating, and after an hour she straightened up and said: Done. It was one of her best.

The studio is on the top floor of the former barracks, in the recruits' old dorm. There's a popcorny smell of sun and fresh ink, and the room is rustic in a way that it's impossible not to be charmed by today. Broad crossbeams are supported by four rows of steel columns, and light floods through the windows and over the worm-eaten boards. In a kitchenette in the far corner, Damian heats water on a gas burner and mixes two cups of instant coffee, which he doesn't offer them because he's busy showing off the photos he's spent all morning tacking on to sheets of polystyrene along one wall. None of the pictures interests Ea. The lighting in them is harsh, and the sitters all stare into space with the same apathetic and suggestive gaze.

'Those two,' says Damian, standing beside her, 'it was the second time they'd met. I only wanted them to kiss, really. Then they asked if it was okay with me if they went at it. I said no problem, just go for it. And they did. I think it turned them on.'

She nods.

'Looks that way.'

The couple are lying intertwined at the edge of a cornfield. The woman's dress has been pushed up to her neck, her head is thrown backwards, and her mouth is open in a moan. He's naked except for his shoes. Yet it's the corn that draws the eye. The plants are large and unnaturally green, with bristling taffeta hair.

Damian surveys her with a melancholy smile.

'I can't help thinking about the first time I met you,' he says. 'You were so young. I remember I just let you talk and talk and talk. I liked your accent. You've lost it, you know that?'

'I still get asked where I'm from.'

'And you think it's the way you talk?'

She turns back to the photograph. Now the corn just looks like corn.

'It's your eyes,' he says, 'the way you *look* at us. Like you're a teeny tiny bit better. That good old European superiority. You shouldn't be ashamed of it, it's actually really sweet . . .'

Damian is about to say something else when Hector calls

from the other end of the room. He wants to know what lens Damian used for the photos of the twin girls.

The worst thing is, she knows he's right.

Ea had thought it would disappear in time, but if anything it's getting worse. She catches herself missing the way people hold their cutlery in Europe. Buildings that are more than a few hundred years old, and the smell of rain on cobbles. More recently, she has tried teaching Coco to eat with both a knife and a fork. Ea loses her appetite seeing the food being shovelled into her mouth.

Ten minutes later, the two men are still deep in technical conversation. Ea wanders over to the bookcase, the only real furniture in the room, and chooses a title at random. She sits down on the floor with the book in her lap, letting naked female bodies in various poses flit before her eyes. Thighs, shoulders, breasts, ears, lips. Not until she's partway into the book's final third does she realise that it's the same person in all the images – Yoko, the photographer's wife – and that she dies at the end. There's a picture of the corpse in its coffin. The body and hair are covered with flowers, the face peeping out between the silky white petals. Then the cat on the sofa and on their tightly made bed. The snowy back yard, a full ashtray, a shirt on a hanger. The last few photographs radiate emptiness. At the other end of the room, she can hear Hector taking leave of Damian in his characteristically abrupt manner, as though the parting were a surprising fact just presented to him via an earpiece. Ea shuts the book and puts it back on the shelf.

~

They walk hand in hand towards the car. The grass by their sandal-clad feet is popping and crackling with insects.

'I don't like him,' says Ea.

'Nah,' says Hector, 'but he's talented.'

'You're more talented.'

He sighs.

'I mean it. All those pictures are *interesting* in the same way. The ones you do are beautiful.'

'Let's not go there now.'

There = Why did you stop doing what you loved?

Working for the realtor was supposed to be a side gig, but these days the jobs for Gabriel have started taking up all his time. Hector spends his days driving around taking wide-angle shots of disgustingly rich people's tasteless living rooms, kitchens, bedrooms. Gabriel maintains that the houses Hector shoots get twice as much traffic as the rest. Maybe it's true, but he isn't taking photos for the pleasure of it any more, and the only poems he writes are the ones in Coco's lunchbox (Ea empties the lunchbox in the afternoon, faithfully preserving the grease-stained scraps in a folder – *Lunch Poems*, literally). She wishes it didn't matter what he does, but when he gave up his spot at the studio she felt a little cheated. She had fallen in love with an artist.

A huddle of eucalyptus trees casts a tufted blue shadow over the car, but they should really have left the windows open. Inside, everything smells of meat and raw, sodden onions. It's like climbing into a mouth.

'He tells me I've lost my accent,' says Ea, fastening herself into the warm seat.

'That sounds like something Damian would say. Does it make you sad? Is that why you're mad at him?'

'Maybe,' she says, switching on the engine and backing out of the parking space. 'Maybe that's all it is. I don't know. Anyway, so what if I have?'

Ea bores her feet through the top layer of pebbles until she feels a damp chill seep into her skin. The day has slipped through her fingers, somewhere between the Headlands Center for the Arts and right now. Beside her, Hector is eating, his head jutting forward between his knees. She isn't really hungry any more. The noonday sun is thudding overhead, making their surroundings seem as flat as a stage set. Ea tears off a piece of tortilla and chucks it towards the silver-backed gull loitering nearby. It puts its head back and swallows the offering without a sound, takes flight and lands further along the shore. A glossy black tree trunk is revolving hypnotically in the surf.

'You shouldn't really be giving them bread.' Hector points with a nacho in the direction of the gull. 'It swells up in their stomachs.'

'I thought that was pasta.'

The waves surge and break, reflected in his smoked lenses.

'Pasta? Maybe. Coco told me,' he says, his mouth full. 'Imagine. All those years you think you're doing them a favour . . .'

A few yards away, a couple of families are setting up a picnic. The sand is cluttered with blankets and sunshades, plastic buckets and Ziploc bags, and nobody pays the slightest attention when a suitcase-shaped Labrador with a sun-bleached head arches its back and does a shit dangerously close to their rush mats. Ea empties her water bottle and shoots a tentative look at the horizon, but her eyes spring back, as though held in their sockets by taut elastic bands.

She's bored. Not the way adults get bored, but the pestering, draining way she recalls from childhood afternoons. She wonders what Coco is doing right now (reading, probably, somewhere on the fringes of the group – Ea saw her stuff a *Dragon Ball* into her backpack). As always when the girl isn't nearby, it feels like a part of them is in shadow.

'I'm going down for a quick paddle,' she says, getting to her feet and brushing bits of pebble off the back of her thighs. 'Want to come?'

Hector nods, but only gets up halfway before he leans forward and puts his weight on his left knee. He staggers a little, but then manages to get his right leg forward and bent into a ninety-degree angle in front of him. Until now, she's only seen this position in movies.

'Hector!' exclaims Ea in horror. 'Get up!'

He's taken off his sunglasses. The wind is blowing his hair into his face. People are staring and pointing. Someone whistles. Afterwards they lie in the sand for ages, holding each other, embarrassed and astonished and happy.

~

He's booked a table at an expensive restaurant neither of them has been to before. There are welcome drinks and a wine list, there's cognac with the coffee, and finally there's champagne on the house when a waiter discovers the reason for their visit. They're home by eleven, way too drunk and full to even consider having sex. Now he's asleep beside her. Each time he inhales, there's a series of clicks from one nostril. Engaged. Maybe it would feel different if she hadn't stuffed herself? More new. Ea rolls on to her back and shoves an extra pillow under her head. Her belly is sore and distended against her ribs; her gullet is burning. She holds out her hand, inspecting the ring, which he's had made specially for her. Damian's sister is a goldsmith, which explains the exhausting trip to the studio. Hector's secretiveness is almost the most touching thing about it. Ea plays with her fingers, making the gold glint. They still haven't put up curtains, and at night the bedroom walls are alive and deep in the light from the street. She's got used to it; by now she's not even sure she could fall asleep in true darkness.

Cashew skitters into his cave with an indignant rustle when the ceiling light comes on.

'Sorry,' grunts Ea, finding the packet of Nexium in the kitchen drawer. Sitting at the table, she drinks the rest of the water in small sips, feeling the fire in her belly die down as the pills begin to work.

It's past midnight, but the light is on in her neighbour's kitchen across the road, and shortly afterwards the dark-haired one turns up and starts fiddling around with pans and chopping boards. As always when he cooks, he's wearing a bandana. For a while Hector and Ea kept track of the various odd things the family did, and now she feels like restarting the game. The piece of paper must be here somewhere. She searches the bulletin board and among the sheaves of drawings that litter the shelves. She pulls out all the drawers from the blue dresser, emptying them one by one until she finds the sheet of paper headed with the words DEVIANT NEIGHBOR BEHAVIOR. The last observation is more than a year old: *daughter, approx. eight, lifting weights while watching cartoons (is that an order?!).* Ea jots down what she's seen, notes the time and date, and tacks the piece of paper up on the board.

Cashew has emerged from his hiding place. He fixes her through the glass with two incensed old-lady eyes.

'Are you hungry?'

Normally it's Hector and Coco that feed him.

Ea grabs the box of mealworms from the fridge. The hike in temperature wakes them from their torpor, and they writhe around in the sawdust. Catching two with some tongs, she lowers them to the lizard. A glimpse of the Barbie-pink mouth, the minuscule, knife-sharp teeth.

'Here, you little gremlin.'

Ea moves the lid back over the terrarium and starts putting all the bits of paper back in the dresser. A photograph falls out of a padded envelope where it had been temporarily filed, along with an expired Clipper card and a few knotted bracelets. All three people are wearing orange life jackets over their swimsuits. The water of the lake below them is black as engine oil. Niels, who has been allowed to sit at the back and steer, is the only one grinning at the camera. Six years old, his curls sparkling in the sun. Sidsel's face is hidden in the shadow of a bucket hat, and Ea herself is in the middle, skinny and huddled, like a piece of kit. She remembers that trip well – it's the last time all five of them were together. Before Russia and her mother's illness, although both must have been in the works by then: grant applications and project write-ups, mutating cells. Once the children had been put to bed, the adults got drunk by the fire. The conversation drifted through the fabric of the tent, carried with the scent of wood smoke. The group discussed politics, gender roles, art; they shouted and talked over one another. She listened out for her mother's voice. Ea hoped every night that she would join the conversation, voice some unexpected opinion – something that revealed her. It didn't happen. Charlotte preferred listening to other people's viewpoints and stories, but her laughter was always the last to fade when something funny or inappropriate was said.

Ea turns the photograph over. The back is smooth and white. There's nothing written on it. Charlotte took it, most likely. Her mother appears in only a fraction of their holiday snaps. Mostly she's the one looking. As the oldest child, Ea was the one who spent most time with their mother, and yet – as though it were determined by some inverse proportionality – the one who felt most alienated from her. Charlotte Gabel was like a house with the lights on in every single room. Everything was what it seemed, with no scope for interpretation, no nooks in which to hide, and Ea couldn't shake a greedy desire for something else, for something more than there was. Their mother lived her life without, apparently, ever wondering whether it could be different. Whether she *wanted* it to be different. The days were welcomed with an equanimity that for years Ea confused with indifference (or, if she was in a nastier mood, with stupidity). The result was that throughout her childhood and much of her adolescence, she had considered herself more on the wavelength of her father, whose presence was felt in stray flashes, than of her mother, who willingly gave away everything she had. Not until far too late did Ea realise how much strength Charlotte's approach to life demanded. Her mother was not simple. She was a giant in disguise, a smiling demigod in an ordinary mortal family of three ungrateful kids and a moody husband, a man in such thrall to his inner life that it seemed as though some malevolent water sprite was living at the bottom of his chest, luring him down into his own depths.

As far back as Ea could remember, Troels had often been away travelling, but in the last years of her parents' marriage he was absent most of the time, so the divorce didn't make much practical difference in the life of their family. By the time their mother got sick and he moved back to Denmark, he hadn't been a stable part of his children's day-to-day routine for years. But, as usual, Charlotte's scrupulous instinct for order made it easy for him, and after her death Troels stayed in the country no longer than absolutely necessary.

Anthropologists aren't good at comforting people, he said one day to Ea. We've always seen something worse. Was it an apology disguised as an explanation? Or an explanation that could function as an apology if needed? Perhaps it was merely a statement. At any rate, as soon as Niels – the only one too young to live by himself – had been settled with their aunt, the house sold and the final papers signed, Troels began preparing to leave.

Ea decided not to forgive him. Not as in never, and when she got a call from a woman during her afternoon shift at Trattoria Ponchielli, informing her that her father had been admitted to hospital in Yakutsk, they hadn't spoken for more than four years. The situation was serious. The infection had spread within a few days from the lungs to the heart (so he *does* have one, muttered Sidsel when Ea called, and neither of them could help laughing, because it was such an awful thing to say). Troels died shortly afterwards, surrounded by his team and the two interpreters who had been there from the beginning.

Ea was living in Trieste at the time, the consequence of a fling that had turned out not to last the season. She had a room with a balcony, a devoted cat she unimaginatively christened Dante, and a job she liked. It was solely for her siblings' sake that she came home for the funeral. They picked her up at the airport, and to her dismay Ea realised all too well how their father must have felt during his visits home. The distance between them was virtually tangible! All the things she recognised in Niels and Sidsel's faces reinforced her sense of alienation, and although Ea did her best to hide it, her thoughts kept returning to the question of when she could get away from Copenhagen. Troels's refrigerated body arrived on a cargo plane four days later, he was buried on a sunny day in May, and before the summer was out Ea had quit her job at Ponchielli and bought a one-way ticket to San Francisco.

Italy no longer felt far enough away.

Sometimes she thinks about Dante, and it tugs at her heartstrings. The cat must be long dead by now. It's been ten years since she saw him last.

Ea lets the photograph fall back into the drawer and stands up on shaking legs. She's overcome with the same dizzying nausea she'd felt at Beatrice Wallens's place. Staggering into the pantry, she pushes the window open, tips her upper body out into the night and vomits loudly. Three, four dreadful waves through her chest, and then it's over. Her abdominal muscles force clumps of air up her throat with a repulsive noise, but there's nothing left. She's empty. Ea spits until the taste is gone. She wipes her eyes and blows her nose into the garden. It's raining. Two storeys below, the leaves are glistening on a tree she can't name. Across the way, the neighbours have finally gone to bed.

The idea seems less obvious as soon as she's out on the street, but she's ready for that. In any case, it won't be as hard as she'd feared. It's late, and passers-by are few. If she jumps from the cast-iron railings, she can haul herself up on to the low tiled roof above the entryway. The chicken mesh and symbolic barbed wire around the wall on the inner side are depressed in several places. She's not the first person to do this climb, but she hopes she's the only one tonight. Ea jumps, hitting the ground with a thud. It was further than she thought; the hard landing is singing in her chest. She's stock still, crouching with her hands on the soil in front of her, listening. She strains her ears to catch footsteps or voices, but all is silent among the graves. The cemetery – originally stretching from Church all the way to 16th Street when it was established in the late 1700s – shrank, as the city grew around it, into a large garden. Few vestiges of the thousands buried here over the centuries remain in the form of headstones: the wooden crosses have weathered, taking the names of their dead Miwok and Ohlone Native Americans with them into the earth, while developers and investment funds have seen to the rest. The gradual parcelling out of the original cemetery has always annoyed Ea, but tonight she's grateful the place is small enough that she can sense the surrounding whitewashed wall.

Once her eyes have adjusted to the darkness enough that she can make out the path ahead, she gets to her feet and follows it between the graves. She's far too alert to be truly afraid. Her surroundings loom with surrealistic clarity; she's aware of the soft slap of her rubber soles, the heavy rain, which releases the scent of the plants, the wind in the tops of the cypresses, a bird or maybe a rat burrowing deeper into the thick ivy around a stela. Ea pauses in front of the statue of Father Junípero Serra. The Spanish monk founded nine of California's twenty-one missions, but here he looks like a child being given a dressing down. Hands clasped behind his back, he's staring guiltily at his sandals, which are poking out from beneath the folds of his stone robe. Ea sits down on a bench a few yards from the monk. The pink flowers on the rose bushes give off the sweetish scent of candy, mingling with the dull odour of rain-washed cement.

What now?

Apart from her visit to the clairvoyant, Ea is inexperienced in attracting the attention of the dead. The tombs at the Mission Dolores Cemetery look like houses, in some cases small palaces, complete with nameplates and hedges between the plots, and as she sits in the darkness surrounded by people who have long since turned to dust, and who would have had nothing to do with her even while they were alive, she feels like an idiot.

On the other hand, might as well give it a shot.

Sitting straighter, Ea places her upturned palms on her knees – although of course it makes no difference how she arranges her body. Then she shuts her eyes.

'*Mor*?'

The Danish word feels obscene in her mouth, which has grown accustomed to a new, smoother language.

She tries again, a little louder this time.

She waits.

Nothing happens, of course.

The night is the same as before.

Ea's eyes blink open. In a way she's relieved.

She isn't sure what she wanted to ask, or whether she can bear to hear the answer. She rarely had use for Charlotte's advice while she was alive.

What does she think has changed?

Ea checks her phone. The background picture of Coco and Hector at their respective ends of the sofa in their matching slippers makes her grin. It's nearly two.

Someone is breathing.

The fact that the person is clearly asleep takes the edge off the shock. Even so, Ea feels her mouth go dry. The person is a few yards away, curled up on the ground inside the traditional Ohlone reed hut erected between the graves to memorialise the many indigenous deaths on San Francisco's conscience. In the dim light she can distinguish the outline of his body, but he's too far away for her to be able to smell him.

She gets up, and the phone in her lap slips off, landing on the flagstones with a clatter.

Curtis blinks. He's pretty nearsighted. Has been since he was a kid. He's still a little groggy with sleep, and in the dark the woman is nothing but a blurry splodge of pale blue. Getting on to all fours, he sticks his head through the gap.

'Hello? Can I help you?'

The woman gets up and shakes her head, already moving away. A thought pops into his head – it's worth a try.

'You don't happen to have a cigarette, do you?'

'I don't smoke. Sorry.'

'Hm.'

'Hang on.' She rummages around in her pocket and finds what she's looking for. 'I've got some gum. You can keep it.' She hands him the pack before he can say he's got no use for it. The mere thought of biting into its hard, crackling surface makes him cringe.

'The easiest place to get over is by Matthew Keller's grave,' he says, pointing. 'From there you can reach the overhang by Maria Dolorosa, and then it's not such a drop on the other side. But watch out you don't tread on the flowers or jump into my cart. It's on the other side of the wall.'

The woman thanks him but doesn't move any further away.

'Sorry about the cigarettes,' she says.

'It's fine, don't worry about it.'

'I quit when I moved here.'

'Oh, right.'

Curtis assumes she's off her head on something – what else would she be doing here? But she doesn't sound drunk or high, and her movements are controlled. Probably no reason to be scared.

'Mind if I ask you something?'

'Fire away,' he mumbles, putting his hand to his cheek. The pain has returned, and it's setting him on edge.

'Have you been sleeping in there very long?'

'Sometimes.'

That's not true, but there's no reason to be foolish. He knows the rules. The woman nods.

'Have you ever felt anything? Anything supernatural, I mean.'

A ghost hunter. Of course. Not the first, either.

'Never. You're the first person to disturb my night's sleep. I get the sense the dead have enough going on already. Sorry to disappoint you.'

'You're not disappointing me at all,' says the woman lightly. 'Thanks for your help.'

He listens until he hears the sound of the wire being bent down and two feet landing on the sidewalk. The rain has subsided. Curtis crawls back into the hut, which he has lined with cardboard and a fleece blanket. He can still grab a few hours' sleep before daybreak, when he needs to be up and out of there, exactly as though he'd never been there to begin with.

*

Charlotte

Just say it, he insists. I won't be angry.

Oh, I think you will.

I had forgotten all about his persistence. It's something he's proud of. The will to bite down until something cracks.

You're underestimating me. Like so many times before, I might add.

Let's talk about something else, I say. It was what it was, that's all.

He sighs, giving up at last.

What do you want to talk about?

I don't know? The beginning. The first time you saw me. Before the children and the house, before everything. When we were two blank canvases bumping into one another. You start.

The first time I saw you, your face was painted green.

That's right, I was dressed as a cactus. What about you?

You don't remember? I was Zorro.

Couldn't really tell though, could you?

Well, at some point I lost my rapier.

And *your mask.*

Probably, yeah.

All I saw was a good-looking, grey-eyed man in black clothing with a ring in one ear. I thought you were very exotic. You were a head taller than everybody else. Luminous, like a stork who'd accidentally landed in a flock of crows.

He nods eagerly, drawing himself up.

We chatted, he says, and I invited you to my birthday the week after. Maybe you weren't beautiful, exactly, but your cheeks were blushing like pomegranates under that green, and your hair was thick and smelled lovely. You moved the air around with your hands when you talked. I really liked all that stuff.

And when I showed up, turned out it was a trap. I was the only *guest at your flat, which was basically just a room. You made pasta with this intense tomato sauce, and I felt like such a hick. Do you remember what I brought you as a present?*

He shakes his head.

Give me a clue.

It was something edible.

Chocolate? No, wait. Did you bring cheese?

I wanted to buy something else as well, or something completely different, but then I panicked and ended up arriving with a whole brie and flowers from the shop. It was incredibly embarrassing.

Well, it ended all right.

You mean we ended up in bed.

Even then, I realised you were different from the women I'd known and loved before. Or made love to. Or wished I could make love to. All those undergrads with cigarettes on their breath and slender necks. You were shy and forthright at the same time, and you didn't seem remotely embarrassed about being naked. In fact, the way you moved, it was like you didn't feel properly dressed until you were in the nude. You laughed a lot, and I laughed with you, although I didn't always get what was so funny.

My sister called you a stick-in-the-mud. Worse, later on.

Your family never liked me.

Nonsense. They loved you until you made it impossible for them.

Troels ignores me.

Do you remember, he says, that your hands were rough and red from working with those wet stalks all day long? When you touched me, it felt like being touched by eager paws.

Paws . . . is that why you tried to tame me?

On the contrary. Every time I saw you with one of my books, I felt guilty. It was obvious you were only trying to make me happy.

You're wrong there, I say, jabbing him triumphantly in the chest. It wasn't for your *sake, Troels. I loved getting recommendations, and I genuinely wanted to experience what other people did when they read. But the magic never happened. I never forgot that the whole thing had simply been made up: word by word, page by page. That some poor sap had sweated blood trying to make it feel like the real world – which only made me itch even more to get out there and look for it. When I finally gave up and clapped the book shut, it was like coming face to face with an oil painting after an endless stream of pencil sketches.*

11
Sidsel

Nothing about Loretta Barry's appearance corroborates Sidsel's hunch that she is an erstwhile punk/squatter/anarcho-syndicalist. The conservator is waiting as agreed by the ticket desk in the Great Court, wearing a knee-length aubergine skirt and matching blouse. Her frizzy grey hair is secured at the temples with two clips, and around her neck is a necklace with a silver owl-shaped pendant. Yet somehow she seems unmistakably hardcore as she greets Sidsel and ushers her through the herds of tourists, leading her towards the World Conservation and Exhibitions Centre. A lift takes them to the second floor, all shining glass and metal, and an area reserved for staff. The centre is only five years old, she explains, and a state-of-the-art conservation facility. They used to work in wretched conditions in the basements of a few ramshackle and unsanitary terraced houses, which had since been demolished to make space for the new architect-designed building.

'Just imagine,' says Loretta, 'cramming labs and offices and archives and somewhere between thirty and forty employees into rooms once intended for servants. Nothing wrong with the equipment, but there wasn't space to use it. Lots of objects were ruined simply transporting them up and down in these stupid bloody lifts, which were much too small. Luckily some of the management saw the foolishness of having one of the world's finest collections but no fighting chance of keeping it in good order. We're down here.'

Loretta passes two colleagues with a wave, and without slowing down.

'In a way I'm glad I've been here long enough to appreciate the improvements. The newbies take it for granted that they've all got their own tables and chairs and decent ventilation and daylight. Just in here.'

Loretta opens the door on to a bright, cluttered room she evidently shares with one other person, currently not at their desk.

'Leave your things there, we'll pick them up later,' she says, nodding towards an already overburdened row of pegs. Sidsel puts her coat on the floor, next to a fern that on closer inspection turns out to be made of plastic – presumably so as not to interfere with the museum's botanical collection.

'And you? Everything all right, good trip?' asks Loretta, and without waiting for an answer she starts rummaging in her bag. Sidsel says it was, although in fact it hasn't been a good trip at all. The fear of death – born at the same time as Laura, though it rapidly outgrew her – had set in as soon as she took her seat and fastened the seat belt over her thighs. She crossed her fingers and shut her eyes, counting to ten in Danish, English, French and German, then back to the beginning again, until the plane levelled out in the air and the pressure in her chest lifted. On their descent into Heathrow, she ran through so many possible scenarios – picturing her own death and what might happen to Laura afterwards – that she felt like she was riddled with holes. Arriving at the hotel, she decided to put the half-day off to good use and take a nap. By the time she was roused by the sound of children's voices in the corridor, it was quarter to ten. Sidsel took a shower, washing with the small, strongly scented soaps, ate a bag of roasted almonds from the minibar, and made herself come twice before falling asleep close to midnight. Beneath her windows sprawled the city of London, huge and indifferent to her good intentions and wasted opportunities.

The next morning she woke up starving and incapable of sleeping longer, and when she made her way to the hotel breakfast room, the only other guest was a woman who'd brought a homemade bean spread in a jam jar, her hair still wet from the shower. But the eggs were well cooked, the April sun set the cutlery gleaming on the table, and as Sidsel crossed the park on her way to the museum a few hours later, she felt light and floaty. Being Laura's mother had proved to be inseparable from a feeling of heaviness that was lifted only in short-lived bursts. But there, on the gravel path between the tulip beds and the blackbirds, she was detached from anyone or anything but herself; a closed circuit, transient and perfect as a soap bubble.

'Here it is,' says Loretta, pulling out a phone from the

grubby Mandarina Duck bag. 'I promised to let Evan know when we were ready. It'll only take a moment.'

It's apparent from the conversation that Evan is the assistant on site. They're discussing how to transport the bust. Loretta suggests a simple dolly would be best, to which Evan responds with something very long that makes her frown and fidget with the bits of paper on the windowsill. Right, she mutters, irritated. Right. Sidsel takes advantage of the wait to check her phone. She hasn't heard from Niels since yesterday, when he replied to her I've-landed-and-I-miss-you-already text with a laconic *All good here*. She knows him well enough to realise that this is true, and that he would text or ring if it stopped being true, and yet she can't repress the urge to know more. It's nearly eleven back home. Laura will almost certainly have been awake since six. Are they having a day out? Sidsel tries to imagine them on the bus, sitting on neighbouring seats. Or has he decided to ride her around on his bike? Niels turned down the keys to her cargo bike, just as he preferred Laura to stay at his place while Sidsel was away. His theory was that the child would miss her mother less if she wasn't constantly being reminded of her by her surroundings. This way, too, she'd have a change of scene – it would be sort of a holiday for her. He might be right, but Sidsel doesn't quite get her brother's fondness for the most difficult, the *least* obvious choices. Like looking after a six-year-old at a seniors' home, with no entertainment besides a depressed flatmate.

'Coming,' says Loretta, without the interrogative

uptick at the end of the question. She's already halfway out the door.

The crimson walls and low lighting in the gallery give it a boudoir-like touch, and compared with the bustle in the Great Court, it seems oddly empty. In the middle of the room is a bench upholstered in leather, and the prosperous citizens of Palmyra are gazing down at the visitors from their plinths with the dignified indulgence of the dead. The gallery's windows have been covered, and every single statue and relief is carefully illuminated with spot lighting that emphasises the detail in the stonework. It's been a long time since Sidsel went to a museum for pleasure, and in a way she wishes she had nothing to do here but join the other visitors and drift through the exhibition.

'Here's the unlucky bugger,' says Loretta, stopping in front of the bust, which is sheathed in plastic on its plinth. Sidsel feels a jolt of anticipation, mingled with the nerves that have been humming away since Thursday.

Loretta shakes her watch out of her sleeve just as a boy who must be Evan appears at the far end of the gallery, pushing a transport crate whose prosaic rattling breaks the burial chamber's spell.

'Sorry to keep you,' he says, hitting the brakes on the wheels. 'I understand you wanted to have a look before we take it upstairs?'

Loretta nods and turns to Sidsel.

'Would you do the honours?'

Moving gingerly as she loosens the wrappings, Sidsel realises it could have been a lot worse. The large chips along the edge of the veil and nose, as well as the smaller ones on the pendant around the brow and the fingers of the right hand, were already there in the late 1920s, when the Beauty of Palmyra came into the possession of Danish archaeologist Harald Ingholt during his excavations at the oasis city's south-western necropolis. Not that Ingholt or any of the French archaeologists working with him had actually found it. The bust had been acquired from a Syrian private collection with funds from the Rask-Ørsted Foundation, and it is the only one of the hundred and thirty sandstone sculptures at the Glyptotek on which the paint is still visible to the naked eye, as shadows on the surface of the stone. The woman's mouth, in particular, glows a vibrant pink, and this, this very thing is the reason for Sidsel's trip to London: an entirely fresh chip, roughly one centimetre by one centimetre, disfiguring the plump bottom lip.

'As you can see, it's a fairly clean break,' says Loretta, standing next to Sidsel with arms akimbo. 'It shouldn't prove too much trouble. We have the piece that broke off back at the workshop. I've not found anything else, and as I understand it, the impact from the edge of the phone was very localised. Right there.' She leans forward and brushes the lip with her forefinger. 'Still, we'd better run it through the scanner to make sure there's no internal damage.'

'The phone?'

'Did no one tell you what happened?'

'I thought it fell. That was what I heard.'

Loretta's brow furrows.

'I'm sorry, do they not think we secure our exhibits properly in place? No. I'm not sure if this is better or worse, but it was a visitor. She was trying to wrestle a phone out of her daughter's hands – I assume the girl wasn't paying attention – but lost control of the movement. Once she'd grabbed the phone, her hand went smashing straight into the bust behind her.'

Loretta demonstrates the arc of the woman's arm. Bang.

'The attendant came running over, the mother was inconsolable. It was extremely embarrassing for them as well, of course.'

'I can imagine,' says Sidsel.

'Well. Considering how many kids and nutters we let through these doors each day, this sort of thing is pretty rare, really. Let's get it upstairs so we can take a proper look. Evan, if you wouldn't mind?'

Tucking his hair behind his ears, the assistant cautiously manoeuvres the bust into the crate, which Sidsel and Loretta pad with tissue paper and sheets of foam.

'There,' says Loretta, giving the lid a pat. 'Off you go, dearie.'

All along the canal, people are lounging with their eyes closed and their faces turned towards the treetops, which glimmer in the air like a shoal of herring. Their coats are dumped in piles between them, next to wine bottles and disposable cups.

Spring has come to London at the same time as Sidsel, and when she turns on to Broadway Market ten minutes earlier than agreed, he's already there, holding up a paperback in the syrupy light, his body arranged in a way at once relaxed and posed.

Sidsel has come to a halt on the corner, outside a bakery. Vicky's back is turned, and she's not ready yet to concede the upper hand – from here she can look at him without him seeing her – by crossing the street and entering his field of view. She glances at her watch. Eight minutes.

A cyclist on a racing bike whizzes past, then takes a right along the canal.

A bell chimes behind her in the doorway, as though to warn her of the gust of sugary air that will engulf her moments later from the shop.

He coughs and turns a page, brushing the skin beneath one eye with his index and middle fingers.

Six minutes.

She can still do it.

Walk away. She doesn't owe him an explanation.

Sidsel clenches her fists in the deep pockets of her jacket, calls his name, and takes a step into the light.

There's a knock at the door, and a woman says something rude that Sidsel doesn't catch. She's not ready to hang up. The sound of Niels's voice dissolves the distance she has begun to feel, the gnawing sense of having misplaced something precious.

'What are you up to tomorrow?'

'Not sure . . . the beach, if the weather's nice.'

She's almost exhausted his patience.

'The wellies are in the tote bag, if you do. Ditto for the hat. Is it still cold back home?'

The woman knocks again, hard.

'Sidsel, I promise you I've got a handle on footwear and clothing. You'll see her soon. Drink a few more beers, take some Molly and have a lie-in tomorrow. I'm off to bed now.'

'Okay, okay,' she mutters, bending her knees to catch a glimpse of her face between the stickers advertising local bands and vegan initiatives that cover most of the already tiny mirror in the loo. All trace of lipstick is gone, and her forehead is glistening. Goodnight, grouchy.

'Goodnight.'

The woman waiting glares as Sidsel walks past and pushes open the door to the bar. The low-ceilinged room is heaving. Sidsel is met by a soup of warm backs and bellies, half-sentences no one hears over the music and sudden bellows of laughter. Folding herself as slim as a knife, she puts her hand on a clammy shoulder and pushes it aside, edging towards the table where she and Vicky have spent the last few hours drinking strong cheap drinks. While she was gone, the lecturer has got chatting to the couple at the next table, and he doesn't notice – or wants to pretend he hasn't noticed – that Sidsel is back until the scrape of chair legs against the floor makes him look up.

'Hi again,' he says, and without batting an eyelid he turns

his back on the couple and the conversation he's just conjured out of nowhere. They stare, disorientated, at each other. The woman reaches for her partner, who lifts his glass as if in reply and drains it angrily. Sidsel feels like telling them she knows exactly how it feels. It's not their fault – it's just the way he is. An artificial sun, a spotlight. You had a bit, and now you want more. Vicky leans across the table until he's so close she can smell his cologne, like incense. The years, two children and his still-recent divorce have left their mark on his face. The black borders of his hair have crept backwards on his skull, and the skin under his eyes and by his ears is knurled with fine wrinkles. The effect of him is the same, and the odour of his body makes Sidsel's pussy open and close in anticipation against the seat.

'Someone was using the toilet as a phone box,' she says, taking a sip of her whiskey sour.

'And have you decided?'

'What do you think? The honest version.'

Vicky narrows his eyes.

'That's a bit longer than the nice version.'

'Doesn't matter.'

He takes a breath and sits up straighter, the way Sidsel remembers from lectures. In those days it meant you had to listen up, because important bits of information would be mingled with irrelevant ones in such an articulate stream you had to concentrate to sort them out.

'She was bored when she was with us,' says Vicky. 'She was so bored she was going out of her mind. Didn't matter whether we were on holiday or at home or with our best friends and their kids. Swimming pools, parents' meetings, birthdays, trips to the woods and the museum – all the stuff other people find natural and interesting enough to do for ten, fifteen, twenty years, it meant nothing to her. Some days she stayed at the office on the pretext of being busy, or she dawdled at the supermarket on the way home, telling herself it was for our sake: she simply wanted to buy the best for our boys. But in reality she wanted to defer the moment she stepped through the door and became part of it all again. It wore her down, and she was back at work five months after Julian was born, even though she had a right to take twice that. We had two kids under three at home, and yet she still accepted all the extra jobs she was offered – if she wasn't actively volunteering to work overtime. I was the one who picked them up and made their food, bathed them and cut their nails. I learned the names of their friends at nursery. Abi had no idea who was who, which made it hard for her to seem genuinely interested when the boys talked about their day. To her, they were just a herd of animals whose other members had no special distinguishing features. I was the one who took time off when they weren't well. Or brought them to work with me. When she did finally force herself to go to the park and kick a football around or sit on the floor and play with their toys, I could practically see her withering before my eyes. Before the children came, sometimes we'd spend hours talking over our empty plates in the evenings. There was always something to say.'

Vicky shakes his head and looks down into his glass, but Sidsel can tell he's not finished yet, and keeps quiet.

'Abigail had two children,' he said. 'She gave birth to them and breastfed them, and then she didn't want to be a mum. Deep down she blamed them for ruining what we had before they came along – the very reason they existed! She never said so explicitly, but before she got pregnant with Xavier, she sometimes used to joke that she always identified more with the crazy professor who spends all day in his study and only gets called in once food is on the table than with the mum who's constantly having to wipe her hands on her apron and shush the kids. She felt like she had more in common with Charles Ingalls, Mr Pevensie and Moominpappa than with their long-suffering wives. Yet somehow it still came as a shock to her. She had expected to be transformed.'

Sidsel tries not to let it show on her face how uncomfortable this new information is making her feel. It's too intimate, too much. Like an expensive gift from someone she only knows peripherally. Vicky is still an excellent storyteller.

'What about the kids?' she asks. 'Does she see them?'

'She has them every other weekend. They're with her now. So you couldn't have timed your visit better, really.'

Vicky takes a sip of his beer and swirls it around in his mouth, then smiles teasingly.

'Were you expecting some other reason?'

'Like what?'

'Like an affair?'

'It never crossed my mind,' she lies.

Because of course Sidsel had imagined Vicky picking a new student every term or two, imagined Abigail living with the liaisons until one day it all got too much, too openly hurtful, too impractical or simply too pathetic.

'I have been tempted,' he says, 'but there's been no one else since you.'

His dark brown eyes have softened, and Sidsel realises that the opening she's been waiting for has arrived. She would be able to reach him, but the thought of bringing Laura into their evening makes her sick. The girl has nothing to do with them, this mismatched couple in the corner of a packed pub that reeks of beer. Sidsel doubts she would ever be able to say her name in here. To get it past her lips.

'What is it?'

'I don't know,' sighs Sidsel, swilling the foam around in the empty glass. 'It was a bit of a sad story, I think. It got to me.'

'You reckon? I hadn't thought about it like that. Sad? Yeah, maybe.'

For a while they let themselves be borne along on the clamour of the other customers, then Vicky clears his throat.

'Let me put the question another way: Why did you text me, Sidsel?'

She looks up, straight at him, and decides to answer in the only way that still feels true.

The flat is twenty minutes away, not ten, as he claimed, and pungent with fresh paint. There are still a few moving boxes along the walls, and despite the furniture and the rug she recognises from his previous home, the living room makes a barren impression. Taking her jacket and bag, Vicky ushers her into the kitchen, where he offers her a seat. Without asking if she's hungry, he opens the fridge and starts taking out various items of food. Ham, two types of cheese, a casserole he made yesterday. Yogurt, plus a bunch of fresh herbs he sets about chopping, all the while keeping up a running commentary about the shops in the area and how well the boys have dealt with everything. Children adapt to new situations much more quickly than adults fear. They're flexible, they have nothing else to compare it with. Mum and Dad aren't going to live together. Why not? Because they're not boyfriend and girlfriend any more. Okay, fine.

'It's mainly grown-ups who end up with bruised egos,' he says, sweeping the herbs off the chopping board into a bowl and drizzling them with oil and lemon. 'The trick is not to project everything on to these little creatures who are still essentially wild. They're basically imps, for heaven's sake. To them the world isn't solid, it's fluid. Until they start school, and we begin fitting systems like *ought* and *should* into their malleable little brains.'

Vicky has warmed to his subject now, and Sidsel, as she has been so many times before, is reduced to the role of spectator. It's the old dynamic, and it works. She lets go, allowing herself to be led, twenty-five years old again, dumb as a post, and wide open. At the same time, something about the situation is stifling. Time machines don't exist. He ladles the food into two shallow bowls and hands her one.

'Thanks,' she says, taking a spoonful. The casserole is tasty, but cold from the fridge, and the herbs have a vague aftertaste. She isn't particularly hungry. Sidsel eats a few mouthfuls then puts the bowl down. She asks to use the loo.

In the bathroom, she takes stock of a growing sense that she's being lied to. Judging by the contents of his fridge, it doesn't look like there are children in this flat most of the time, and apart from the two toothbrushes on a shelf next to the sink, she hasn't noticed any sign of the boys. There are no small shoes jumbled across the hall, no toys, no books with thick paperboard pages. Her own flat, by contrast, is suffused with Laura and her things in a way that's impossible to camouflage. You can smell it and see it; it would take days to eradicate those traces. Julian and Xavier are magically present solely in the telling of them, two small boys whose names might really have been anything. Come to think of it, wasn't there something contrived about Vicky's story more generally? He spoke as though he knew the most intimate details of his wife's motives, as though he were able to dissect the intricate emotional cause and effect behind her struggles with motherhood. He described in detail the thoughts going through her head, whether she was with the family or dreading being with them. This despite the fact that the problem (according to him-as-her) was precisely the *breakdown* in communication between them after the children came along. The more Sidsel considers it, the more likely it seems that Vicky, like a ventriloquist, has grabbed his ex-wife out of the suitcase and stuck his hand up her skirt. By using Abigail as a stand-in, he presented the collapse of his family without giving himself away.

She opens the bathroom cabinets one by one, noting what soaps he uses, that he keeps his hairbands in a chipped coffee mug emblazoned P.R.O.S.E., and that at some point he has battled with, or still battles with, dandruff. Sidsel sits down on the edge of the bath. It's past midnight, and she still needs to drop by the museum and supervise the reinstallation of the bust before she leaves tomorrow afternoon. The pulsing desire she felt at the bar has shrunk to a stupid, horny puddle – something she could easily have dealt with on her own. Mostly she's just tired. The last few hours they've talked and talked without saying anything. Did she really think that it would be possible to leapfrog six years of accumulated silence in a single night? That one of them would manage to be honest?

She doesn't know any more what she hoped to get out of their meeting.

When Sidsel opens the door, she's surprised to find him waiting on the other side.

'May I?'

She nods. Arousal has made his saliva thin and metallic, like sucking coins. It's a long kiss. Sidsel has time to step out of it several times, picture how they must look – two tipsy idiots, not exactly attractive – before vanishing back into the sensation of liquid mouths and tongues. His hands in her hair and around her face.

'But afterwards I'll go,' she says.

Vicky nods and strokes her forehead again and again, until suddenly he pinches her earlobe hard and pulls. She shuts her eyes and gives a creaking moan. With his other hand he has opened her trousers and tugged them down over her buttocks. He slips two fingers inside her and keeps them there. The matter-of-factness makes Sidsel gasp. She's wet, has been for a while, and when he pushes her ahead of him into the bedroom and on to the bed, there's no resistance left. Having Laura has changed her body, just as age has changed his, but it's the same drastic desire, the same urgency as before, and as he presses her face into the mattress and thrusts himself inside, she feels the familiar craving, the wish that they could do everything at the same time, multiply themselves and the act. Perform it a thousandfold and over and over, with undiminished ferocity.

12

Niels

It's daft, but Niels can't help feeling let down by Laura's behaviour. She hasn't mentioned Sidsel all day, but just like yesterday she turned into a wild, snivelling animal as soon as she got into her pyjamas. I've got a bad feeling in my tummy, she whined, twisting and writhing until the duvet was damp with sweat. I miss my mummy. I *can't* shut my eyes. They *want* to be open. She struggled bitterly, not giving up until ten, and then only on the condition that Niels remained in a chair beside the bed, one hand resting on the mattress at a specified distance from her pillow. Bedtime has cancelled out all the pleasant hours they spent in each other's company: the visit to Efie and the playground; going back to the flat, where he showed her how to roll pizza dough with an empty wine bottle and taught her to lay out the cards for solitaire. All gone. Tomorrow they'll have to start from scratch, he understands that. Everything will be new.

Niels recognises the sound of Cosmo's dragging slippers. He puts the book down on the desk and nudges the door ajar.

His flatmate is, for once, fully dressed, but his hair is crushed flat on one side, and there's the stale odour of unwashed bedding on his body.

'Am I disturbing you?' he asks.

Nodding towards the sleeping girl, Niels motions Cosmo towards the living room.

'Laura will be staying here until tomorrow,' he explains. 'Sidsel's in London for work.'

'Oh, that makes sense.' Cosmo slumps on to Barbara's sofa. 'I thought I was imagining things.' He smiles sheepishly.

'What things?'

'Well, I assumed I was hallucinating when I heard her yesterday afternoon, and again tonight. The funny thing is I wasn't scared. I just thought: a kid? Guess I'm imagining things.'

'I thought you were asleep.'

Cosmo shook his head.

'No, no,' he says, 'I heard you loud and clear. Or I didn't think I did. If you follow me? I heard you, and I didn't hear you. She's really grown. How old is she now? Eight? Nine?'

'Almost. She's six.'

'Six. Wow.'

As they talk, Cosmo picks at a hole in the sleeve of his jumper, pinching the loose threads with his long, light brown fingers and pulling, expanding it systematically.

'By the way,' he says, 'I'm probably heading down to the Lamb on Monday. Dino's trio is playing, Johansen's back. You in?'

'I've got posters to do.'

'Oh yeah,' says Cosmo, looking worried in a way that makes it obvious he's not quite cut to the chase. Niels senses the impatience he couldn't let himself show Laura spilling over, even though this is someone who needs the exact opposite, and it's frustrating to recognise this failing in himself. He and Phillip have known each other since the first year of primary school, and Niels has always found it easy to be in his company. With almost everybody else, sooner or later he rubs off on them, and once it's happened he starts to feel uncomfortable, restricted in his movements, as though wearing a shirt that's too tight. But not with Cosmo. There's no danger of Niels seeing his expressions mirrored in Cosmo's face, of hearing his phrases repeated or noticing his fitful gestures manifested in this delicate-limbed body. Like Niels, Phillip seems to have set early, arriving in the world in a state of finality.

'Come on, out with it,' he says, sitting down opposite his friend. 'What's this really about?'

Cosmo raises a smile that reaches halfway up his cheeks before sagging back, and his face stiffens into an exhausted grimace.

'I need to talk to Fernelius. He asked if we could do it at the Lamb, and I said yes before I thought about it properly.'

He mutters something else that Niels can't catch.

'Fernelius? That Fernelius?'

'There's only one Fernelius, as far as I know.'

'What do you need to talk to him about?'

'I've been thinking about it ever since I got home. It makes no sense to leave it standing there, given the situation.'

'Leave what standing where?'

'The guitar,' says Cosmo. 'I sold it to Krister. It's over. It's not good for me. Obviously, I mean, look at me.'

He pauses, as though to let Niels actually do it. Look at him.

'It's time people realised that they should stop waiting. That there's nothing to wait *for*. I'm tired of that life.'

It's not the first time Niels has heard Cosmo declare he's finished with music, but something is different now. He's more resigned, less angry. Cosmo surveys Niels, who to his own surprise is filled with grief at the thought of never seeing Phillip Tibbett on a stage again.

'Which one?' he asks, but knows the answer.

'My Gibson. The other isn't worth anything. We haven't, you know, figured out the practical stuff. The deal isn't done, but it will happen. He's got the money, anyway. Rich pig,' he adds, laughing mirthlessly.

Niels thinks of the cases that have been relegated to a corner of Barbara's study for so long, those two secret sarcophagi, and realises Cosmo is right. Niels probably imagined it would pass of its own accord. That one day he would wake to the sound of Cosmo practising, and find his friend curled around the instrument, swallowed up in the motion of his fingers over the strings. Lost to the world in one of his wild, proliferating improvisations. Then a thought comes into his head that perks him up.

'Fernelius is a trumpeter. What the hell does he want with your guitar?'

'Krister can play most instruments,' says Cosmo, 'and he's not a bad guitarist. If he'd put his mind to it, he could have been one of the best.'

Niels doesn't reply. He's thinking about the night he first heard Krister Fernelius's name. He had been washing up after dinner at Linn's collective when Cosmo arrived, soaking wet and twitchy from the coke. He'd started pacing around the kitchen, incapable of sitting still, cursing the Swedish trumpeter who, according to a mutual friend, had seduced Helene: until the break-up a few weeks before, she and Phillip had dated for four years. The body isn't even cold, he spluttered, his eyes black. Graverobber, he sobbed, fucking bastard Swedish necrophiliac arsehole; then he collapsed on to the sofa and fell asleep, still wearing his jacket and muddy boots, exhausted by jealousy and what smelled like several days' intensive drinking. The collective decided to let him sleep it off, and next morning Niels dished up a bowl of porridge to both Linn and a mortified Cosmo. After a shower and a few cups of strong coffee, he explained to Niels that it hadn't come as a surprise, of course, that Helene would be with someone else. He wasn't that stupid. What had floored him was the thought of that Swedish pretty-boy being the next one to stick his dick inside the only woman he'd ever loved. Anybody would have been better than that, he hissed. If he'd had a brother, he'd have chosen him over Krister Fernelius – even Niels he could have lived with. And now here's Cosmo calmly saying he wants to sell his beloved guitar to Fernelius. The Swedish pretty-boy.

'How did that even happen?'

'Through Johansen. He texted and asked if I was serious about selling, because if so he might know someone . . . He didn't say it was Krister. Fuck it. As long as he can pay what it costs.'

'What are you getting for it?'

Cosmo's eyes are evasive under his thick lashes.

'We haven't landed on a number, but it will be enough for a deposit and the first month's rent somewhere.'

Niels can't hide his surprise, and Cosmo is fast.

'I wasn't planning to live with my nanna for ever. I hope you didn't think that of me.'

'I don't know what I thought,' shrugs Niels. 'Seemed like a pretty good situation, until you—'

He had been going to say, 'until you got better.'

'Until what?'

Niels changes tack.

'So you'd rather be ripped off by some country bumpkin who finances his nights out by renting out the broom cupboard in the apartment his parents have bought him in Amager?'

Cosmo doesn't laugh. He merely throws up his long arms in resignation.

'Niels, buddy. I'm sorry if it's inconvenient for you. Honestly.'

Niels can't curb his frustration any longer.

'What are you on about?'

'Well, you pretty much live here.'

'Right now I do, but probably not for much longer. I've been talking to Luken about visiting him in Tübingen, hanging out over the summer and travelling on from there.'

It's not true. Niels has thought about it, but Luken hasn't actually invited him yet, and he's not the type to impose.

'Luke?'

'Bloke I met in Italy last summer,' he snaps. 'Listen, Phillip, if you want to move, do it. I can be out of here in a day. I mean it. Just say the word and I'm gone.'

Niels gets up and fetches the tobacco from his jacket. He's restless and tense, weary after spending all day with a child. The constant attention Laura demands is hard to get used to. He hasn't had time to think two coherent thoughts since picking her up from school the day before. The book he's been carrying around in his pocket he might as well have left at home. There hasn't been one free second – not one idle moment. He doesn't get how Sidsel does it, day after day after day. Out over the sea the darkness is close-packed, greenish at the waterline. He pushes the window open and lights his cigarette, drawing the smoke deep into his lungs and exhaling. It helps. Cosmo has risen from the sofa, and comes to sit now at the dining table behind him. The chair legs squeal against the parquet.

'I can talk to Barbara,' he says. 'Maybe you can stay here? She and Hugo are only home for a few weeks over the summer. I'm sure she wouldn't mind.'

'Don't do that.'

'Fine. I'll leave it.'

Niels gets the prickly urge to make it plain to Cosmo that it was partly for his sake he moved into this rotten old dump in the first place.

'Don't you ever get sick of it?' asks Cosmo.

'Of what?'

'Don't you ever feel like just staying in Copenhagen for a while? Taking it easy?'

For some reason, Cosmo is talking as though it's Niels, not him, who has barricaded himself in his room and survived the winter on a diet of strawberry yogurt and Tuc crackers. As though it's Niels who has fried his brain with American-produced shit and set up camp in his bed, suspending the border between day and night until the hours are nothing but a grubby grey sludge. As though it's him, for fuck's sake, who's planning to sell his most precious possession to a person he hates. Niels doesn't answer the question. Instead, he says:

'I'll probably come along to the Lamb on Monday.'

'You mean it?'

'It's no problem. I'll go out a bit earlier.'

'Most people think I've been away. You're one of the only ones who knows . . .'

'I'll be there.'

Niels's gaze is fixed on a point on the Swedish coast. He's in no mood for talking any more. It feels like two liquids that are meant to be kept separate have intermixed inside him. As though he's leaking somewhere.

‘Anyway,’ says Cosmo at last. ‘I think I’ll have a lie-down.’

The door closes, and minutes later Niels hears the interminable voices resume their rapid dialogue.

While he’s been out of the room Laura has rotated ninety degrees, and is now lying lengthways across the bed with her arms flung out to the sides. Bending down, Niels tucks his hands under her back and knees and carefully shifts her nearer the wall. As always, he’s astonished by how light she is. A bit of fluff. A flame. Once he’s sure she isn’t about to wake up, he lies down beside her, still fully dressed and not remotely sleepy. The blood is hot and churning in his ears. If it weren’t for Laura, he wouldn’t go to bed at all on a night like this. He would take advantage of his frame of mind and channel his energy into studying, read until daybreak, and finish with an inspired email to Luken; or, better still, he would go for a run along the beach. The mere thought stirs something inside him. To open the door and simply step out into the cool space of the night, to set himself in motion. Slowly, at first, then faster and faster. To sprint until his lungs ache and his legs buckle beneath him. He’d let himself collapse into the sand, half fainting, and wake next day to the squalling of the birds. Beside him, Laura rolls on to her stomach with a sigh. Drawing her knees up to her chest, she burrows her warm feet under his ribs. Niels retreats to the edge of the mattress. He isn’t used to sharing a bed. He couldn’t even get comfortable with Linn; most nights at the collective he ended up in an armchair in the common room. She couldn’t see it as anything but a rejection, and in the end Niels got tired of defending himself. People can think what they like. He gets up and grabs a quilt from the living room, folds it once and positions it on the floor beside the bed. Sometimes it helps to recreate conditions on his backpacking trips, where sleep felt like a duty. The knotted earth through the camping mat beneath him and the night sky above. Sleep was the necessary short circuit that allowed him to set off again the next day, ready for the many miles waiting to be put behind him. Niels settles down on his back and folds his hands over his chest, supressing the urge to pluck at his thoughts, letting them pass like traffic. But he can't go under, and after ten minutes he's still on precisely the same level of consciousness. Niels opens his eyes and stares up at the same grey ceiling.

Surrounded by the same lapdog darkness.

For every breath Niels takes, Laura manages to breathe in and out and in again. She breathes like the historyless being she is.

A bird on a branch in a forest.

Pure potential.

Niels, meanwhile, feels like a lead weight. It's as though everything behind him weighs twice as much as the present and the future combined, as though he'd keep falling if he let himself relax, even for a moment.

Each day is a field to be cut.

An ever-growing stack of posters.

Niels has long since accepted the fact that life requires strength, so where has this new urge to give up come from?

To sink.

Before he's even opened his laptop, he can hear her voice in his inner ear. His brain responds to the auditory mirage by shooting pulses of well-being down his spine and into his buttocks. Niels turns down the brightness of the screen and plugs in his headphones, then he types her name into the search bar and chooses a video at random (*Spring Special*).

Same room, different day, different time.

The fairy lights, for instance, are gone.

She's wearing a lime-green cami. Her hair is gathered into a bun on the top of her head, fastened with a clip that is somehow also a big orange flower.

Hey. It's me, Miss Fessonia.

She giggles, drops her gaze, then looks directly into the camera again.

Thank you so much for joining me, beautiful. I want you to relax, to have your body be completely relaxed, your mind completely relaxed.

Niels knows the *you* is an illusion.

He knows it's a rhetorical trick – that it has nothing whatsoever to do with him or any of the other thousands of sleepless souls out there.

He knows this, but it doesn't matter any more what he knows.

Miss Fessonia is speaking only to him.

13

Sidsel

Through the gap in the headrest she's staring at the driver's neck, as criss-crossed with wrinkles as a crumpled sheet. For a few minutes she gazes blankly at the map of skin, as though searching for the answer there, somewhere between the hairline and the collar of his shirt. At first, the older man's lack of interest in her was a relief. Apart from a perfunctory exchange of civilities and addresses, he has left her to her own thoughts, but now she longs to be distracted.

Sidsel curls up on the smooth seat. If only he'd put the radio on, at least! Her overtired brain is acting like a faulty slot machine – first a violent whirring, all possibilities open, and then *ding ding ding*: she's back in Vicky's bedroom. Last night's movements, its vile animal noises, are spiralling round and round in her head. Sidsel clamps her eyes shut, squeezing them until searing patterns bleed through the dark. When eventually she opens them she meets the driver's worried gaze in the rear-view mirror. Don't worry, sir, she feels like sneering, I've got no intention of passing out or throwing up in your shiny black coffin of a taxi. Instead she turns her face towards the window, hoping to catch sight of something interesting, but the roads on this early Sunday morning are mute, wrung dry of life. Apart from two crows hopping in ritual circles around the remnants of a takeaway, there's nothing . . . nothing that interests her in the slightest . . .

'We're here,' says the driver, pulling up outside the hotel, which she recognises by the two replica Assyrian jugs either side of the entrance. Sidsel finds her wallet and puts the notes in his outstretched hand, unbuckles her seat belt and shuffles to the edge of the seat. She's eager to get back to her room. After a shower she's going to lie clean and alone in the big bed, sleep for a few hours, wake to the sound of her alarm and start the day from scratch. She's going to put on clothes, eat breakfast in the restaurant, and get to the museum and later the airport in good time. And by the time she goes to bed tonight, all of this will already be nearly a thing of the past.

'Miss . . . *miss*, you forgot something!'

He's taken the trouble to lean over the passenger seat and roll down the window.

'It was on the back seat,' he grunts, dangling the little green-and-white-striped jumper in front of her like a treat. The effort, together with the belt chafing against the heartbreakingly soft neck, reveals him as wholly and perfectly human. There's nothing to be done about it now. It's too late, and they've been equally to blame for ignoring it. Sidsel shakes her head.

'It's not mine,' she says.

'Are you sure?'

The driver jiggles it again, a little less enthusiastically. Sidsel swallows and takes herself in hand.

'Someone else must have left it,' she says. 'Don't you have a grandchild you could give it to?'

He gives her an offended look, then straightens up and jerks his arm back through the window.

Vicky had gone to take a shower as soon as they were finished, and for a while Sidsel lay in the churned bed, listening to the water splashing. Some impulse made her get up, scrape her clothes off the floor and slip into the boys' room. She wasn't prepared for the sight that greeted her: the room seemed cosy and lived-in. There were pictures and fairy lights on the walls, and a few low shelves housed wooden boxes labelled with handwritten, neatly decorated stickers: Cars, Blocks, Magnets, Musical Instruments, Animals. The ceiling above her glowed with a sea of tiny luminous stars. It took Sidsel a few seconds to realise they weren't placed at random. Vicky had recreated the constellations, and not just the ones everybody knew, but the rare ones as well, the ones almost nobody could see or name. Sidsel dressed, her hands trembling. Her inner compass was spinning like a baffled weathervane, hither and thither, detached from any underlying principle. A few hours ago she'd been sure Vicky was lying, but the boys were more apparent in here, more themselves. She could almost smell their warm, drowsy little bodies. The jumper – judging by the size, it had to be the youngest's – she had grabbed almost in passing before letting herself out into the grey morning.

It was easiest for them both that way.

Sidsel had hoped to leave something, to make some mark; now she had, in the shape of an absence.

It's been fifteen minutes since Loretta went to get 'refreshments', and Sidsel is too afraid the conservator will return and think she's nosing around to risk leaving her seat by the window. Nor does she dare succumb to the urge to close her eyes. The hangover has worsened as the morning has worn on. Hopefully she can get a few hours' sleep on the plane. It takes off in less than four hours, but Loretta's invitation was not one that brooked refusal. Your first conservation job at the British Museum, she'd said, once the Beauty of Palmyra was back in the gallery fifteen minutes before opening. We've got to celebrate! At long last, the door of the office opens and Loretta appears with two cans of Coke and a packet of biscuits.

'The café didn't have anything ready yet, but I found a few bits in our kitchen. I had a choice of coffee or Coke, and if you don't mind me saying so, you look like you could do with the sugar.'

Sidsel accepts the can gratefully.

'I couldn't sleep yesterday,' she explains once she's taken a sip of the ice-cold drink. 'And I was really looking forward to a whole night of uninterrupted sleep. My daughter's an early riser.'

Settling into her office chair, Loretta rolls it over to the window so that she and Sidsel are facing one another. The packet of biscuits she sets on the carpet between them.

'Was it very noisy?' she asks. 'A lot of hotels like to build their walls out of cardboard.'

'The hotel was fine,' Sidsel assures her. 'It wasn't their fault.'

'Well,' says Loretta, 'that kind of thing is always unreliable. Sleep is like love – it's either there or it's not. You can't force it.'

She smiles grimly and reaches for the biscuits.

'Sorry, but I just got divorced,' she explains. 'It's a subject that's on my mind a lot. Love, not-love.'

'I'm sorry to hear that,' says Sidsel, and Loretta waves her hand dismissively.

'God no, don't be. It's very undramatic. There's just a whole lot of, what do you call it, *practical* stuff involved when two people split up after so many years. What do we do with the house and the car, insurance, wills? The first time it was more existential – back when we were still harbouring certain illusions. Michał is my second husband,' she adds, tearing open the wrapper and taking a biscuit out of the pack, 'my second ex-husband, I should say. More accurately.'

She eats the biscuit in a single mouthful.

'Do you have children?'

Loretta chews for a moment before answering.

'Michał and I? No, we each had our own. Bloody mess to begin with, and now they're all so grown up they don't care what their parents get up to. I called my eldest daughter to tell her, and you know what her reaction was? Good for you. She said she was amazed it hadn't happened sooner. And I thought we'd pulled off seeming happy, in a solid, faintly boring sort of way. Ha. They probably knew before we did.'

Loretta takes another biscuit, which breaks and is caught in her lap.

'After my first husband and I separated, I read a book recommended by someone I thought was a good friend,' she says, brushing crumbs off the taut fabric of her skirt. '*Love's Striving*. Absolutely made my blood boil! The author divided up marriage into phases and talked about how you should and shouldn't behave during each one. *In phase one your acknowledgement of the other person happens of its own accord, but this is something you must remember to bring with you into later phases*, etcetera, etcetera, etcetera . . .'

She shakes her head irritably.

'There are a lot of things I'd have done differently, that's for bloody certain. But I couldn't! It was too late. Anyway, I was basically alone with the kids – it wasn't like I could just head off into town and try again. Do it over, and better. My ex and I agreed we'd leave it up to them where they wanted to stay and for how long. They both chose to be based with me, apart from the odd weekend they spent at their dad's *significantly* larger flat. The most grotesque thing is that now they're grown up, I have to remind myself how much I longed for freedom – my own freedom – during those years. I tried talking to Michał about it – he had three sons himself – but I'm afraid he didn't understand me. Like my husband, he never really had much to do with looking after the boys when they were little. I'm not pointing fingers here, that's just the way it *was*. One of us had to be the breadwinner. But that also meant that my first husband could pick up after the divorce more or less where he'd left off fifteen years earlier, while I had no idea who I even was after my youngest daughter left home. The kids had virtually consumed me. I was like a city that had been under siege for the last twenty-two years, completely out of touch with my old ways and customs . . . Do you want one, by the way? Otherwise I'll eat the lot.'

Loretta holds out the packet towards Sidsel, who takes one to be polite.

'Don't misunderstand me,' continues Loretta. 'I'm not a biological determinist. This isn't to say that men always get off scot-free. That it's necessarily the way it has to be. My point is just that it's either one parent or the other who deals with the actual bond with the children, who bears the actual responsibility. Never both. It can't be done. That said, in my own experience, it's almost always the mother who lets herself be anchored. But maybe that's a generational thing?' She stands up to put her ringing telephone on mute. 'It strikes me that the wind is changing. When I talk to my children about this stuff, they always make me feel terribly old-fashioned. Perhaps you think so too?'

The conservator is looking directly at her.

'I don't know,' says Sidsel, and she feels heavy, as though carved out of a single block of stone.

Loretta widens her eyes and clicks her tongue.

'No, I suppose it's all rather complicated. You should probably get going now, by the way, if you want to make your flight. Getting across London is a nightmare.'

~

Sidsel remembers that trip better than the others, because her father had never been away for so long before, and because the night before he left he got out their atlas and showed her where he'd be staying over the coming months. In this entire area, he explained, tracing a finger over the empty stretch of grey, there's just under a million people. If they were distributed evenly across the republic, there'd be two and a half miles between each person. He and the rest of the research team would be based in Yakutsk, the capital of the Sakha Republic. Sidsel had asked him to explain several times what he was going to do up there, but as always when it came to his work, Troels's explanations were so imprecise that they struck her as secretive. Well, first, he might say, we need to look at the bigger picture. Of what? Oh, I mean the overall situation. That evening Sidsel had asked him again, receiving yet another answer of the contentless, generalised variety. But he must have changed his mind, because later, when she was reading in bed, he knocked on the door and sat down in the chair by her desk. He glanced around with curiosity, praising her choice of posters, then started to talk. He talked about the project's interpreter, Aleksander, who had been born in a village in the northernmost part of the republic but studied in Yakutsk. About how they would drive further and further north on the frozen Lena River, the ice road, trying to get the local fishermen to talk. These were people who'd had the rug of their existence pulled out from under them overnight. Their fishing licences had been handed to large national corporations, who sold the precious white salmon and sturgeon eggs to Asia and Europe at a staggering mark-up. The fishermen never saw a kopek. But the order had come from Moscow, and they were more afraid than angry. The interpreter was indispensable in that regard. Having grown up in a village among fishermen and reindeer hunters, the young man knew their cast of mind, their habits and ways of speaking. He would assure them that Troels was there to help, that they could trust him and the NGO he worked for. Without Aleksander, Troels explained to his daughter, he was nothing but another dubious European with intentions that were, at best, murky. Troels told her about spending the night in the fishermen's tin huts with their families and their dogs. About the darkness and the ill-tempered cracking of the gas stoves, the huts' only source of heat. He described the thousand teeth of the cold, and the sense of being in a landscape without end, like a character trapped in a story abandoned by its author. When he was done he stood up and stroked Sidsel's hair, then left the room with an awkward wave. Six months later their mother filed for divorce, and not long after that a birthmark on her lower back began to itch. By the time she finally got a referral (there'd been no one to cover for her at the shop), the cancer had spread to the lymph nodes in her groin and under her left arm.

Among their family friends, the general consensus when it came to Troels was harsh. Most people were united in the suspicion that he had developed a drinking problem or fallen in love with a local woman, if not some combination of both sins at once. Sidsel wasn't so sure. There had always been something captive about her father, as though inside him was a prison, and wherever he was on Earth there were bars across his eyes. Preparing for a trip, he would convince himself that *this* time he would manage to escape, to *be* and *see* for real, but each time he came home crestfallen – more trapped than when he'd gone. With Charlotte it was the other way round. She rarely left town, but her nature found free rein even where space was tight: alone in a terraced house with three kids, behind the counter at the florist's on the square, as a patient on an oncology ward. For the last few months of her life she was bedridden, yet she made Sidsel feel that she could, if she wanted to, simply stand up and walk.

Some people are good at living, the priest had said, and Charlotte Gabel was one such person.

If her mother was a city under siege, she had learned to love the encircling force without reserve, a willing Gulliver lashed tightly to the ground by throbbing umbilical cords.

'I'm getting off here.'

Sidsel looks up. The man jerks his head towards her feet, which have slid out into the aisle and are now blocking his path. His hair is set with glossy wax, his eyes angry and blue. She draws back her legs and he edges past without a word, stepping down on to the platform and melting into the crowd. How vanishingly little we can get away with giving one another! The train jars into motion once again. On the other side of the window, the chimneys of London march past in a seemingly endless parade that dwindles, nonetheless, before petering out altogether, replaced by factories, lawns and low-rise blocks. The past has eased its grip on her attention, and she turns it now to her fellow passengers, admiring how smoothly they adapt to the motion of the train, how every single one functions as the vessel for a whole sea of thoughts without ever making an issue of it.

14

Beatrice

Several of the guests turn unobtrusively in their chairs, startled by the sight of the little princess who has arrived at the chic Italian restaurant this Saturday afternoon. She returns their stares with a charming smile, but to her mother it's obvious something's wrong. Fifi's immaculately made-up face tightens into a worried grimace as she smooths her skirt and sinks on to the bench opposite Bee with a rustle.

'I don't get it,' she sighs. 'Who's half an hour late to a meeting *they* scheduled?'

'Have you tried calling them?' says Bee, taking a sip of the overly expensive red wine. You can get used to having money in no time. It's the other way around that's the problem. Fifi hasn't touched her lemonade, merely batting the ice cubes around disconsolately with her straw.

'Of course I haven't called them.'

'And they didn't call you either?'

'Nobody's called anybody, Mom. People don't do that.'

'So what's that for, then?'

Fifi looks at her phone, then out through the large windows. Is she already regretting letting Bee come along?

'I sent a text,' she said at last. 'They haven't read it.'

'Do you want to go? We can go. When my clients are this late, I consider the session cancelled. They usually accept that.'

Bee sounds a little overeager. She doesn't like the idea of her daughter selling her voice to an app. Fifi shakes her head, then straightens in her seat.

'There they are.'

The two men are younger than she had expected, but otherwise they look like everyone else in this town. The man with the full beard and tattooed knuckles introduces himself as C.P. (sea pea?), while the other, a man of East Asian appearance in a hoodie and a sleeveless jacket with lots of pockets, says a name she doesn't catch and can't bring herself to ask him to repeat.

Fifi is all smiles as she makes room for the app men at the table and graciously declines the offer of something to eat. Bee says she'd like another glass of wine. Same again is fine.

'It's really nice here,' says Fifi, turning to the man with the sleeveless jacket, while his friend goes up to order. 'Good choice.'

He thanks her, explaining that it's his girlfriend who opened the place and that she's thinking of repeating the success in Cole Valley.

'I've tried to warn her,' he says, dropping something that looks like a USB stick into one of his many pockets. 'It's not as simple as you might think. You risk watering down the concept. She needs to tread carefully.'

He turns to Bee, smiling.

'Beatrice, right? I didn't quite get *who* you are? Relationship-wise.'

'Oh,' says Fifi, reddening beneath her powder, 'I brought my mom along. I hope that's okay with you guys?'

'Sure, sure. That's awesome.'

He doesn't look like he means it, and Bee is relieved to see C.P. pay and move in the direction of their table, carrying a tray.

'There, something for everyone,' he says, setting down two espressos and the glass of wine. Coffee? Bee seems to be the only one planning to enjoy herself. Pauline insisted on serving alcohol at her meetings, including the morning ones. Not too much, nothing inappropriate, just enough to make you drop your shoulders.

'Fantastic,' says the other man. 'So, how about we start by telling you what we're thinking, Seraphina? Broad brush, I mean. Ideas, user interface, target audience . . .'

So far neither of them has apologised for arriving forty-five minutes late, and Bee doesn't like the way Fifi is smiling at them. Like a child at an orphanage. Far too anxious to be loved. *Pick me.* She's already given them too much, and over the next fifteen minutes it becomes apparent that they want more. Miss Fessonia is going to lend her face as well as her voice to Dreamon. Fifi will move into people's phones. She will allow herself to be summoned as they lie there staring into the darkness.

'Cards on the table, we've been through a whole list of

potential candidates,' says the man Bee now knows is named Jeff, 'and you're really something special. Your followers are hyper-dedicated to *you* specifically, Seraphina. It's not ASMR they're after, it's the feeling of being with Miss Fessonia, and we want to make that feeling as authentic as possible – to get rid of all the unnecessary stuff. You won't be available on a platform with a bunch of other people. Your videos won't be preceded by commercials. You will have your very own universe, somewhere that's one hundred percent you.'

C.P. has already taken out an iPad, and now he puts it on the table between them. Fifi is gnawing excitedly on her bottom lip. Bee feels like reaching out to grab her daughter, hold her back, protect her, but now C.P. has opened the beta version of Dreamon. Fifi gazes at the screen, where an animated version of her face appears against a backdrop of stars. Jeff is watching her discreetly.

'Okay, so the concept is to build this kind of realm of sleep,' says C.P. 'The app functions as a gateway to this place, and you're the user's friend and helper.' His finger skates across the screen. 'In here, people can define their goals and track their progress. So let's say I sleep five to seven hours a night, waking up two or three times, but I want to sleep a minimum of seven hours, waking up once at the most. I type it in here, boom. Now I'm not going it alone any more – Miss Fessonia is holding my hand the entire way.'

'How pretty,' says Fifi. 'Were you the one who made all this?'

'Me and a couple others. And this is only the beginning.

Once you're on board, we'll start integrating your videos and voice-overs and sounds into the background structure. There'll be menus that let people curate the exact experience they want. What works for one person won't necessarily work for someone else. I'm sure you know all about that. People are incredibly specific when it comes to ASMR. It's actually a lot like porn in that sense. Not that I'm comparing them otherwise,' he adds, fatuously.

'We're envisaging that you'll create original content for the app,' says Jeff, 'stuff that's not on your channel. You'll have access to professional equipment, lighting, a make-up artist. It will be a deluxe version of the brand you've already created.'

'Miss Fessonia 2.0,' adds C.P., switching off the tablet.

Fifi stares longingly at the black glass.

'How does that sound?' asks Jeff.

'It sounds really good,' she says breathlessly.

'Yeah? We think so too,' he laughs. 'There're already a bunch of sleep apps on the market, but they're all very clinical. With Dreamon we want to build something that people actually look forward to interacting with every night before they go to sleep.'

'May I cut in here? Quick question.'

All three turn to Bee in surprise. Fifi shakes her head imperceptibly, but Bee doesn't care. This stinks to high heaven.

'Yeah, sure,' says Jeff grudgingly. 'Fire away.'

'My understanding from Seraphina is that she has a pretty good business going with her channel. But it's reasonable to assume that she'd lose a lot of, I guess you call them viewers, if there was an app where you could get the same thing but better. Or am I completely off base?'

Jeff has kept up a vehemently obliging smile while Bee has been talking, but now his face is as buttoned-up as a doctor's.

'That part isn't fully in place yet, but the idea is that Seraphina will be paid a lump sum for the content she creates for Dreamon.'

'So in principle you're buying Miss Fessonia,' says Bee. 'You're buying Fifi's project for a lump sum.'

Jeff turns to Fifi, who's turning one of her earrings nervously.

'Obviously you'll still be free to run your channel. In the vast majority of cases, more platforms just mean more traffic, more views. Maybe it would be best to think of this as a spin-off from what you've already built. An expansion—'

'Or a watering-down,' says Bee. 'Isn't that what you were talking about earlier? When you take something good and overexploit it.'

'Mom.'

Fifi is wan with embarrassment, but Bee has no intention of sitting here and watching her be conned. Isn't this what a mother is for? To stand between her child and the world like a sieve, filtering out all the bullshit. And now Fifi is facing two massive piles of shit who are clearly out to make a quick buck from something she has spent years building up. Alone in her room in Bondurant. Without any help from men in sleeveless jackets.

‘Think it over,’ says Jeff, getting to his feet. ‘And if you need to talk it through again, you can always call.’

‘Oh, so now she’s allowed to call your *secret, secret* phone line?’

He stares uncomprehendingly at Bee.

‘Yeah. If she has any questions, she’s welcome to contact me.’

‘But she won’t. She won’t contact you.’

He slings on his backpack, darting Fifi a smile.

‘Sounds like your manager has spoken.’

‘Thanks,’ says Fifi, rising to take his outstretched hand. ‘I’ll call.’ Her skirt snags on a nail in the bench, and the tulle rips with a brittle noise.

‘Oh no,’ she gasps, evidently on the verge of tears.

C.P. says goodbye and follows his partner, who’s already on his way out.

‘Hey!’ yells Bee. ‘Forget it!’

The men are gone. The meeting is over.

Fifi is stock still, standing as though turned to stone, then she rushes to the toilets, the ruined skirt flapping in her wake. Bee sits back down. The couple at the next table have been gawping, and now she turns to them.

‘Can I help you with something? Anything at all?’

‘No thanks,’ replies the woman curtly, and whispers something to her boyfriend. They look away.

‘That’s right. No thanks,’ mutters Bee, emptying her glass.

They exchange an indulgent smile.

Happy that they aren’t her.

Bee isn't too drunk to understand why Fifi is angry. But that doesn't change the fact that she did the right thing. Dreamon will have to find another mermaid. Her Seraphina still has her voice. She is free to sing as she pleases.

Fifi puts her computer down and sits up in bed.

'You mean it!?'

For the first time in several hours, she sounds like her usual bubbly, easily enthused self.

No. Bee doesn't think it would be a good idea to go find a man she had sex with one time twenty-four years ago and let him know, after as many years' delay, that he's a dad. On the contrary, she thinks it's a bad idea, and possibly dangerous, who knows? But Fifi will soon be off home to Bondurant and Marianne, and Bee doesn't want to leave her daughter with the impression that she's out to ruin her life. After the meeting with the two app developers, Fifi spent so long in the bathroom that Bee had time to order and eat a tiramisu the size of a man's shoe. The dessert made her feel sick, but it tempered the effect of the booze, as she'd hoped, and all the way home she tried (in calm, balanced language) to explain why she thought it would be best if the Dreamon guys found another candidate. But Fifi was beside herself, and nothing Bee said made any difference.

She'd had it under control!

Didn't Bee understand it was a negotiation? A proposal?

What right did she have to stick her oar in?

Back at the house, Fifi went to bed without saying

goodnight. Bee dawdled in the living room, hoping that her daughter would have a change of heart and come back down to talk things through, but after an hour and a half, when this still hadn't happened, she went upstairs herself and knocked. Bee regretted the words the moment they were out of her mouth. At the same time, it was impossible not to be delighted by the effect they had on Fifi: like a sparkler catching light and starting to fizz.

And maybe it wouldn't be so bad.

It might even be nice to see him again.

'You mean it?' she repeats, switching on the bedside lamp. The light scorches Bee's eyes. 'Tomorrow?'

'Yup.'

She hasn't worked out all the details yet.

For instance, it's still unclear who's going to drive. Fifi isn't allowed to because of her epilepsy, and Bee had her licence revoked around Thanksgiving last year. It wasn't an altogether bad experience. The officers were friendly, and she needed someone to talk to. She'd begun to hope they would keep her at the station overnight, but then they sent her home after all. Pauline paid the fine; obviously there wasn't much she could do about the licence.

'Morning is probably best,' says Fifi. 'Half ten? Or would after lunch be better?'

Her eyes are radiant, and Bee doesn't have the heart to say that no time is better than any other when it comes to shaking people to their core. Or possibly ruining their lives.

'Eleven sounds good.'

‘Then it’s a road trip!’

Leaping off the bed, Fifi throws her arms around her mother and kisses her on the mouth. The last time that happened, they were living in a camper van, and Fifi had her own eyelashes.

Just like before, the house in the ad seems bigger and brighter than the one she lives in. With each click a new and gorgeous room bounds into view, rooms she recognises but has no idea existed. Like in a dream. She’s amazed it’s worth taking shots like these. How can anyone not be disappointed when they walk into the actual house? But his name doesn’t appear anywhere. He has no copyright on his images, nor is he to be found on the list of Gabriel’s smiling employees. Bee is about to give up when *For fire for warmth* pops into her head. He mentioned in passing his abortive career as a poet, possibly to make her feel like less of a screw-up. She types the name of his debut into the search bar, and there is its author: Hector Nunez, ten years younger and many pounds lighter, photographed during a reading at the bookstore on Bonita Avenue. He’s holding the poetry collection in his left hand. The book casts most of his face into shadow, but there’s no doubt that it’s the man who came to the house with his camera and his tripods. Who told her, ‘That sounds rough. Let me know if there’s anything I can do.’

Bee is well aware that this is something people say.

That they don’t mean it like that.

But then they should think of something else to say.

There are plenty of encouraging platitudes that don't involve a concrete offer of help.

And anyway, she does intend to pay him.

The first time she calls he doesn't pick up, and Bee leaves a short message that's supposed to make it sound like the call is work related. Then it occurs to her that it's Saturday night, and that he probably won't deal with that kind of message until Monday. She calls again, and again gets his machine. The third time he picks up straight away.

'Good evening,' she says, 'this is Beatrice Wallens from Park Hill.'

'Just a minute.'

She can hear him moving, a door opening. Bare feet on flooring, slap slap slap.

'There. Okay, Beatrice, what's up?'

Yep, what's up, Beatrice? 'Do you remember me?'

'Of course I remember you.'

'Am I disturbing you?'

He laughs, not unkindly.

'You woke me up, so I guess you could say that.'

Bee looks at the clock. It's half past one. What is it with her and time these days? It's getting her all turned around.

'I'm so sorry about that,' she says. 'I didn't realise it was so late, but it really couldn't wait.'

Hector clears his throat.

'Is it about the pictures? Is there something you're not happy with, or . . .?'

'The pictures are perfect. They make me want to buy my

house, and I live here already. It's about a . . .' She casts around for the right word without finding it, '. . . a transport job.'

He doesn't answer.

'I noticed you had a car, you see, the last time you were here.'

'I do have a car.'

For the first time there's a vein of coolness in his voice. He's keen to get back to bed, understandably. This is no time to beat about the bush, not now she's come this far.

'My daughter is visiting me for the first time in years,' says Bee, 'and I've just ruined a business meeting for her. I got drunk and said some things I shouldn't have. She was really mad at me and she might have, maybe, lost a – kind of a client. I mean, it wasn't something I thought was a good idea, but still. I crossed a line, and now I'd like to make it right.'

'I'm sorry to hear that,' he says, 'but I don't think I—'

'Yes. Yes, you can. Because I ended up promising her that we would drive to Kentfield and visit her father tomorrow morning, and the thing is that neither of us has a licence, and we don't have a car either. She has never met William. Her father's name is William,' she adds.

There's silence at the other end.

'How did you get my number?'

'Your poetry collection,' she says. 'I remembered you were a writer. There was a website with contact information.'

'And now you're asking if I'll drive you to Kentfield?'

'I'll pay, of course. For the inconvenience.'

'I'm sorry, but I don't think that's going to be possible.'

Bee lowers the phone and takes a deep breath.

'Isn't there a bus?'

'If we take a bus it's not a road trip,' she hisses, 'plus he lives on a fucking mountain. There aren't any buses going there. People like that have cars.'

She doesn't mean to; she's not trying to make him feel bad. It just comes tumbling out of her.

'Sorry,' she hiccups as soon as she can catch her breath. 'Sorry, I don't know what I'm doing. That's the problem, really.'

15

Hector

Hector is too unsettled to go back to bed. He sits at the kitchen table, naked apart from his glasses and a wine-red T-shirt that says *Wish I hadn't bet on the hare.* He's trying to figure out what just happened. Was it because she called him a writer? Could it really be that simple? Nobody has called him that for a very long time, and Hector felt a bolt draw back in his chest before he heard himself promising to collect Beatrice and her daughter at nine o'clock the following morning. He *has* been thinking about her since the visit a few weeks ago. Not in an obsessive way, just enough to be noticeable. Usually, the people and their homes are erased from his memory as soon as he's sent a selection of images to Woolhouse, but the beautiful, drunken Ms Wallens and her half-empty rooms had lingered in his mind. Something about the way she left her troubles on view, like shining, deep red wounds, like a gash across her chest. Most people try to hide when he comes round, but she let him see all the way down to the bone. Hector slumps forward, resting his cheek against the waxed cloth. It's Sunday tomorrow, and he's agreed to meet up with Ea and Coco after swimming. They were going to tell the girl the big news afterwards, over waffles. Wedding! Bridesmaid! But he can't bring himself to call Beatrice and say he won't help after all. Besides, he's not sure Coco will like finding out that way. The first thing she'll do is ask how long they've known, and why they didn't say anything before. Coco isn't like the nine-year-old girls he remembers from his childhood: shampoo-scented, gum-chewing little witches who moved in packs and scrawled the names of their future babies on each other's forearms. His daughter doesn't care about make-up or stickers, or who plays with whom. She prefers to be alone or in the company of adults. Even when Coco was tiny, Lola used to proclaim merrily to anyone who would listen that Cordelia Lucia Nunez was something special, that she had given birth to a total little freak. Like so much else Lola did, it had annoyed him at the time, but today he's inclined to agree with his ex-wife. You can't compare Coco to anyone but Coco.

'William in Kentfield,' mutters Hector, looking at the pygmy iguana, which is glimmering palely in the light of the neighbour's ceiling lamp.

'Can't sleep?'

He didn't hear her come in. The old parquet creaks and grumbles under everyone but her. She was slim already, but over the last month she's got thinner still. There's something bothering her, but Hector hasn't dared ask what it is. He's afraid of the reply. Afraid she'll say what's been lying like a gun beneath the pillow of their relationship from the beginning. There's a distinct possibility that the proposal was related to this fear, and now his fiancée is standing in the doorway, twisting her engagement ring with a worried expression on her pretty goat's face.

Hector holds up the phone.

'It was only Lola.'

Lola's long since stopped calling him at all hours, but that's what popped into his head.

Ea looks sceptical.

'What did she want?'

'To talk about the summer vacation. You know what she's like. Once she gets an idea in her head.'

Ea gives a snort that he knows means they don't need to talk any more about it.

'Aren't you coming back to bed?' She strokes the hair from his forehead. Kisses it.

'In a minute. You go back in.'

He watches her walk down the hallway and slip into Coco's room, re-emerging seconds later and vanishing into their bedroom. Coco has a habit of kicking off the duvet, and Ea is always scared she'll get cold. She grew up in a country where the cold was a perpetual threat, one that had to be combatted with heaters, mittens and hats that made them look like little bank robbers. He's seen a picture of her as a kid, dressed in just that sort of hat. But that was ages ago; he doesn't know where the album is now. Ea doesn't like to talk about her childhood, he's grasped that much. In the early days of their relationship, Hector enquired about her past cautiously but with interest. The dead parents, the years in Italy, the two siblings back home in Denmark. He let himself patiently be fended off and tried again, certain it was only a matter of time before she opened up to him. Until one day it dawned on him that Ea would rather be free.

Free like a carrot you pull out of the ground once it's ready.

Nobody asks the carrot what it was like growing sweet and orange in the dark.

As soon as Hector understood that this was how Ea wanted to be seen, he did his best to think of her that way: as a creature who had begun the moment she stepped into his apartment, applying for the job of Coco's babysitter.

Now, for the first time, he's not sure this was the right tack.

Ea seems afflicted by the same melancholy that overcame his senile grandma towards the end. As though after years of self-imposed amnesia, she has in fact forgotten something she wishes she could recall.

16

Niels

'The white pigeons are the queens. Do you know why they're white instead of grey, or only a little bit grey? A bit of grey on the throat or the wings. But there are some that are white all over, and that's because they eat flowers and leaves instead of trash. Ordinary pigeons eat all sorts of rubbish and old stuff and they don't get sick. They can eat bread that's been lying in a puddle of mud and they don't get sick. Isn't that crazy? If I was a pigeon, I'd only eat flowers and leaves until I was completely white.'

The voice is rapping against his consciousness like a teaspoon, and he registers that she's been talking for a while. With a powerful effort, he bundles and archives his thoughts for later use and focuses on Laura, who is dangling her legs off the front of the bike, strapped in place with the strong elastic belts that normally secure the bucket of paste.

'What about wood pigeons?' he says. 'They live out in the woods but they're still grey, almost purple on the chest. And they don't eat rubbish.'

Laura shrugs.

'I'm talking about the rules for *ordinary* ones,' she says graciously, turning towards him. 'When are we getting there?'

'When we don't feel like cycling any more.'

'But where are we going?'

'I don't know,' says Niels. 'Sometimes it's okay not to have a plan.'

'Fine. But Mum usually has a plan.'

'I can imagine.'

'My fingers are freezing.'

'Then pull them into your sleeves.'

'But then I can't hold on.'

'You don't need to hold on, Larva. You're strapped in. Look.'

Pause.

'I'm getting hungry, too.'

'Hang on just a bit longer. Can you do that?'

She nods bravely.

It's not true that he doesn't have a plan. Niels has no intention of spending any more of his life on one of Copenhagen's playgrounds. It must be possible to hang out with a kid in a way that doesn't wither the soul. He's had a chance to study the parents at those playgrounds, and in all their faces he has glimpsed the same murky fantasy: that something or someone will come along and carry them off, like in the cartoons when an eagle swoops down and grips its victim's collar before it rises in two elegant loops and is gone.

'Why does he sleep so much?'

'Cosmo?'

Little by little, Niels has got used to the way Laura assumes he can read her mind, beginning most of her sentences in medias res.

'Whenever we're home he's asleep.'

'He's sad. It can be tiring.'

'Is his mum dead?'

Niels doesn't remember having said anything that could have given her that impression, and assures Laura that Cosmo's mum is in perfect health.

'She's just not very nice, but that's another story. That's not why he's sad.'

Laura's interest is piqued.

'Why isn't she very nice?'

'Being nice is harder than you might think. I mean, you're not always nice, are you?'

'No,' she admits, 'but why is he *that* sad?'

'I think it has something to do with the fact that he can't play his guitar right now.'

'Why can't he?'

'Well, he can, but he doesn't feel like it.'

Laura considers this.

'That's a pity,' she says as they turn the corner on to Sundkrogsgade. 'When will he be happy again?'

'I don't know. This stuff is hard to predict.'

'Maybe when it's his birthday,' suggests Laura, and Niels doesn't contradict her, why not? They're making good headway. It's a gorgeous morning, and the sight of the industrial landscape in the spring sunshine is perking him up. Nothing here is decorative; everything is as it is because that's the best and most practical way. Compared with the familiar scale of the city, the proportions out here are intoxicating, and he takes in the view with satisfaction: containers stacked like enormous Lego bricks, grey and blue and green, yellow and red. They form a labyrinthine and windowless city, criss-crossed by miles of alleyways through which the wind howls and staggers. You can easily get lost in here if you don't keep your wits about you. There are no people to be seen, no ships docking today. The cranes are summoning their strength for the next heave. The containers guard their cargo jealously, or wait to be refilled. It is a place where the global economy takes physical form – and makes itself vulnerable. If you really wanted to start a revolution, you could begin the destruction here, and blow all this shit sky-high. Niels accelerates, then lets the bike roll the final stretch down to the quay.

'Here we are,' he says, getting off.

Laura stares at him in amazement. A streak of clear snot is dribbling from one nostril. He wipes it away with his finger.

'Ouch. Your mittens are scratchy. Where are we?'

'At the end of the world.'

It was Cosmo who used to call it that, although the poetry of the name doesn't really suit this brutal concrete place, which first appeared on the map of Niels's life when the two friends started coming here aged twelve instead of going to school. They would sit on the quay, smoking cigarettes and slurping yogurt drinks, setting off firecrackers among the containers. The infernal din as the bangs ricocheted between the corrugated metal walls felt like an omen, or so they tacitly agreed. But an omen of what?

17

Ea (and Coco)

As soon as the woman in the black swimsuit has left the sauna, Coco turns to Ea and asks if she *still* doesn't want a baby. Her voice is disbelieving, as though the ponderous body were such an appealing advert for pregnancy that no one in their right mind could remain unmoved. Ea has been preparing for the question ever since she caught sight of the woman doing her sedate laps of the pool. She smiles and says, well, she's got her: Coco. The girl snorts at the glib response. Ea ought to know better, and she does, but she's become aware of the two older women on the bench below them. Their voices have gone quiet, and she can almost see their ears prick up under the damp grey hair and swivel in her direction.

'A child of your own,' sighs Coco. 'Why don't you want a child of your own? Everyone else in my class has a little brother or a little sister.'

That's not true. It's the land of the only child, this city. It's expensive and difficult to have kids here, and not many parents can afford a house big enough for more than one. Ea can only think offhand of three of Coco's classmates who have siblings. She doesn't say so; instead she asks if that's something Coco wants, a sibling?

'Nah, not really. It sounds kind of stressful.'

Ea is relieved, but it's too soon to let down her guard.

'I was asking *you*,' says Coco, 'why you don't want a kid. Most women your age would love one. A child of their own, a baby,' she adds pedantically, in case Ea once more has the nerve to play dumb.

'Coco,' Ea says softly, 'that's quite an intimate question.'

'Fair enough. You just said I was basically your daughter. So.'

Coco hops down from the bench and squeezes past the two women.

'I'm going to grab a cold shower. Sorry if I hurt your feelings.'

The two women beneath her reluctantly resume their conversation. Ea ought to follow Coco and give her a proper reply. The girl is allergic to the elastic, roundabout way that adults talk, and can nurse a grudge for hours if she senses that's what's happening. One of the women says something Ea doesn't catch, forcing her to repeat the words that had felt moments earlier like a sudden impulse. The woman clears her throat uneasily.

'There's nothing for it but to jump in feet first. A baby is hard work, but after the first six months it gets easier.'

Her friend clucks in agreement, and Ea says she can imagine, which is obviously all it takes to restore the first woman's confidence.

'And if it's your body you're nervous about,' she nods towards Ea's flat belly, 'then let me tell you it won't look like that forever, no matter what you do. It's no good worrying about that. Gravity doesn't care if you've given birth or not. I've got two kids, two big boys, and I had a wonderful body until a few years ago. Narrow waist, firm boobs, fantastic arse. And then one morning I woke up looking like a pudgy rectangle. Boom. Overnight – and it was all hormones.'

'I can't have kids,' says Ea, 'but thanks.'

'Oh God, shit, I'm *really* sorry,' says the woman, turning her back. A few minutes later, they both get up and leave.

It's not something to lie about, but they deserved to be embarrassed.

Ea lies flat on the bench and stares up at the wooden ceiling. For as long as she can remember, the thought of one day having a child has felt like a hand over her mouth: like a house without windows. As a child she never played with dolls or stuffed pillows under her top, and her younger siblings only began to interest her once they had learned to walk and talk. Infants bored and frightened her with their wet, open mouths, their simple, pressing needs. For years, Ea expected to start craving one of her own: one of the creatures her friends would occasionally introduce her to. It didn't happen. Even Laura prompted nothing apart from astonishment, and although Ea had imagined she'd stay for several weeks getting to know her black-eyed niece, the old restlessness quickly found her again. She returned to California, leaving her sister with the puckered little body and a weariness that seemed as private and impenetrable as a new romance. There was nothing to be done. Motherhood vibrated at a frequency she didn't pick up, and by her late twenties Ea began preparing to make a terrifying compromise with her body:

For what man could love a woman who refused to carry his child?

It was Hector, good, good Hector, who without knowing it had set her free.

He'd said it on their second real date.

That night they'd made love in a way that put a definitive end to the employer–employee relationship. Sitting across from her in bed, he told Ea that he didn't want any more children.

That he thought she ought to know, before things went any further.

He didn't want her to look back and feel cheated.

As he spoke, he kept his head down; then he looked up.

Ea still remembers the puzzled mix of relief and shame that rose up in her chest like a black balloon.

I'm very fond of Coco, she said carefully.

Hector scrutinised her face before deciding she was telling the truth.

Lola is crazy, he said, but she's a good mom.

And that was that.

Or it had been until a few months ago, when the intolerable doubt that had driven her into the arms of the medium had come prowling in.

It started with something as mundane as a late period.

The blood, usually so reliable, had missed the appointment they'd had for more than twenty years.

For six long days, Ea expected to feel the grip loosen in her lower abdomen, and every time she looked down at her unstained panties, she felt more bewildered.

Was this *hope* she was feeling?

Was it childish anticipation keeping her awake at night?

It must have been, because when she woke on the seventh morning to the familiar sticky warmth between her legs, Ea felt her heart sink.

She was disappointed, and the disappointment had an unforeseen effect.

Like a changing wind, she began turning towards Denmark. She listened to Danish radio and read articles about the upcoming elections, looked up her brother (though Niels didn't exist on the Internet) then her sister, and dropped the orange Google Maps guy outside her green front door somewhere in north-west Copenhagen. The photograph had been taken on a day in spring; the roses were in bloom. Left of the door was a red bike with a child seat and a plastic bag over the saddle – why *shouldn't* that be Sidsel's? When she got tired of counting on her fingers, she added Central European Summer Time to the clock on her phone, and this new attention to the time-shift made her West Coast days feel moonlike, the nights thin and false. As the colour ran out of everything, Ea was seized by a previously unknown urge to communicate. Having not written a proper letter since her early teens, she now composed long emails and texts that she somehow couldn't bring herself to send. The sentences crumbled in her hands until they were nothing but rubble, strained attempts at contact. She couldn't help but wonder whether it was all one big red herring, an inelegant attempt by her conscious mind to cover up for her *true* lack, her *true* longing.

So when Sand – fucked-up, fundamentally muddle-headed Sand – attributed her own newfound zen to a visit to Beatrice, Ea had been desperate enough to give it a shot herself. She would have given anything to feel a little of the peace she thought she saw in Sand's green eyes.

How naïve that strikes her as now!

Ea drapes her arm over her eyes and laughs sourly, for there they are again, the voices. Near and far, but undeniably present.

Is this how it feels to go insane?

The laughter makes Coco hesitate. She was about to sit down, but now she's not so sure. As far as she can see, there's nothing to laugh about. There's no one in the sauna but the two of them. The girl wavers a few yards from the person she learned to regard first as an extension of her teachers, then as a fun, engaging big sister, and now . . . well, what now? As a part of her dad, like the doll she got from Grandma, where there's a head under the dress as well as on the top. No legs at either end. It's all right to spy by accident, but she still doesn't like it.

'Do you remember, when I was little, I thought your name was Ear?' she asks.

Ea sits up with a jerk. Her face is as narrow and white as toast in the dim light.

'In a way I wish it was.'

'Why?'

Coco clambers up on to the bench. Ea's skin smells of chlorine and the moisturiser she uses. It occurs to her that she's hungry. Her stomach is an empty bucket. Ea promised they'd go to Buttermilk afterwards; she'd forgotten about that. Lucky, lucky – now the day is woven through with a thread of gold.

'Why not?' asks Ea.

'Because Ear isn't a name.'

'If I was called that, it would be.'

Coco rolls her eyes but allows herself to be drawn towards the damp shoulder. The kiss feels as light as a butterfly on her hair, the mouth landing and taking flight again in an instant.

*

Charlotte

In the end I accepted that I was someone who preferred more tangible pursuits, I say.

What?

I knew it. You never listen.

I lost the thread. I'm sorry. No, I mean it. Sorry.

He puts his hand on my knee. His face is a long mask, the cheeks grey and sunken, the eyes watering.

You know, you look terrible, I say.

Hey, come on.

But you do. This isn't how I remember you at all. So . . . shrunken.

What about you, then?

I run my hand over my face, but it feels exactly as it always does, smooth and fleshy.

You don't look well, that's all I meant. How did it happen, exactly?

Does it matter?

He gives my knee a squeeze and moves his hand away. Hurt.

Behind us, the membrane emits its peculiar noise. A soughing that's at once as gentle as the waves and as threatening as the drone of a wasps' nest that's only just been sprayed.

In an attempt to lighten the mood, I ask:

Do you remember the first place we moved into together?

Troels nods, smiling to himself.

That studio on Ryesgade with the toilet in the hall. It smelled different every time I came back from the university. Of blackberry jam or toasted hazelnuts, paint and benzine. There'd be bits of fabric strewn across the floor, and the table was covered with pictures you'd cut out for your colleagues. The whey would be dripping through a cloth into a bowl, and on the stove there'd be the yellow cast-iron pot full of stock, boiled using the bones the butcher insisted on giving you. Since he was so in love, and all.

You think so? I ask, trying to recall the young man's cheery, vapid face.

I know so.

Well, anyway, I say, when I think about it now, I realise I spent my youth and a decent chunk of my adult life ploughing through the world in search of something to call mine. Everything I claimed to be interested in, everything I told myself I found fascinating, it all felt like it was tacked on as loosely as the bits of blue and yellow and pink fabric that were supposed to be feathers on Ea's parrot costume. I fastened them with pins that kept pricking me. Unlike that costume – which, by the way, I put the final finishing touches to with my swollen hands about a week before Lent, when I was heavily pregnant with our second daughter, and suffering from oedema and heartburn – nobody came along to give me *final form. My life was random chance on top of random chance, until, given the sheer weight of evidence, it looked like that was the point – or at least it could have been. Listen to me, now we're right back to the costumes.*

I envied you, Charles, but I doubt you'll believe me.

Do you understand, I say a little impatiently, because I can sense I'm close to something, a type of core, all my life I was trapped in this nerve-racking place between work and play. Like an otter.

Troels frowns.

Like an otter?

Yes, I say, the way it smacks mussels against stones to get at the salty goodness inside, but it still can't help tossing them up in the air and catching them again.

And then we fall silent.

The glossy animal a seal in the soft wax of our youth. It's hardening now. Now we don't have access any more.

18

Beatrice

Their surroundings during the second half of the journey are becoming more affluent with every mile they put behind them, and after a while Bee has to ask Seraphina to stop sighing in that exasperatingly rapturous way.

'I just can't believe anyone actually *lives* here,' she protests. 'That they go to bed and wake up in a house like this every single day. I wonder if his is as big?'

'I don't think there are any small houses in this part of Kentfield,' says Hector glumly. 'I don't think there's anything small here at all.'

Bee eyes him gratefully. Thus far their driver has said no more than strictly necessary. So he doesn't hate them, then, as she was beginning to worry. Fifi chatters on about cars and bay windows, fountains and glazed roof tiles, indifferent to their lack of enthusiasm. Nothing can touch her today. She's put on daughterly clothes for the occasion: navy blue slacks and a short-sleeved shirt with a lace collar, and a black silk ribbon tied in a bow at the end of her braid. If Bee had to be honest, she looks more like an enchanted porcelain doll than ever, but Bee doesn't have to be honest, not necessarily, and now that they're so close to their goal, even Fifi must surely realise that clothes won't be the deciding factor. Bee had thought she would spend the whole trip regretting this. She hasn't. Moving so ruthlessly from thought to action is actually downright invigorating.

'Here it is. Number 660.'

Hector parks the car at the end of a cul-de-sac, ten yards from the gate that shields William Catchpoole's property from the rest of Kentfield.

So he really does live on a mountain, thinks Bee, rolling down the window with the crank handle. Hector switches off the engine. The air up here is still and fragrant, like a forest. Beyond a row of cypresses is the distant view over Phoenix Lake and Mount Tamalpais. Insects whir around the crowded purplish-blue clusters of lupins in the verge. There are no people to be seen anywhere, nor is there any sign of them, apart from the grilles around their secluded domiciles.

Leaning forward, Bee pokes her face between the front seats.

'What do we do now?'

'I think it's best if I go in alone.'

Bee doesn't disagree; she's just surprised, because until now Fifi has been saying *we*.

'Are you sure? I can come with you part of the way.'

She shakes her head.

'No, Mom.'

'Okay.' Bee drops back into her seat. 'But promise me you'll call if something happens.'

'What could happen? He's my dad.'

Fifi unfastens her seat belt and opens the door.

'Wish me luck.'

She walks up to the intercom, presses a button and leans forward.

What is she saying?

What *can* one say?

Oh, there's no way this is going to end well!

For a long moment nothing happens, then the gate splits in two. On the other side, the driveway narrows to a flagstone path that winds through what can only be described as a park, complete with benches and hillocks, and a water feature set between two perfect palm trees. The house is not visible from the road.

'Damn, he opened it,' mutters Hector.

Fifi pulls an excited face and gives them two thumbs up, then she slips through the gate, which closes soundlessly behind her.

After an unbearable ten minutes have passed in the silence of the car, Bee abandons the idea of letting Hector speak first.

'Do you think this is a bad idea? What if he gets mad? Maybe we should have warned him after all.'

'Yeah, you definitely could have.'

Bee stares at him in dismay.

'Poor Fifi. She'll be so disappointed if he won't at least talk to her. He's in for a shock.'

Hector opens the door but doesn't get out.

'We'll see,' he says. 'He hasn't chucked her out yet. People can surprise you.'

Is that a veiled implication?

Has Bee surprised Hector?

She wishes she could think of something engaging or interesting to say to him. Something that will make him forget he's wasting a sunny Sunday morning loafing around in the car with a middle-aged woman he doesn't know, purely because she shouted at him on the phone. She's still casting around when he catches her eye in the mirror.

'She didn't seem angry.'

Bee blinks, confused.

'Your daughter. You said she was angry with you. Something to do with a meeting?'

'Oh no,' says Bee. 'No, she's not angry any more. That's the trouble with Fifi. She forgives everything way too easily.'

Bee hopes he understands how this might be a problem. And perhaps he does, for now he changes the subject and asks if she ever considered telling Catchpoole about the child.

'Never,' says Bee, sticking to the truth, or to the past as she remembers it, as she has told it to herself. 'I felt that Seraphina had come to *me*. His world seemed so bizarre, so cold. In those days I'd never even used a computer, and there was this man talking about them as though they were the only things that mattered. Anyway, we were only together one time. It would have complicated his life unnecessarily. Do you have any kids, Hector?'

'A daughter.'

'So you know that children complicate things. How old is she?'

'Nine.'

'Oh, nine. That's a good age. You're always happy when you're nine, aren't you? That's how I remember it.'

'Hm,' says Hector. 'I didn't like being a kid. I spent most of my childhood fantasising about growing up.'

'And has it lived up to your expectations?'

'Most of the time it does.'

He strokes his hand over his beard, then adds in a subdued voice:

'But it's pretty extreme, isn't it, being a parent? Nobody tells you how horrible it is to love someone in that way. How scared you are of everything. It wasn't until I had Coco that I started noticing how crazy the world is. How dangerous people are. It drove me nuts thinking of the terrible things that could happen to her, if not now, then later. My ex hated it, and I understood, but what was I supposed to do? I couldn't let go of these thoughts about all the stuff just waiting to crush my girl.'

'Was that why you split up?'

'It was part of it. Around Coco's second birthday it dawned on me that the coldness that had appeared between us was permanent. She felt pretty much the same way. So we got divorced. Just when you think everything is about to begin.'

Bee locks eyes with him in the mirror. Under the shadow of the cap they're close-set and dark, wreathed with long lashes.

'I've been a bad mother,' she says. 'I did my best at first. I guess everybody does, but it was like the only decisions I could make were the wrong ones. I led us down some dark, dangerous roads that weren't right for a kid. My idea of a good life made it impossible for her to be happy, even though she really, *really* tried. At some point I gave up and left her with her grandmother. Luckily, my mom still has all her instincts intact. It's the only good decision I've ever made on my daughter's behalf.'

Hector is still for a while, not speaking, then he turns to look at her.

'You admit it. Not many people would be able to do that.'

Bee snorts.

'Once you get used to being honest with yourself, it's not so bad. It's the charade that grinds you down. I meet lots of different people in the course of my work, people who are stuck, at least in a metaphorical sense. And the best thing that can happen to them isn't that they get to talk to whoever they think they need to talk to. The best thing that can happen is that they stop lying to themselves and—'

Bee falls silent as suddenly the gate opens and out comes Fifi, walking beside her father with a look on her face like that of a child who's been allowed to choose the biggest and shiniest balloon of them all. William Catchpoole waves in the direction of the car, then hurriedly puts his hand back in the pocket of his shorts. Bee grins, startled, because now she remembers him perfectly! The years have softened the freckled face, and the once flaming red hair has faded to a sandy grey. But the smile is just as boyish as it was back then, on the windswept terrace. He looks like what he is, thinks Bee: a very well-off computer nerd in his early fifties.

'Here comes the bride,' says Hector, unbuckling his seat belt.

Fifi can't stop telling the story, and as soon as she's got through the whole thing (there's not all that much to tell), she starts again from the beginning, each time emphasising some new detail: his reaction when she revealed her errand; the housekeeper, Wilma, who didn't seem remotely fazed and insisted on serving mango juice and a chocolate cake that neither of them touched; the fireplaces and the walnut parquet; the pool; or the unlikely trip to Italy.

'He'd virtually already left! If we'd got there just an hour later, it would have been too late.'

William, as he apologetically explained to Beatrice and Hector, had been on his way to the airport when Seraphina pressed thc buzzer. He was off to Venice, and from there to Rome and Florence. It was a vacation he'd been planning for a long time. The plane was leaving in a few hours, or he would have invited all three of them indoors. Bee does not doubt he's telling the truth. Odd as it sounds, he seems genuinely pleased to see them.

'His suitcase was so small,' says Fifi, showing how small with her hands. 'Seriously, half as big as mine. No – smaller than that. I asked if he was planning to buy all the clothes he was going to wear over there, but he said he took pride in travelling light.'

'That sounds like something a very rich person would say,' says Hector, without taking his eyes off the road.

Fifi looks at him, wounded.

'Why do you say that?'

'Because I think it does. There's nothing wrong with it.'

'Is he travelling alone?' asks Bee.

Fifi's expression grows sorrowful.

'I'm pretty sure. He got divorced three years ago. He and his wife had been together since they met at university. She took their two cats when she moved out, so now he lives alone. He's thinking of selling, because he says he uses maybe ten per cent of the house on a daily basis. The rest is empty, apart from when Wilma comes over and cleans.'

Hector grunts.

'You got all that out of him in less than half an hour?'

Fifi ignores the mocking tone.

'I think that's how it works when you're family. The bond is already there. Anyway. He promised to get in touch when he's back in the country. I'm thinking of inviting him to Nanna's,' she says, and looks out of the window. 'I'd like to show him where I grew up.'

Not entirely accurate, thinks Bee, as Hector merges on to Highway 101, which will lead them over the bridge and back to the real world. You want to show him where you *wish* you grew up. But he's your dad. You decide.

Her phone vibrates. The client from last Thursday wants to know if she has time to talk. It's urgent.

A complaint, bound to be. Her money back, and a few days later: another snide Internet review.

Of course. You can call tonight.

Bee presses send, heavy-hearted.

As she watches the city and all her unpleasantly concrete problems coming closer, Beatrice regrets nothing. What good would it do anyway? At the same time, it's clear that both her life and Fifi's would have turned out rather differently if she hadn't waited so long to give her daughter a dad.

19

Sidsel (and Cosmo and Niels)

It's beating down and, apart from the nervous-looking teenager who confirms that the sea is *that* way before jamming her earbuds back in under her hood and calling her Pomeranian to heel, nobody knows that, right now, Sidsel is stepping off the pavement and on to the muddy track, holding her phone aloft like a lantern. According to Google Maps, the quickest way from the station runs through the woods, and although it can't be more than ten minutes at the most, Sidsel doesn't want to waste any more time. She could have strangled the young man at the airport desk who had repeated with hermetic amiability what she already knew but was refusing to accept: that a technical fault had barged in ahead of her reunion with Laura and extended the waiting period by four unbearable hours. We do apologise, said the man, raising his smile from her face and aiming it at the next person in line. She left the desk with her hands itching to smash something and a voucher that covered the cost of bottled water and a Greek salad. By the time she'd eaten, sitting at a tall, wobbly table near the gate, sixteen minutes had passed. The rest of the time she spent in a state of indecision, drifting in and out of the terminal's shops until at last most of the Sunday lay wasted somewhere behind her and the plane rumbled into motion on the tarmac.

The light of the screen hits the ground and the nearest trees like a floodlight, and after a few minutes of walking she slips the phone back into her pocket. There's nothing to be afraid of. The way the darkness and the sleek grey beech trunks surround her doesn't feel menacing. The buds on the trees smell freshly of nuts, and everywhere around her the rainwater clicks and trickles in its runnels. The woods at night! It's so easy to forget these places exist after spending most of the day at an airport. Spring, dark, silence. But this isn't a large forest, and before long the lights of Strandvejen are peeping through the trees. Pausing at the wood's edge, Sidsel consults her phone, then turns right and continues south along the coast.

The pulsing blue dot that both is her and symbolises her is moving across the digital landscape. She's 458, 450, 410, 380, 320 yards to her destination and to Laura, who has fallen asleep on the sofa, so determined to stay awake until her mother came home that Niels gave up trying to persuade her otherwise. Now, scooping up the girl into his arms, he carries her to bed. She slips through his hands like fine sand, smacks her lips and dozes on. The dishes from this weekend are waiting in the kitchen. Niels rolls up his sleeves and watches, whistling, as the water fills the bowl they had used for the whipped cream. The dot turns down the garden path and continues past the dining hall and common areas before it stops outside number eleven and disappears from the map. In Barbara's study, the sound of the doorbell rouses Phillip, who had been half asleep. Climbing out of bed, he goes over to the window and pushes the slats aside. The woman goes back down the steps and looks around the garden. For a few moments, Phillip gawps at the moon-shaped, rain-wet face. The heavy lids, the round, slightly downturned mouth. Then he remembers what Niels said: Sidsel. From London. Has she always looked this much like her mother, or has it come with age? She makes a tetchy movement towards the door, which opens at that very moment. The muffled sounds of the siblings' voices fill the hallway, and Phillip lets himself sink back on to the mattress, sapped by the shock and the momentary confusion.

'She's in here,' says Niels, ushering Sidsel through the living room and down a short corridor. He stops outside a closed door. 'I'm just in the kitchen.'

The light that hits the back wall makes Laura flinch in her sleep. Sidsel exhales with relief, for there she is. Warm and real. The intervening days have not distorted her. She gets into bed beside her daughter and strokes the hair away from her damp face. The heat from Laura's open mouth taps her neck in small, rhythmic puffs, and Sidsel feels the sense of urgency that has propelled her forward over the last many hours dissolve and melt away.

Gone is the urge to eat her, to bind the two of them

together with thick ropes and lots of knots, to never, ever let her go.

They've not lost anything.

Everything is the same as it was just before.

Sidsel lies there until her eyes have got used to the darkness, then she does a lap around the spartan room. In the wardrobe are a few items of clothing and a stack of clean towels in various colours. Apart from the books and the French slogan taped firmly to the wall above the desk, there's nothing to give away that it's Niels who lives here and not a wealthy older couple. Her brother would be able to pack up his life in less than ten minutes: he can fit everything he owns into the waterproof rucksack waiting in the corner for the next bout of restlessness. Sidsel closes the wardrobe. If she ever heard an explanation as to why Niels is currently staying in an exclusive sheltered development near Charlottenlund Fort, she doesn't remember it. His chronically unstable housing situation is the subject of a recurring discussion between them, and Niels is unbudgeable. Unlike his sisters, he refuses to have anything to do with the inheritance, and the only reason he hasn't given the money away already is that he thinks Sidsel should have it. Take the Larva out of school and go travelling for a year, he says, whenever she brings it up. I'll meet you somewhere.

It sounds great, but of course she can't do that.

Sidsel isn't even sure she could cope. Besides, it's reassuring to know he has something to fall back on if he buckles under the weight of his ideals some day.

She's wise enough to keep that last part to herself.

'To say thank you for your help,' she says, handing him the black drawstring bag with the museum's initials stamped in gold. He shakes out the contents into his hand and widens his eyes theatrically. He's always been dreadful at accepting gifts.

'Hey, a scarab.'

Sidsel laughs resignedly.

'It's a magnet.'

'Then all I need is a fridge. Is that for Laura?' he asks, snatching the uniformed bear out of her hands and plumping down on the sofa.

'It was the cutest thing that—'

'Like hell it is. It's bloody perverse. Someone needs to explain to her that the police are deployed by the state apparatus to ensure the submission of the individual and transform the population into a depoliticised mass. Otherwise she can't have it.'

'It's all on the card,' says Sidsel defiantly, taking the bear back, 'and while I remember . . .'

She grabs the medication from her bag and puts the box on the table next to the scarab.

'Ovex?'

'For threadworms, although I'm not sure you have them. It's just three pills. One now and then at weekly intervals.'

'Think I'd almost rather have the teddy-bear cop,' he mutters, turning the box in his hands.

'The pharmacist said that all adults with regular access to

the household should take it. I'm sorry. They've got it down at the school.'

'It's not your fault, and I'll take it, I guess,' says Niels.

'You're sweet. Thanks.'

Sidsel glances around Phillip's grandmother's living room. On the wall above the sofa hangs a genuine Lundstrøm. The naked woman is painted with wide, assured brushstrokes. She looks as strong as an ox, with one foot resting on a stool and her hand on her hip. But her face is as blank as an egg. There are no eyes, and no nose or mouth.

'We went to visit Efie.'

His expression is not as challenging as his voice, but he looks curiously, childishly eager to see how she reacts.

'When?'

'Yesterday. I promised her I'd go round ages ago. Before I knew I was looking after Laura.'

Elisabeth's birthday. Of course. Sidsel's phone had reminded her of it over breakfast at the hotel – she couldn't bring herself to delete the annual notification.

'We talked last night. Why didn't you tell me then?'

Niels takes out his tobacco and begins rolling a cigarette.

'It sounded like you had other things on your mind. Shall I roll one for you?'

Sidsel shakes her head. She's not angry. In a way it's a relief that it's happened without her having to make a definite decision one way or the other.

'What did you say to Laura?'

'Just told it like it was. That we were visiting my aunt

because it was her birthday. She didn't think it was weird. Then we ate some pastries and drank squash, and funnily enough she was fine with that too. And Efie was happy to see her.'

Sidsel looks past him, into the woman in the painting's featureless face.

'Do you want to know how she's doing?'

'Not really, no.'

Niels stretches noisily and jumps up from the sofa.

'Didn't think you would.'

'Where are you going?'

'Smoke. Come outside and keep me company, if you like. It's stopped raining.'

Sidsel doesn't move, feeling the cold from the open doorway steal around her ankles, then she gets up and puts on her jacket.

He's standing in the middle of the garden with his back turned.

Narrow and hard.

Niels was still a child when their father died. Elisabeth was the only adult he had left.

She knows that – but what's she supposed to do?

You don't just forgive something like that.

Her daughter. The loveliest, the *only* one she had!

She won't.

She can't.

Not even for his sake.

'Hey, did I tell you what happened to the bust?' she says,

brushing fat raindrops off a deckchair. 'It didn't fall over, like I thought.'

She lays it on with a trowel, exaggerating the damage, and like Loretta she imitates the arm movement, stupidly proud as always of making Niels laugh. As a child, she and Ea used to compete to see who could do it fastest, and because she was more beautiful and less self-conscious than Sidsel, Ea usually won.

'Christ,' he says, wiping his eyes, 'Christ, that's so dumb. Do they hand out fines for stuff like that?'

'The museum has insurance. I'm not even sure they got told off.'

Niels stubs out the cigarette in the upturned flowerpot.

'I'll assume they were ashamed of themselves, though. Anyway. I'm off.'

'*Now?* Where to?'

'Don't know. Out. I'm not used to being in charge of a kid for more than a couple of hours at a stretch. I've just got to—'

He shakes himself like a dog with fleas.

'Okay. Has it been that bad?'

'Nah, not at all. You shouldn't take it like that.'

'But we'll say goodbye tomorrow?'

Niels adjusts the scarf around his neck.

'If not, then I'll drop by sometime this week and say hello. Anyway, I owe her a game of Monopoly.'

'Sure,' she says. 'Enjoy your walk.'

Imagine being like that.

So free.

Sidsel knows not everyone can stand it, and she hopes with all her heart he's one of those that can. She remains sitting on the doorstep until she can't hear his footsteps on the gravel any more, then goes inside and grabs her toiletry bag, fumbling for the bathroom switch.

'Sorry.'

She doesn't recognise him immediately. Phillip has always been thin, but now she wouldn't hesitate to call him skinny. His thick black curls are down to his shoulders, and he's grown a tangled beard. The collar of his dressing gown is like a stole around his neck, making his features seem somehow more outdated.

'I think your daughter's awake,' he says, jabbing behind him with his thumb. 'I heard her calling a minute ago.'

Sidsel thanks him and hurries in to see Laura, who has kicked off the duvet but is sleeping like a log. When she returns to the living room, Phillip is on the sofa, eating a piece of cake with a fork. Sidsel settles beside him. The odour of sweat is strong but not unpleasant.

'Who's been baking?' she asks.

'Niels and Laura. They celebrated my birthday three months early, with flags and balloons and the whole shebang. I think it was Laura's idea. It's really good, you want to try?'

'Yeah, okay.'

Phillip disappears into the kitchen, re-emerging with the cake and two beers on a tray. Sidsel eats greedily: the sweet layers, the cold, fatty cream. She hasn't had anything since the airport salad.

'But what's up?' she asks, when she's finished chewing her mouthful. 'Niels says you've been a bit down lately.'

'Is that what he says?'

Phillip rolls the beer can back and forth between his hands, wondering how much she can stand to hear.

'I'm not sure if you knew I went to New York?'

'For college. Niels told me.'

'For a while I was staying at a friend of a friend's place, but his girlfriend was eight months pregnant, so they were pretty keen for me to find something else. She knew someone who knew someone who had a room in an apartment in Harlem. There were two other people living there already. An Italian guy and a girl from Iran. Perfect, I thought. I'd rather not live by myself, and Leila and Matteo seemed cool enough until I realised they didn't talk to me, or to each other. They both acted like they were alone. No saying good morning, no how was your day or *anything*. When they got home from work they went straight to their rooms. There'd be three people in that tiny little kitchen sometimes, each of us making dinner and not exchanging a word. I think they just preferred it that way, but I got a bit weird about it. I got this idea in my head that everybody knew something I didn't. That that's why they were acting like this. One night when I got home late from a concert, I suddenly felt absolutely convinced that there were surveillance cameras in the lights in the hallway, and that they'd been put there to keep an eye on me. So I grabbed a bicycle pump and smashed the lights out the whole way down. There were shards of glass all over the place. After that I was kicked out, of course. People were pretty freaked out. I had no place to go, so I ended up sleeping in one of the rehearsal rooms. The cleaning crew spotted me, and someone must have called my parents. Barbara offered to let me stay here until I found something better.'

'Hang on,' says Sidsel, 'when did all this happen?'

'I got home at the beginning of the year.'

'So what now? Have you found something better?'

Phillip massages his woolly knees, which are sticking out from underneath his dressing gown.

'Fuck, I dunno really. I'm trying to figure out what I want. You know how in the old days the blacksmith's son became a blacksmith, and the carpenter's son became a carpenter? It's the same with me and my parents. I've never imagined myself being anything other than a musician. And now it might be too late? That's what I'm figuring out.'

Sidsel wants to contradict him. The trouble is, though, he's right to be doubtful.

'Sometimes I think I should have gone the whole hog. Gone totally, genuinely bananas. All this,' he throws out his hands as though to encompass his body, his situation, his grandmother's flat, 'it seems a little half-hearted.'

'I think it's a very good thing you came home.'

He smiles broadly beneath his beard. His teeth are crooked, but healthy and wide.

'There's something I need to show you.'

Phillip goes into his room and returns with a sheet of paper.

'My present from Laura.'

Sidsel stares at the drawing. She must have lost interest halfway through; one of the butterfly's wings still needs to be coloured in. The sun, like all her suns, is wearing sunglasses.

'It's lovely,' she mumbles, sensing the heat behind her eyes.

A little white wing.

Of all the things to cry about!

'Hey.' He takes the drawing gently out of her hands and puts it on the table. 'Come here. Come on.'

Sidsel has known Phillip Tibbett since he was seven years old. Charlotte could smell a neglected child a mile off, and whenever she thought it had been too long since Niels had last brought him round, she invited him herself. One day, when he'd wanted to go to the swimming pool with Niels and Ea instead of to his guitar lesson, she simply called his teacher and pretended to be his mum. Unlike most other grown-ups, she was stunningly indifferent to his talent – to talent in general.

Sidsel turns her head, raising it to his. Her lips graze his neck. It's a moment before he understands what she wants. The kiss is polite, almost a question, and he tastes like she does, of beer and vanilla cream.

Dawn materialises as a pale streak along the curtains, and outside the sparrows burst into exuberant twittering only to suddenly fall silent. Sidsel drapes the towel over the back of a chair and crawls into bed with Laura, putting her arm around the agile little body.

'Your hair's wet,' says the girl drowsily, and turns so that their noses nearly touch. 'Hey, Mum, when did you get home? Your hair is wet.'

Sidsel shushes her, kissing her forehead.

'It's still nighttime, we've got to sleep a little more. Close your eyes.'

'Oh!' Laura sighs delightedly, poking her feet between her mother's thighs. 'Your skin's so cold.'

'Good night, Larva.'

'Good night. But . . .'

Sidsel reluctantly opens her eyes. She's desperate to be allowed to sleep. Laura has sat up in bed, alert as a meerkat.

'Mum, listen, he's playing,' she whispers excitedly. 'It worked!'

20

Curtis (and Coco)

The meshes of the dream have come so loose that after a couple of attempts the loud, ugly sound slips through and wakes him up completely. Curtis remains lying on his stomach, listening to the monkeyish screams of the gulls. His eyes stay closed. Just after midday, he, like so many others, had sought shade under one of the pot-bellied palms in Dolores Park. He can tell he hasn't been asleep long. An hour, maybe? It's already a hot day. Someone's smoking weed, and the distinctive smell makes him look up. On a bench a few yards away, three boys are sharing a joint and commenting on the women walking past. They've pulled off their tops. Their chests are smooth and hairless – not a day over fifteen, any of them, and yet this is how they talk. The tits on that one, the ass on her, what they'd do to that girl if they got the chance. Split, snap, stab. Obscenities. Curtis swiftly loses interest. One of them is actually quite good-looking, as far as he can make out, a light-skinned black boy with pale eyes. Forget it. Over, over. He shuts his eyes again and lets his head loll between his arms. The grass is cool against his throbbing jaw. A bad molar, rotten to the bone. It should have been taken out ages ago. The taste – of cabbage – he's used to, but the pain, constant and insistent, he can find no sensible place for in his mind. In a minute he'll get up and spend a few hours with the sign. He's found a good spot, and has sat there long enough to make it his. Most people respect that. Curtis's spot, leave it be. The staff at the café are left-leaning and still young enough to practise their ideals. They leave him to his own devices, maybe asking him to shift a few feet or not to smoke when all the tables outside are busy. He's explained that he prefers a cup of coffee with cream and sugar, if they insist on serving him something. They don't get that he isn't hungry, but once you look, you realise the city is overflowing with food. People always buy more than they can eat.

The boys start to move raucously away. They've tied their tops around their narrow hips. Curtis follows them with his eyes across the sloping plane of the park, watching their slovenly, elegant movements, the way they shamble forwards, the spluttering outbursts of laughter that force them to stop and put their hands on their knees. A woman lying nearby looks up, and like Curtis, she doesn't let them out of her sight until they reach the bottom of the park and vanish south along 18th Street.

'What's wrong with them? Were they drunk?' asks her daughter, without raising her eyes from her book.

'High, I think.'

Curtis smiles. He takes a shine to them immediately. They look like two movie stars, the way they're lying on their stomachs in the grass, wearing sunglasses and eating something that smells like pancakes out of a big pink paper box.

'Let's keep the rest for your dad,' says the woman, closing the lid. The girl opens it again.

'He should be here on time, then.'

The woman pokes her in the ribs.

'You're such a meanie. He's doing them a favour.'

'There's always food when you help someone move. That's how you get people to come,' she protests, but leaves the box alone.

The woman checks her phone, then sits up and squints in the direction of the path.

'He'll be here in a minute. He just needs to find a parking spot.'

Curtis hopes that he's a good man.

That he's not a destroyer. Over the course of his years on the street he has seen many families, and it's all too rare that they're happy. The image of those two and their gigantic box is a lovely thing to take with him, an amulet for the rest of the day. Jesus, but that goddamn tooth! Like the devil himself making a racket in his jaw. Curtis suppresses a moan and presses his cheek into the grass. The bad root thuds, thuds, thuds like a heart in the middle of the bone.

By the time they roll up their blanket, the shadow of the palm has stretched long and thin, and there's no longer anything to protect the sleeping man's head from the sun. Past burns have made the skin peel, and underneath the deep dry brown it's as pink as a tongue.

They're calling for her impatiently now. Coco counts to three, then she darts across to the man and puts her water bottle near his elbow. If someone doesn't come and take it, it will be there as a gift, a miracle in fact, when he wakes up.

21

Beatrice

Are you there? Let me know if you're there.

I'm here.

Good.

And are you alone?

He was here just now.

Who?

My ex-husband, but I think he's gone now, actually. He went so thin and papery all of a sudden. The damp got into him. Why? Can't the two of us just talk?

We're not going to talk today.

How funny. I feel like a horse in a field – just right.

I'm glad to hear it. In a minute I'm going to ask you to let go.

A tub of water and bobbing flowers.

Don't be scared.

I wasn't scared. You're the one making me nervous.

I'm here on your daughter's behalf, to ask you to let go. You're caught in her aura.

Is that what this is? Her aura?

I'm going to ask you to let go now, Charlotte.

Charlotte.

Charles.

Lottemama.

You'll feel a slight push. Follow it.

The woman you'd see waddling through the park in winter, kids in tow behind her, wearing a sheepskin coat with banana-shaped buttons down the front and her hair in a bun under her hat. Proud and fervent as a she-bear, pugnacious as a goose. It was for their sake I dressed like a pragmatic flower. I passed over the black and elegant clothing in the shops in favour of patterns and colour combinations I thought would make them happy. I wore footwear that allowed me to break into a run without twisting my ankle and falling.

Yes. Good.

I was the one who got up an hour before everybody else and drew faces on the hard-boiled eggs with a felt-tip pen, picked flowers in the dewy garden for the birthday vase, cleaned the dog's menstrual blood off the floor and cried when it was put down one morning in December. I sliced fruit and placed it in Tupperware boxes, cupped my hands into a bowl when they needed to throw up, and wiped their noses with the inside of my blouse; I gave them thousands of kisses, and every now and then I gave them money. I never hit them even once, although I'm sure I must have felt like it.

Just follow it.

Wait, there's more! I was light and nimble once, often alone and almost never sad. I liked to brush my hair for ages, to sit in my bed with my legs crossed, upright as a hyacinth, and sing songs we'd learned at Girl Guides. I loved ymer yogurt with a thick layer of sprinkles and the foxish scent of the blackcurrant bush at the bottom of the garden. The hedgehog's friendship with the twilight. The two went together like the halves of a clasp. My little sister's regal name and brown curls made my insides quiver with envy, and yet I liked showing her off to my friends. You'd have thought my parents would love each other even more for having made a child as good and beautiful as she was, but it was the other way round: the goodness and the beauty had been taken from a box no one had realised was nearly empty. My mother's smell was different, and in the new houses everything was aslant, like on a ferry. It was the first of many mysteries. I wrote the initials of the boy I liked on the bottom of my gym shoes in a fit of enthusiasm, then changed my mind and had to drag my feet for the rest of the season. And I used to go bounding around like a gazelle! So, they're ruined, said my friend about the vinyl records I had lent her, and which she had been thoughtless enough to leave on a windowsill in the sun. They were as crinkled as crisps. We were both eager to see if I could forgive her. I could, but the effort made me almost a grown-up, and with my new-found patience and broad hips I travelled to different countries, wept down telephone lines with my fist full of sweaty coins, and came back to a profusion of red-and-white flags. It was hard to know if I was just pretending, with my grazie mille*s or English* thank you*s. I dreamed of something that might have been fame, and swiftly forgot that dream again. I met a man who taught* *me bliss, and I cut my hair short and tied a scarf tight around it when he left. I met other men, and other men and others, and they left me too, or I left them when I got sick of waiting. On New Year's Eve I held up a sparkler in the dark and wrote my name in light. I swore it was the start of something new. It was decided: I would resurrect the happy empire of my solitude. Only, it was never very long before my hankering for others grew so strong that I abandoned my promise, desperate to bump into anyone at all, to touch an arm or a cheek that was not my own. The truth is, I was made to love. My life was lived according to the crazed mathematics of affection. Once something has been added, it can never be subtracted again. Children's hands and stomachs and necks and gemlike faces. Men's voices and the smell of their jackets in the hall. The dopey names we gave the animals, and which they bore with so much dignity. It filled my heart to the brim. Mummy, can I, can I please, from you, can I borrow a handkerchief from you? My answer was a yes as long as life. By the way, shall I tell you something mind-boggling? The scanner they put me in was made by the same manufacturer as my sewing machine. That huge contraption tilting and rotating on its own axis like a fairground ride. They said it could see right through me – could predict the breadth and the extent of my suffering and pain. But this isn't the story of my death. Of how it grew strong inside me, as my children grew strong outside. The trumpeter unscrews the mouthpiece and raps it empty of spit; cables are wound around a forearm. My drawers, my pockets are empty. What I want is to forget all this, to turn my back, be light and scattered as the snowfall once again.*

Now. Let go.

Like a flock of starlings, one and many.

Bee blinks, looking up. The client is sitting on the edge of the sofa, her hands clamped between her bare knees.

'Was that it?' she asks.

Bee nods.

'Can you sense it?'

She takes a deep breath.

'I think so. It's quiet now. Or, sort of, empty.'

'Empty is good.'

'I was scared I was going crazy.'

Bee gives a placatory smile.

'You're not the first person to say that. It doesn't happen often, only every once in a while.'

There's a knock on the living-room door. Bee's already spoken to Fifi about waiting until they're done. She apologises and slips out into the hall, closing the door discreetly. Her daughter's eyes are wide and agitated behind her glasses.

No more talk about William, Bee pleads inwardly.

'What is it? We're just wrapping up.'

'It's just – I think your neighbour is dead.'

'Who? Fifi, what makes you say that?'

'I saw it from the window. An ambulance came, and a few minutes later they carried him out in a bag. Sorry, but I felt so weird. I couldn't help thinking about Nanna.'

'Oh, Fifi, come here. Marianne is fine. And if it's any

comfort, my neighbour wasn't a very nice person. To be honest, he was a bit of a cold-hearted—'

'Mom.'

Fifi pulls back from the embrace.

'A cold-hearted prick. He was – you didn't know him.'

'Yeah, so you could show a little respect.'

'Yes, you're right. Stupid thing to say. Would you like a cup of tea with us? We're pretty much done.'

Seraphina follows her into the living room, where the client is standing by the window, gazing down into the street.

'I think someone's died,' she says, without turning round.

'Take a look for yourself!' exclaims Fifi, hurrying over beside her. 'Now they're driving him away.'

Bee goes into the kitchen and puts the water on to boil, then empties the Pissing Strawberry of leaves and cold tea. As always after a session she's exhausted, opened like a can of peeled tomatoes, but she doesn't want to be alone, not yet.

'Green or white?' she calls, splashing a little cold water on to her face.

'Green,' answers one of them.

As she comes back into the room, the two women detach themselves reluctantly from the window. The gingko leaves slip back into place, shielding them from the darkness outside.

'Sit down,' says Bee. 'It just needs to steep. Have you introduced yourselves?'

They nod, arranging themselves at opposite ends of the sofa. Bee manoeuvres the pouffe up to the coffee table, sets it on its edge and sits astride it.

‘Thanks again for letting me come over at such short notice,’ says Ea.

‘Of course. I’m glad you texted. Although I think they would have figured it out for themselves sooner or later. Neither of them was particularly insistent. As far as I could tell, your father had already moved on.’

‘Right, yeah. That sounds like him.’

Fifi is paying no attention to either of them. She’s immersed in something on her phone. Bee leans forward to pour the tea. The pressure of the firm pouffe against her pubic bone, the warm tingle, reminds her of something she had forgotten existed. Since Pauline moved out, the desire to do anything but drink and sleep has lain dormant. Distant and inaccessible.

‘I guess I’ve always imagined that dying does something to you,’ says Ea, accepting the cup with the stiff awkwardness that always grips people when it comes to the more technical aspects of Beatrice’s trade, ‘that it changes you in some way. But perhaps that’s a misconception?’

Bee deliberates. She doesn’t want to hurt anybody, but then again, there’s no reason to use kid gloves.

‘I’m not sure it is. I usually tell my clients that they can’t expect to repair something that broke on this side by reaching into the other. Their tools simply don’t work here, that’s one way of putting it. Imagine hitting a nail with a hammer made of smoke. You can try, but you’ll never succeed.’

‘Mom,’ says Fifi determinedly, ‘I still think I should call Nanna.’

'You realise it's nearly eleven?'

'She'll be up reading,' says Fifi, but doesn't move.

'Okay, then go ahead.'

Ea looks from one to the other.

'I didn't realise this was your daughter.'

Bee sips her tea.

'It is.'

'You must have been young when you had her.'

'Is twenty-seven young? Maybe these days.'

'My mother was twenty-four when she had me.'

'There you go, then.'

'I've been thinking about it,' says Fifi, and starts polishing her glasses on the seam of her T-shirt, 'and I figure I won't have any kids.'

Bee has no particular wish to be a grandmother. Even so, she's struck by the throwaway tone.

'You've never said so before,' she says.

Fifi pushes her glasses into place.

'Well, we've never talked about it, have we?'

Ea is staring at her, fascinated.

'How old are you?'

'Me? Twenty-three.'

'Have you felt this way for long?'

'A few years, I guess. Most of the things I dream about have nothing to do with kids. And it's not like there's any shortage of people on the planet. Far from it. It's scary not knowing what kind of world my kid would grow up in. What kind of life they'd have. Will there be clean tap water in fifty years? Clean air? I get that it sounds harsh, but I know loads of people who feel the same way. Or loads of people online, anyway,' she adds, blowing innocently on to the steam rising from her tea. 'And there are more and more all the time.'

'You might change your mind,' suggests Ea.

'Maybe. I don't think so.'

At that moment Pita leaps up from her basket and starts to bark. A second later, the doorbell rings.

Pauline?

Bee loses her balance, but manages to break her fall with her elbow before she hits the floor.

'Are you okay, Mom?' asks Fifi, helping her into a sitting position.

The doorbell again. All three of them jump.

'I'll go see who it is,' says Fifi composedly. She disappears into the hall, reappearing a moment later followed by Mr Pistilli, who flops down on to the sofa with his hand over his heart. He is, as ever, well dressed and freshly shaved, but the way his pomaded grey hair is dangling over his eyes gives him a deranged look.

'Ms Wallens,' he groans, 'you cannot imagine the evening I've had. It's been too dreadful for words.'

'And here we were thinking you were dead,' says Fifi, so ingenuously that Bee can't help but laugh.

Mr Pistilli gives her an aggrieved look.

'Me? No. It was my guest who died, and in a very irresponsible and insensitive way at that. Tell me, if you please, what kind of individual with any respect for themselves or others would lie down and die in the home of a complete stranger?'

'Did they do it on purpose?' asks Ea, who can't bring herself to leave this bizarre gathering and go home. Hector thinks she's at the movies with Patti.

'She didn't take her own life, if that's what you mean. But it turns out the woman was eighty-six years old. Surely she must have sensed which way the wind was blowing? Think of all the trouble her family will have now, getting her back to England. Oh my God, what a mess. What's someone like that even doing here? At that age, what's wrong with staying put? Or at least within the borders of Europe. Well, I'm done playing hotel, at any rate. My sister did warn me, and you hear the nastiest stories. Orgies and animal cruelty and theft I was prepared for, but the idea that someone would travel all the way over here just to up and die in my home – that's a new one on me. That's a new one,' he repeats, and giggles before immediately turning pale and earnest once again. The poor man is obviously distressed, but Bee can't help herself.

'This might be a stupid question, but how can the police be sure you're not involved?'

'Me?' he whispers.

'I mean, isn't she going to be autopsied so they can find out the cause of death? They probably can't rule anything out until then.'

Mr Pistilli stares into space, then he puts his head in his hands with a low wail.

'That was totally unnecessary, Mom,' hisses Fifi, patting

Mr Pistilli on the shoulder. 'Of course they know you didn't do it.'

'There are a million places she could have died,' he moans, 'she had all day to die. It's been hot – she could have keeled over in the street or on the bus, but she waited until she was tucked up safe and sound in my guest bedroom. You should have seen my house earlier. Swarming with police, doctors, paramedics. Tramping around everywhere! Up the stairs, down the stairs. Some of them ignored me, some of them peppered me with questions. I felt so, I don't know . . .'

The skin on his face is moist and flushed.

'Naked?' suggests Ea.

'Yeah, that's it!' Mr Pistilli pounces on the word gratefully. 'Naked is exactly right.'

'Hang on,' says Bee, feeling guilty now. Of course it was a shock to find his Airbnb guest dead in bed. Even more so for a man like Mr Pistilli, who sets such store by calm and orderliness. Going over to the corner cupboard, Bee takes out the bottle and four glasses, arranging them on a tray that clinks enticingly as it travels back across the room.

'I'd say this calls for something stronger than tea.'

Ea protests half-heartedly as Bee hands her a glass of Armagnac. 'One for the road. Just one, for Mr Pistilli's sake.'

'I don't normally drink,' says Fifi, 'but tonight I'll make an exception. Cheers.'

'Cheers.'

'Cheers. You too, Mr Pistilli.'

'All right, cheers.'

'To – what was her name? Your guest.'

'Day. Enid Day,' he says. 'I must have heard that name at least a hundred times tonight.'

'To Enid,' says Bee, raising her glass, 'an adventurous soul who has now found peace a long way from home.'

'Oof, that burns.' Fifi puts a hand to her throat.

Ea pulls a face but drains her glass.

'I'm going straight home to throw it out. Mattress, topper, the whole caboodle. All ruined.'

'Chin up,' says Bee cheerfully, 'you're not the one who's died. You can handle losing a mattress. Another one?'

Mr Pistilli nudges his glass towards her.

'One last one, then.'

'You know what, you shouldn't be drinking alone. There we go. How about you two?'

'I'll be off home after this one,' says Ea.

Bee fills her glass to the brim.

'You do whatever you want. In fact, everybody do whatever they want. Agreed? Everybody does whatever they want. Fifi, sweetheart?'

'A little half.'

'You can have an ordinary half. There. Cheers.'

'Cheers.'

'To what?'

'To my dad,' says Fifi, 'my dad, who I met for the first time today, and who's currently on his way to Italy. He might have landed already, actually.'

They clink glasses to William Catchpoole, who might

already have landed. Then Ea gets to her feet and says thank you for a lovely evening, and Fifi leaves to call Marianne, as previously announced. Beatrice and Mr Pistilli are left alone in the room. Pita has curled up in the corner of the sofa, exhausted by the unusually lively evening.

'Well, then. One last, last one?' asks Bee, holding up the bottle. 'No point holding on to this tiny little drop.'

This time they drink without clinking glasses, and more slowly.

'My daughter doesn't want children,' says Bee, and she can hear that it sounds like a non sequitur. Mr Pistilli raises his furry eyebrows.

'Is that right?'

'So she says. Out of consideration for the planet. She's obviously joined some sort of group, I didn't quite understand it.'

'But she's so young,' he says, sounding reassured. 'She could still change her mind.'

'Yeah, that's true.'

'She will, you'll see. The urge to have kids is like a switch being flipped.'

'So you don't think it's something about me that's done it?'

The alcohol has made their voices deep and confiding.

'You?' says Mr Pistilli, stroking two fingers across his upper lip. 'Well, since she says that's not what's going on, perhaps you should just believe her.'

It sounds so appealing that Bee feels better at once. Just believe her. Why not? Balancing his glass on the armrest, Mr Pistilli looks from one white wall to the next.

'Forgive me if this is an indiscreet question, but is it usually this empty in here?'

And now we're even, thinks Bee. Fine.

'Yep.'

'You're moving, perhaps? You and your—'

'Wife,' Bee helps him.

'Oh, I wasn't sure if you were married.'

'We were. We aren't any more. The house is for sale with Woolhouse.'

'He's supposed to be good.'

'Pauline says he's the best.'

'Oh, right? The best.' Mr Pistilli yawns discreetly into the back of his hand.

'I saw that,' says Bee. 'You should go home and sleep.'

'No! Sleep? I won't get a wink tonight. My system is much too shaken. Some rest, maybe. It's just the whole *thought* of the way she was lying there with her hands gripping the edge of the duvet—'

He shudders.

'You're welcome to spend the night here.'

Bee means it. She'd be happy to find him in her living room the next morning, to lay the table for three.

'I can make up a bed for you on the couch.'

Mr Pistilli surveys the comfy upholstery, then gives a dignified nod.

'But first let me just nip across and grab my toothbrush.'

PART THREE

Acqua alta

22

William (and Siew)

It's summer break, and the Catchpoole family has visitors: an aunt and her thirteen-year-old son. The two boys don't know each other, but they're cousins and the same age, and the adults expect them to get on. Things are dragging a bit. The cousin is sulky and withdrawn, but then William remembers the air rifle he was given as a birthday present. They can have a go with that! He jumps up and asks his cousin to wait while he grabs it from his room. As expected, the other boy's face lights up at the sight of the gun. Exhilarated by his success, William points at a blackbird hopping around underneath a small hazel tree at the bottom of the garden and asks, can the cousin see that? He can. Good, says William calmly, because now I'm going to shoot it. He's not a good shot – he only hits the empty cans when he stands humiliatingly close – but this time there's a strange, somehow final sound, and the blackbird falls to the grass. The cousin, who doesn't understand a thing, is already running across the lawn. Setting the rifle down on the garden table, William follows hesitantly. His knees and hands are shaky, because now he vaguely remembers someone saying something about a nest. The closer he gets to the bush and to the dead bird, the more positive he is that his younger sister mentioned it over breakfast. She promised to show it to him. But then the guests arrived, and his sister – still little and not lumbered with a cousin – snuggled up on her aunt's lap and let herself be petted and praised. The nest was forgotten. William reaches the boy, who is stooping a little, prodding at the smooth, brown-speckled bird with his shoe. It's dead, he declares unnecessarily. Nice shot. Thanks, says William, swallowing with relief. There's no nest! It must have been some other bird, some childless and irrelevant female that he hit. These things happen. Blackbirds – he now allows himself to verbalise the thought – aren't exactly in short supply. He's about to turn round and follow his cousin when he hears the noise. A thin, penetrating cheeping, unmistakable. Heart jumping, he pushes a branch aside and gazes straight down the six orangey-yellow funnels.

The film runs out, and despair scatters through William's body like cold ashes. He clenches his fists, commanding the tears back into their ducts.

Siew Wuong taps him on the shoulder.

'Are you okay?'

'Yeah, just jet-lagged,' he mumbles. For how can he explain to his Malaysian fellow tourist that the memory of the blackbird tends to haunt him at times of emotional pressure, like now? The curtain in his internal cinema simply drops, and the pictures emerge. Impossible to fast forward, impossible to switch off. His therapist calls the blackbird's death a *Personal Myth*, which makes sense, but it hasn't made a blind bit of difference. There is no prize at the end of the trauma.

'It's always worst on the second day,' nods Siew sympathetically, and they trudge on in silence across flooded St Mark's Square, chilly and drenched, wearing the fluorescent yellow disposable waders that the hotel porter handed them with an inscrutable expression that morning: *for the acqua alta*. She's crook-backed, and so short that they come up to her groin, and in places where the water is especially high, William – the only man in the group who can walk unaided – carries her on his back. The guide brandishes her umbrella and shouts at them to keep it moving.

'She's worse than my old schoolmistress,' groans Siew as they join the others. The guide scowls at them, then continues talking about the bell tower and the basilica, which have just been hit by the sixth biggest flood in twelve hundred years.

'It's not unusual for water to get into the narthex,' she says, gesturing towards the barricaded church. 'They took that into account when it was built, incorporating various drainage systems. This time, though, the water has made it all the way to the nave.'

'Ooh,' they say. 'Aah.'

The killing of the blackbird had ripped him to shreds. All that once was solid and secure turned to poisonous fumes. What was harmless became dangerous; what was soft, caustic and stinging. The bird was dead, and before long its young would die too, one by one, of starvation or a predator's claws.

The inexorability of it went through him like an electric shock. For the better part of a week, William refused to eat or talk, and when he started back at school after the vacation, he felt like a stranger to his old friends, to his old, unworried life. Numbers were his salvation. He had always liked math, but it wasn't a matter of liking any more. Numbers were eternal; numbers were pure. They kept no grim secrets, and in their mute company he could finally relax. Over the years, the wisdom of his decision has been reaffirmed in various ways, most recently when his wife walked out. She'd said she 'couldn't see herself in their life together any more'. He didn't try to understand what was behind those apparently meaningless words, sure that the answer would cause him far more pain than the uncertainty.

'The water itself isn't actually all that dangerous,' says the guide, chivvying the group past the marble arch of the main entrance. 'It's the salts it carries with it that are the biggest problem. When the brackish water is absorbed by the marble cladding, it seeps into the walls and columns and creeps higher and higher up the internal structures of the basilica. The water dries, but the salt crystals are deposited in the stone, and they make it porous. The worst damage isn't always the damage you can see, you know? We're going down this street here. William, if you wouldn't mind?'

She nods towards Siew, who is already preparing to climb on.

'This is the saddest guided tour I've ever been on,' Siew murmurs, clambering up on to William's back. He wedges his arms under the hollows of her knees and follows the others without much effort. Siew weighs no more than a twelve-year-old child.

The makeshift footbridge that the hotel has erected for its remaining guests lurches alarmingly as William passes from the streaming road on to the terrazzo tiles in the vestibule. Stripping off his waders, he takes his key from the porter with a ceremonial nod. On his way upstairs, tempted by a half-open door, he pokes his head into the library, temporarily closed because of the flooding. Beneath the vaulted ceiling, it's a peculiar sight: velour chairs and heavy mahogany tables stacked on a raised platform at one end of the room, and hastily covered with tarps. He can hear the rumble and drone of dehumidifiers, and through an open window a tube pumps milky green water back into the canal, where humans insist it belongs, but where it refuses to stay. A few loose pages and solitary paperbacks are still bobbing on the surface, but the rest of the books have been gathered into large sacks, ready to be carried out and away. A woman in a swimsuit and proper waders catches sight of him and wearily waves him on. *È chiuso, signore!* William apologises and hurries up to his suite, where he slumps on to the bed, exhausted by the marble-grey sky and the stinking torrents. Someone else might have cancelled their trip when the city entered a state of emergency, but the thought never crossed his mind. William doesn't like it when plans change at the last minute, and anyway, it suits him just fine to be at arm's length from the misunderstanding that happened two days ago, when a young woman bestowed on him a biologically impossible title: *Dad*.

William was born with Klinefelter syndrome. A genetic mutation that equipped him with an extra X chromosome, it means he cannot get a woman pregnant. So although he remembers quite clearly the night when Seraphina believes her conception took place, William can say for sure that it did not. The question (the mystery within a mystery) is why he didn't just come straight out and tell her so. He could easily have put an end to the whole charade, but instead he let the woman talk. She told him about the good years at various collectives and the less good ones in a self-sufficient village, about her violent stepfather and the move to Iowa, about growing up with a beloved grandmother. He listened with interest as she explained how, using the records of the retreat and a relatively brief online search, she had deduced that the retired programmer and creator of Pictor was the man she was looking for. That William Catchpoole was her father. Before she left, he had returned her hug and promised to call when he got back from Europe at the beginning of May.

In the taxi on the way to the airport, he had composed a short email informing Seraphina Wallens that she was mistaken.

He decided to send it once he was on the plane.

Then put it off till he'd had something to eat.

Read it again and changed the wording.

Shortened it, lengthened it.

Elaborated, apologised, deleted the apology and most of the elaboration.

Deleted the draft.

Switched off the phone.

There's a knock at the door. Three short knocks in swift succession.

'Yes?'

'It's Siew, open up.'

'One second.'

William smooths the bedspread and adjusts the heavy pillows, pulls a sweater on over his polo shirt.

'Good evening,' he says, stepping aside as she walks into the room without waiting to be invited.

'The Ruskin. Good choice. One of the best rooms.'

William thanks her. He hasn't yet taken the time to find out what this Ruskin did to have the suite named after him.

'I brought soup,' says Siew, handing him a searing hot foam cup in a plastic bag. 'All the restaurants are shut, so when I finally found one that was open, I thought I should buy something for you too. This was the only thing they had left.'

'Thanks, that's really kind of you.'

She shakes her head, irritated.

'Just eat.'

'I don't have a spoon.'

'Do it like this.' She makes as though to drink. 'It's not very thick. Good for the body clock.'

William drinks the aromatic, salty fish soup while Siew

watches patiently from the spot she has claimed on the edge of the bed.

'So you've been here before?' he asks when he's done.

'Oh yeah,' she says, laughing. 'This is my third time in Venice. First time alone. My husband died last year. We used to travel together.'

'I'm sorry.'

'You know what, sometimes it's actually like he's still here.' She waves her hand next to her right ear. 'Right around here somewhere.'

'Uh-huh,' says William uneasily.

Siew picks a bit of fluff off her grey slacks.

'But I won't lie, the evenings can get pretty long. During the day there's the trips and the group, all these things to do.'

'I understand.'

They fall silent. The hand-blown Murano lamps bathe the room in a golden light.

'Shall we see if there's anything on the TV?' asks Siew, passing him the remote. For a few long minutes William channel-hops, until they land on Rai 1.

'Stop,' says Siew. '*L'eredità*. It's Italy's biggest game show. Huge prizes, super suspenseful.'

'You speak Italian?' asks William, after listening to a couple of the host's incomprehensible questions and the contestant's incomprehensible answers.

'Nope. But it's thrilling anyway, don't you think?'

'Sure,' he admits. 'I guess.'

After half an hour it's clear that the contestant will leave with a hundred and twenty thousand euros. He's sobbing with joy, hugging his wife and two teenage sons, who have joined him on stage.

'Just look at them,' sighs Siew.

'Yeah. They're really happy.'

'Do you ever wish you weren't rich, William?'

The narrow eyes are scrutinising him intently from the other side of the bed. She's not kidding.

'Because you are rich, aren't you?'

He confirms that he is.

'It's odd,' says Siew, letting her hand glide over the padded headboard, rapping a knuckle on the carved wood, 'but the older I get, the more I feel like I'm lugging all my money around in a big invisible backpack. After my husband died, there was no one to share the burden any more. I met him late in life, and it was just us, you know. You got any kids?'

'I have a daughter,' says William.

The impossible word quivers in the air between them.

Siew pats his arm.

'Good for you.'

In the studio, silver confetti flutters down over the host and the dancing family. The prize-money total is flashing madly in the right-hand corner of the screen.

'This conversation reminds me of a story I used to beg my grandmother to tell. Do you have time to hear it?'

'A true story,' says William sceptically, 'or a fairy tale?'

Siew smiles and turns off the television, settling back among the pillows.

'Depends how you want to take it, I guess. Let me think for a moment. Okay. It begins like this: long ago, the living could see the dead, and the dead could see the living. Both the living and the dead came to the market. On one side of the road the dead sold their wares, and on the other side, the living sold theirs. In those days, people used copper money, not paper. The dead cut coins out of paper that were identical to the copper coins of the living, but the living weren't fooled. They put the coins in a bowl of water: the real ones made of copper sank, while the paper coins of the dead floated. They gave the dead their forged money back, and little by little the dead could no longer trade with the living, only with the other dead, and it was no longer permitted for the living and the dead to speak to each other. The dead were punished if they talked to the living – their officials would fine them – and the living grew afraid and took to beating them. Dissatisfied with their lot, the dead resolved to erect a screen of woven bamboo between themselves and the living. The living could now see the dead only indistinctly, while the dead, who were closer to the gaps, had a clear view of the living. The living didn't like that much, for the screen was too thick to beat the dead through. But the living were stupid: one day they asked for a screen of paper to be put up instead. Now they could beat the dead through the paper, but they couldn't see them any more.'

Siew sits for a while with her hands in her lap, watching the American man sleep. He's friendly enough, but quieter than she's used to. Like a big, shy boy. From the canal outside, the siren of a police boat is heard and disappears again. There is only the sound of his breathing now, and the Adriatic slopping softly against the palace walls. *Lap, lap, lap* . . .

'Yes, you're right, my love,' she answers in their own language. 'It's getting late.'

She slips off the bed and sticks her feet into her velvet slippers. He's waiting like a shadow by the door as she steals around the room, switching off the lights. With a nod he reminds her to take the empty cup and plastic bag before she leaves.

Thank you to Louise and the people at Gutkind. To Rosinante, and to Iben and Anna for having been there from the very first pages. Thank you to Martin B, Hanne, Minna, Lea and Ida for reading and sharing their thoughts. Thanks to Martin F for telling me about the ice road and to Kasper, who tried to explain to me what it feels like to code. Thanks to Sofie and Anne Marie from the Glyptotek. Thanks to the philosopher, my friend and my muse. I hope the white trousers are still just as white, that the *Weltgeist* does not let you down. Thanks to Malene and to Sara and Rod for letting me live with them in San Francisco. Thanks to my parents, and to you, Ivan, Dunia and Nitesh.

(At least) three passages in the book have phrases or images that have been borrowed from the work of other people. These include Charlotte's pomegranate cheeks, a simile that can also be found in the New Danish version of the *Song of Solomon*, the 'waterfall of images', which can be found in Inger Christensen's *Brev i april*, and 'Once more, my soul, the rising day', which is drawn from 'A Morning Song' by Isaac Watts. The story about the market of the living and the dead is a retelling of a Chinese myth I found in Eric Mueggler's monograph *The Age of Wild Ghosts* (2001). The title of Part II and of Hector's only collection of poems so far is taken from a line from Ted Berrigan's *Sonnets* (1964): 'For fire for warmth for hands for growth. / Is there room in the room that you room in?'